HOW TO BE FAMOUS

ALSO BY CAITLIN MORAN

How to Be a Woman
Moranthology
How to Build a Girl
Moranifesto

HOW TO BE FAMOUS

A Novel

CAITLIN MORAN

HARPER

An Imprint of HarperCollins*Publishers*

HarperCollins books may be purchased for educational, business, or sales promotional use. For information, please email the Special Markets Department at SPsales@harpercollins.com.

Originally published in Great Britain in 2018 by Ebury Press, an imprint of Ebury Publishing, a Random House Group Company.

FIRST EDITION

Designed by William Ruoto

Library of Congress Cataloging-in-Publication Data has been applied for.

ISBN 978-0-06-243377-0

18 19 20 21 22   LSC   10 9 8 7 6 5 4 3 2 1

To Georgia—not only the greatest agent and friend, but also the best font. We've been very brave.

AUTHOR'S NOTE

This is a work of fiction. Real musicians and real places appear from time to time, but everything else, the characters, what they do and what they say, are the products of my imagination. Like Johanna, I come from a large family, grew up in a council house in Wolverhampton, and started my career as a music journalist as a teenager. But Johanna is not me. Her family, colleagues, the people she meets, and her experiences are not my family, my colleagues, the people I met, or my experiences. This is a novel and it is all fictitious.

PART I

1

When I was eleven, I formally resigned from the family dream.

From the earliest moment I can recall, the family dream was simple: that, one day, we would get money from somewhere—win the pools, discover a medieval chalice at a jumble sale, or, least likely of all, *earn* the money—and leave Wolverhampton.

"When the bomb drops, we want to be on the other side of *those*," Dadda would say, at the end of our street—pointing across the flat fields of Shropshire, to the distant Black Mountains, on our left. We practically lived in the country.

"If they nuke Birmingham, the fallout won't reach Wales—those mountains are like a wall," he would add, nodding. "We'll be safe there. If we get in the van and drive like fuckers, we'd be over the border in two hours."

It was the mid-eighties, when we knew, for a fact, that the

Russians would launch a nuclear war against the West Midlands at some point—the threat was so visceral that Sting even had written a song about it, warning that it would, by and large, be bad—so we were absolutely braced for it.

And so we made our plans for escape. Our dream house was a survivalist bolt-hole, with its own water supply—a spring, or a well. We'd need enough land to be self-sufficient—"Get some polytunnels up, get your fruit in," Dadda would say—and we'd have a cellar full of dried grains, and guns—"To shoot the looters, when they come. Or commit suicide," he added, still cheerfully. "If it gets too much."

The dream house was talked about so much that we all presumed it was real. We would have passionate, hour-long arguments about whether to keep goats or cows—"Goats. Cows are fussy fuckers"—and possible names for the property. My mother, who had been made simple by many pregnancies, favored a ghastly option: "The Happy House." My father didn't want to give it a name—"I don't want any bastard to be able to find us in the phone book. Come the apocalypse, I'm not going to be feeling *sociable*."

We were poor—which was a normal thing; everyone we knew was poor—so we all made each other Christmas presents, and that Christmas—Christmas 1986—I had drawn a picture of the Dream Survivalist House, as a present to my parents.

Because it was just a drawing, I had spared no expense on this house: there was a swimming pool in the garden and an orchard at the back. The front room was painted the color of a peacock's wing, all the children had their own bedroom and Krissi's had a slide in it, that went out of the window, and straight into his own fairground. The house was magnificent.

My mother and father looked at it with tears in their eyes.

"This is beautiful, Johanna!" my mother said.

"This must have taken you ages!" Dadda marveled. And it had. The roof was covered in fairies. Their wings had taken hours. I'd drawn veins on them. Wings, I reasoned, must have veins. There must be a vascular system.

Then my mother looked at it again.

"But where's *your* bedroom, Johanna?" she asked. "Have you forgotten to draw it?"

"Oh, no," I said, eating my breakfast mince pie. The pastry was very tough. My mother was not a gifted chef. I was glad I had topped it with a slice of Cheddar cheese, by way of precaution. "*I'm* not going to live there. *I'm* going to live in *London*."

My mother cried. Krissi shrugged: "More room for me." My father lectured me. "It's absolute certain death to live in a city!" he said, at one point. "If the Russians don't get you, the IRA will. Civilization is a trap that will blow your knickers off!"

But I didn't care if the Russians, or the IRA, did drop a bomb. They could drop a million billion, and I still wouldn't want to live on the side of a mountain, with goats, and rain. Even if it was radioactive and full of mutants, and would lead to my certain death, London was still the place for me. London was where things happened, and I wanted—with utmost urgency—to happen.

AND SO AT nineteen, here I am in London—and London, it turns out, *is* the place for me. I was right. I was right that this was the place to go.

I moved down here a year ago, to a flat in Camden, to pursue my career as a music journalist. I brought three bin bags full of clothes, a TV, a laptop, a dog, an ashtray, a lighter in the shape of a gun, and a top hat. That was the sum total of my possessions. I didn't need anything else.

London provides everything else—even things you'd never dreamed of. For instance, I'm so near Regent's Park Zoo that I can hear the lions at night, fucking. They roar like they are trying to let the whole city know how sexual they are. I know that feeling. I want to let this whole city know how sexual I am. I see them as another one of those unexpected London bonuses—en suite sexy lions. This is something Wolverhampton would never give you. Although the downside is that the sexy lions drive the dog crazy. She barks until I order a Meat Feast pizza, and I give her the meatballs whilst I eat the crusts, and cheese. We are a good team. She is my pal.

If I imagine the dog is a horse—which is easy, as she's very large—I live a life that could largely be described as "that of Pippi Longstocking, but with whisky, and rock music." To live in a city at eighteen, alone but for a pet, is to engage in adult pursuits, but with the vision of a child.

I spent three days painting my flat electric blue, because, in *Sound & Vision*, that is what David Bowie did, and there is no better person to take interior decorating tips from than David Bowie.

I then tried to paint white clouds on the wall—to make it *celestial*—but it's surprisingly hard to paint clouds with a big paintbrush and some white emulsion. The clouds look like empty speech bubbles—the walls look full of spaces where things should be said, but I don't know what those things are yet. That's part of being eighteen. You don't yet know what your memorable speeches are. You haven't said them yet.

When I have money, I have takeaway spaghetti bolognese for breakfast, every day, because that is the most treat-y meal, and children buy themselves meals that are treats. When I don't have money, I live on baked potatoes—because they are treat-y, too.

I wake at noon, and stay out until 3:00 a.m., and then I have a bath, when I come home—because I can. It doesn't wake anyone up. Every single one of those baths makes me happy. You leave home to have baths in the middle of the night. That is true independence.

My phone is regularly cut off, because I forget to pay the bills—they come so often! Who opens their post in the month it arrives? Only the dull—and, when the phone is cut off, people ring my local pub, the Good Mixer, and leave messages there for me. The landlord complains about this often.

"I'm not your fucking secretary," he will say, handing over a pile of multicolored Post-it notes, when I come in, with the dog, for a pint.

"I know, Keith. I know. Can I borrow your phone?" I will reply. "I just need to get back to the most urgent ones. They want me to interview the Beastie Boys in Madrid!"

And Keith will hand over the phone, from behind the bar, with a sigh, because it is the responsible thing to do, when a lone teenager needs to make a call. It takes an inner-city village to raise a child!

I keep all my dirty clothes on the floor—because who

would waste their money on a washing basket, when you could spend it on roast chicken, and cigarettes?

Once a month, when all the clothes have made it to the floor, I put them in my rucksack, and take them to the laundrette. One of Blur uses the same laundrette. It's nice to use the same laundrette as a pop star. We nod at each other, silently, and then read the music press, whilst popping out every so often for a cigarette. I once watched him read a bad review of Blur, as he was doing a whites wash. I have never seen anyone transfer their underwear from a washer into a dryer so sadly. It's hard to combine being a public icon with your day-to-day domestica. The disjuncture is jarring. Grace Kelly never had to unclog lint from a tumble-dryer filter while Pauline Kael shouted abuse at her.

AND WHAT THIS makes me aware of is that London isn't just a place you live. London is a game; a machine; a magnifying glass; an alchemist's crucible. Britain is a table, tilted so all its loose change rolls toward London, and *we* are the loose change. *I* am the loose change. London is a fruit machine, and *you* are the coin you put in—with the prospect of it coming up all cherries, and bells.

You don't *live* in London. You *play* London—to win. That's why we're all here. It is a city full of contestants, each chasing one of a million possible prizes: wealth, love, fame. Inspiration.

I have the pages of the *A-Z* stuck to my wall—so I can stare at the entire of London, trying to learn every mews, alley, and byway. And when you take four paces back from the wall—so you're pressed up against your chest of drawers, staring at it—what that network of streets most closely resembles is a computer circuit board. The people are the electricity jumping through it—where we meet, and collide, is where ideas are hatched, problems solved, things created. Where things explode. Me, and the sad man from Blur, and six million others—we're trying to rewire things. We're trying, in whatever, tiny way we can, to make new connections between things. That is the job of a capital city: to invent possible futures, and then offer them up to the rest of the world: "We could be like *this*? Or *this*? We could say *these* words, or wear *these* clothes—we could have people like *this*, if we wanted?"

We are Henceforth-mongers, trying to make *our* Henceforth the most enticing. Because the secret of everyone who comes to London—who comes to any big city—is that they came here because they did not feel normal, back at home. The only way they will ever feel normal is if they hijack popular culture with their weirdness; inject themselves into the circuitry; and—using the euphoric stimulants of music, and pictures, and words, and fashion—make the rest of the world suddenly wish to become as weird as them. To find a way to be a better rock star, or writer. To make the rest of the world want to paint their walls electric blue, too. Because a beautiful song told them to. I want to make things *happen*.

2

I am trying to explain all this to Krissi, as he sits on the
sofa of my flat, in Camden, in August 1994. It is difficult,
for the following reasons: (1) Krissi viscerally hates London,
because (2) Krissi loves Manchester, where he is currently at
university, and (3) Krissi is very, very stoned, because (4) he
and my father have spent the last two hours smoking a massive Sunblest bag full of weed.

Krissi and my father are visiting me, in London, because
tonight, Oasis are playing the Astoria, and they want to see
them.

At any other time, I would be surprised by both of them
wanting to see a band like Oasis—they're not jazz enough
for my father, who so regularly refers to Charlie Parker that,
until I was twelve, I presumed he was someone he knew

from down the pub—his name really does sound like someone who works in the warehouse at B&Q—and Krissi is currently so deeply into dance music that he regularly shouts "Bring the BASS BACK!" in the middle of conversations he finds boring.

But in the autumn of 1994, Britain is in the middle of a collective, homoerotic love swoon over Oasis. They're like the rough, cool boys at school you fancy, even though they're beating you up—because they look so handsome while they're kicking you. There's nothing more intoxicating than a swaggering gang coming into town, who have a plan, and Oasis have a plan—"To be the best rock 'n' roll band in the world."

The last greatest rock 'n' roll band in the world, Nirvana, ended when Kurt Cobain became so unhappy with the pressures of fame that he shot himself, which put the world on a massive downer, to be honest.

By way of contrast, Oasis are loved because it's understood that they will not put the world through that kind of trauma again. No more rainy vigils, no more turning the radio off at sad news.

This upswell of Britpop—gathering speed in late-summer 1994—is all about bands whose unspoken vow is to be as *alive* as it's possible to be. In reaction to the cold rains and angry songs of American Northwest grunge, they are about the simple brilliance of life in Britain: football in the park, booze in the sun, riding a bike, smoking a fag, fry-ups in a café, dancing at a wedding reception in a workingman's club, playing a new record over and over again, getting pissed on a Friday, getting loaded on a Saturday, hugging your friends as the sun comes up on Sunday morning. They have turned everyday life into a jubilee. They have reminded us that life is—above everything else—a party. They have rewired the circuit board.

And Britain has fallen in love with this simple promise. To celebrate the everyday glorious. There is a sudden, tremendous hopefulness. All the news is good—the Berlin Wall comes down, Mandela is free, and Eastern Europe has walked out of the Cold War, and into the sunshine. There is a lot of sunshine. When I think back to that time, it feels like it was always sunny—like you were always walking out of the house without a coat, and with nothing more than keys, money, and fags. Every week, the radio pumped out more treasure. Every weekend, there was some new, big anthem to sing.

You could rent a flat in London for £70 a week, at a push; coffee was 20p a cup, in a café, and fags were £2.52 for twenty. It was cheap to live. It was cheap to slowly kill yourself. What better time to be a nineteen-year-old girl?

"PARKLIFE!" MY FATHER says, rolling another joint, and then leaning back on the sofa.

And, unexpectedly, what better time to be a forty-five-year-old man? For my father has taken to Britpop with the startling glee of a child waking in the middle of the night, and wanting to play.

"It's like the sixties, all over again," he said, approvingly, watching *Top of the Pops*. "Same hair, same trousers, same chords. They're all ripping off Bowie, the Beatles, The Kinks, The Who. The best shit. It's Mods vs. Rockers, all over again.

I, of course," he said, taking a drag on the joint, "was always a Mocker."

He wasn't. I've seen the pictures. He was a classic hippy. He had an Afro like a sunflower, and wore bell-bottoms that would have been hazardous in strong winds.

And, just like a child waking in the middle of the night, he has become a problem. For this sudden cultural shock wave, rolling out across Britain, has unleashed his dormant tendencies. Like King Arthur being roused from his sleep by a blast on a magical trumpet, my father's rock 'n' roll tendencies have resurrected. Always a regular and chaotic drinker, my father has now stepped things up a level by reverting to his teenage habits: he's started smoking weed again. He's started buying the music press again, and getting angry about certain things: "The Wonder Stuff—what a bunch of fucking jesters," he would shout, rattling the paper around. "I thought we got rid of this shit with Jethro Tull." Or: "The Lemonheads—nice tunes but fuck me, that bloke fancies himself. He needs to piss off and surf for a bit." He's asked me if I can get him some E: "That Ecstasy—is it good stuff?" he inquired. "The name suggests so," even as I tried to explain I had never done it, didn't have any in the house, and would always be unwilling to procure some for a parent with such rampant genes for addiction.

Most crucially, however, my father has started rebelling against authority again. In 1994, the biggest authority figure in his life is my mother, and he has rebelled against her by taking out a huge bank loan, and buying himself a second-hand MG sports car, for "nipping around."

The rows about this have lasted months—my mother screaming about the repayments, versus my father's disingenuous claims that it's "improved" their credit rating—and have resulted in the inevitable: my father getting in the car, and driving down here to see Oasis.

He is, in short, having a midlife crisis, prompted by Britpop.

"Hey derrr Rasss-mon," my father says, in an appalling Jamaican accent, whilst dragging on the joint. "Smoke de 'erb."

"Krissi!" I say, brightly. "Ptarmigan!"

"Ptarmigan" is our code word, for "we need to have a crisis meeting *right now*."

One minute later, I am locking us both in the toilet. I sit on the edge of the bath, whilst he sits on the toilet.

"I am uncomfortable with our father being stoned and racist in my front room," I say, lighting a cigarette, and flicking the ash down the plughole. "This is not why I pay rent."

"I *want* him to stay stoned," says Krissi, who is already quite stoned. "He was straight all the way down, and kept banging on about how much he hates Mum. I don't want some hippy being continuingly emotional. Racism is far easier to deal with. Racism won't make him cry. Have you ever seen him cry?" Krissi asks. "He started just outside Coventry. It's horrible to watch in a man of that age. His wattle vibrates." Krissi shudders.

"Mate," I say, sympathetically.

"I know. He *also* tried to tell me how good Mum is in bed."

I put my hands over my ears.

"Do *not* pass your trauma on to me, Krissi," I say, warningly. "My head must be kept free of my parents' sexuality."

"Too traumatized to hear what you're saying, old friend," Krissi says. "Gotta share the trauma by making you think about Mum and Dad having sex."

"I can't hear you," I say, pressing my hands tighter.

Think about Mum and Dad having sex, Krissi mouths. "I am making you think about that."

I throw a towel over Krissi's head. He leaves it there.

"This is calming," he says, reflectively. "I like it. It's like a cheap sensory deprivation tank."

"I don't want to take Dad to this gig," I moan. "I hate it when he meets people I know from work. Remember when he met Brett from Suede?"

I've interviewed Brett a few times. When my father met him, at a gig, he greeted him with "Mate, I'd shake your hand—but I've just had a wazz, and my hands are pissy 'cos the sink's bost." It's not the kind of vibe I want to project to sexy rock stars.

"Oh, he won't be coming to the gig," the towel said, mysteriously.

"What?"

"I top-loaded that joint with skunk weed—he won't be able to move for a week," the towel continued.

And, indeed, when we got back into the front room, Dadda was lying splayed out on the floor, listening to *Abbey Road* very loudly, and staring at the ceiling.

"You coming to the gig, Dad?" I said, cautiously.

"No, no, my love," he said, rubbing his stomach dreamily. "I'm going to while away the afternoon in my sunshine playroom. Leave your old dadda here, with his dreams."

Krissi bent over, to pick up his weed. A hand shot out, with the terrifying power and rapidity of the Terminator, and clamped down onto the bag.

"Those are my dreams, mate," Dadda said, in a slightly pained voice. "Leave them here."

3

Walking toward the gig, Krissi explains that he's got "too stoned," and needs to "get very drunk," in order to counteract the weed. We go into a pub and knock back several shots, in a businesslike manner, but the booze—contrary to Krissi's theory—doesn't seem to "straighten him out," but merely—as I predicted—just makes him even more smashed. Still, it's a happy smashed. He keeps hugging me, which is very un-Krissi-like, and telling me I'm a "dude," which I graciously accept.

When we get to the Astoria, there's a huge queue for the guest list. We stand in line, smoking cigarettes, and are chatting away about Liam Gallagher's unique walk—"It's like an aggressive baby, in a nappy"—when Krissi suddenly nudges me in the ribs.

"Look! Look!"

Six ahead of us, in the queue, is comedian Jerry Sharp. It's the nineties, when comedy is "the new rock 'n' roll," and Jerry is one of a slew of young, hot comedians telling story-jokes about sex, love, death, and their obsession with The Smiths. His sitcom, *Jerry Sharp Will Die Alone*, is about his continuing inability to find love in the modern world. Every week, he meets a new girl he falls in love with, who bins him off by the end. It has made a whole generation of teenage girls desperately believe *they* could be the ones who could make him happy. Obviously, I believe I *really* could. Who would not be delighted by me?

"Oh my God," Krissi says, staring. "I really fancy him. I can't believe he's here!"

Jerry is pale—troubled young man pale—with blond hair, shades, and a leather jacket, despite the heat.

"He looks like a hot Nazi," Krissi says, longingly.

Krissi has never talked to me about who he fancies before. This is a novel and delightful thing.

"Like Rolf, the evil postboy in *The Sound of Music*," he continues.

"Oh—are you Rolf?" I say, surprised. "I thought you'd be more Captain von Trapp. I'm Captain von Trapp. *I* would come when he whistled," I add, longingly.

Krissi stares a bit more.

"Would you not do him?" Krissi sighs. "I would."

"He's *all right*," I say. "Seven out of ten."

We have further chance to observe Jerry Sharp when he gets to the guest-list booth, and announces his name, in a faux-modest way.

"Jerry Sharp," he says, in an "I'm pretending it's a normal name—but, yes, it is a famous name" way.

The woman on the guest-list booth, however, is having none of it.

"Sorry, love—you're not down," she says.

Jerry can't believe this.

"I'm pretty sure I will be," he says, with a dangerously self-deprecating smile.

"Nope," she says, briskly.

Jerry pushes his sunglasses onto his head, and points at his face.

"Does this change anything?" he says, pointing at his face, and smiling in a tightly charming way.

The woman looks at him.

"No," she says. "Do you want to stand to one side, love. So I can serve other people?"

Furious, Jerry stands to one side, gets out a mobile phone, and starts punching in numbers, sighing heavily.

He's still standing there by the time Krissi and I get to the booth. I can feel Krissi vibrating with the joy of standing near Jerry Sharp.

"Dolly Wilde—it's plus two, but I'm only using one," I say.

She's just started to tick me off on the guest list when something occurs to me.

"Er, 'scuse me," I say, turning to Jerry Sharp. He ignores me. "'Scuse me."

He looks up, in a "Fans, please—I'm off duty!" way.

"Erm, I couldn't help but hear you're having problems with the guest list," I say. "I've got a spare plus-one—you can have it, if you'd like? And then I will have done my noble deed for the day. I'm currently on a 'noble' tip."

Jerry's expression changes in a second—from tetchy hostility to a fully charming, grateful, and hot reverence.

"You're Dolly Wilde, aren't you?" he says, like he's just realized I'm actually a human being—and not a farm animal, getting in his way. "From the *D&ME*? You're the *positive* girl. You love everything!"

He says this in a way that conveys that "loving everything" is an eccentric and foolish position to take—but whilst beaming, hotly, at me, from behind his sunglasses. It's quite discombobulating.

"I am one of Jesus's sunbeams, yes," I say.

"Good job I've got my shades on, then," he says, still grinning.

The woman in the guest-list booth makes an annoyed sound: "Hrmff?"

"So I'll give Mr. Jerry Sharp my other guest-list place, then, please," I say, to her.

"Well, this is extremely convenient," Jerry says, with a rakish smile. "I don't think the Gorgon there is a comedy fan."

He gestures to the woman in the booth. She gives him a sour smile.

I hand him his ticket. There a pause. His hand is still out.

"Don't you have an aftershow pass, as well?" he prompts, in a slightly pained way.

"Of course!" I say, and take the spare pass out of the envelope.

"See you at the party, cheerful Dolly Wilde! I owe you a pint!" he says, disappearing into the crowd.

I expect Krissi to say, "He asked for a pass, as well? How

presumptuous! How rude!," which is what I'm thinking—but instead he just says, "So hot," again, so I change my thoughts, and just think, *So hot*, like Krissi. I am a woman. I am open to other people's thoughts. The more the merrier!

THE GIG IS one of those gigs that's not so much "a band playing their songs whilst people enjoy them," and more like "people turning up to vote for a new future." This is a rock election; a landslide victory; a coronation.

The sound is ferocious—tight; fierce; like something trying to claw and swagger its way out of a small space.

Coming from the same kind of place as Oasis—a small, dull estate in a run-down industrial town—I know this feeling: it sounds exactly like getting the bus, uptown with your friends, on a Friday night. Already half-drunk, shouting "Come on!" at each other as the bus bombs past the tiny houses—all lit with the blue of the TV—and accelerates down the dual carriageway, and the orange street-sodium blurs, and you can't wait to explode into the white lights of a club, and spend the next five hours swaggering around the place like a king or queen of misrule.

Krissi—in his drunken, euphoric state—is both amused by, and immersed in, the man-ness of it all.

"We're the LADS!" he roars, grabbing me, and jumping up and down to "Shakermaker."

During "Live Forever," he cries—but then, everyone does.

"Oh my God—you haven't cried since Harriet Vale refused to go out with Lord Peter Wimsey in the Dorothy L. Sayers mysteries!" I shout into his ear.

"Shut up!" he roars back. "We're gonna live forever!"

It's nice to see him so in touch with his feelings. Well, Liam's feelings.

When the gig ends—Liam staring at the audience, blankly, as "I Am the Walrus" spirals to its conclusion—the sweaty shuffle for the aftershow party begins, everyone sticking on their passes, and saying "That was amazing!," whilst everyone else replies "What? Sorry—I've gone totally deaf."

"We going to the aftershow?" Krissi wobbles slightly, under the impact of so much booze.

"But they're collections of the worst people on God's Earth, herded into a mosh pit of cuntery, all blahing on about how brilliant they are," I tell him.

"Who said that?"

I'm so happy he asked.

"You," I reply. "Last time I took you to one. You were not gracious."

"But, Johanna," Krissi says, looking deadly serious, "I done it with a doctor, on a helicopter."

At the aftershow, upstairs, in the amazingly named Keith Moon Bar, I bump into a couple of people I know, and Krissi disappears.

When I find him, an hour later, he's standing by a window, looking both triumphant, and slightly furtive.

"What are you doing?" I ask.

"It's a free bar!" he says, triumphantly. "FREE! I asked them what the most expensive drink was, and then asked for 'a trayful.'"

He stands back, to reveal that the windowsill has four-teen glasses of booze on it, arranged in neat rows.

"What's that?" I ask.

"Double brandy and orange—three pounds twenty each," he says, proudly. "I am a honeybee—and I have gathered my nectar," he says, owlishly—taking one, and knocking it back. "I have laid in provisions. We are ready . . . for the winter."

We've only drunk three alcoholic pods of our honeycomb when a voice next to us says, "Is this a shop? A booze shop? Are you selling it to fund the *Guides*?"

We turn around—and Jerry Sharp is standing next to us, looking amused.

"Well hello, Plus One," I say.

"Hello, Jesus's sunbeam. I was going to buy you that thank-you pint—but it seems you are several steps ahead of me," Jerry says, amusedly, gesturing to our booze shelf.

"Would you like some of our provisions?" Krissi asks—offering him a glass. I've never seen Krissi's "fancying face" in action before. It's amazing—like rainbows are coming out of his eyes.

"What is it?" Jerry asks, politely.

"It's three pounds twenty—yet free," Krissi says, proudly. Jerry takes one.

"What did you make of that, then?" he asks—gesturing to the recently vacated stage.

I'm just about to reply when Krissi—who has just lit a fag, and taken a drag—says, very quietly, "Oh, dear," and does a small bit of sick into his glass.

"It's okay!" he says, nobly—and then does a bit more.

"Is that how you filled the glasses in the first place?" Jerry asks, looking into his.

Krissi starts laughing—and then clamps his hand over

his mouth. He's gone pale green, and is sweating profusely. I go to put an arm around him, as the first part of some manner of alcoholic triage—but he pushes me away, urgently.

"Whitey. Home. Now," he says, and starts walking away.

"Our coats are in the cloakroom!" I shout after him, fumbling around for my rucksack. "We have to get our coats!"

"Can't," Krissi says, briskly—breaking into a rapid trot, and reeling down the stairs.

I fish my cloakroom ticket out of my pocket. "Oh God, look at the queue," I say. There must be fifty people in it, waiting. The Astoria coat queue is legendary. It would be easier to queue for the last chopper out of Nam.

"Your boyfriend looks like he needs to get home," Jerry says, taking a calm sip. "Let him go. Have these"—he looks at the shelf—"twelve drinks with me, and wait for the queue to die down. It's the only sensible thing to do. It's what the *Guides* would recommend."

"He's not my boyfriend. He's my brother," I say. "I don't have a boyfriend."

"Well, then," Jerry says, eyes lighting up. "Let's drink to . . . waiting for coats with unattached girls!"

We clink glasses.

TWENTY MINUTES LATER, Jerry and I are smoking fags, and I've asked him what his favorite albums are at the moment—because the rules are that the nonfamous person asks the famous person questions. The nonfamous person is in charge of effortful Conversation Admin—they must lay on the schedule for the more well-known. And the conversation should be about, of course, the famous person. That's just a given.

We've mutually enthused about Julian Cope—"Oh my word, 'Safesurfer'!"—and Jerry's tried to tell me I should like Slint, which I am resistant to, as, to me, they sound like people who are deliberately making horrible music that will make their mums sad.

"The album's called *Spiderland*," I say. "Spiderland would be the worst possible place you could find up the Faraway Tree."

And Jerry laughs! I've made a famous comedian laugh!

I am still high on the laugh when Jerry starts to explain to me that—despite my loving them—I should actually hate R.E.M. now, as, "They've sold out, now they're on Warner's. We've lost them."

"But four million people bought *Green*, and twelve million people bought *Out of Time*. So quite a lot of people have *found* them," I say. I am proud of having remembered these statistics. I saw them on *The Chart Show*. They were the first "fact caption" on the video to "Shiny Happy People." The second was "Michael Stipe once ate fifteen packets of crisps." I love the fact captions on *The Chart Show*.

However, Jerry dismisses all this with a wave of his hand.

"They're for sad fat mums in Oklahoma now," he says, as if this is a bad thing.

Personally, I thought making music for sad fat mums in Oklahoma sounded like a *lovely* thing to do. I mean, they are a hard audience to write for! They only have the time and money for one album a year. If it's yours, you *must* be good.

I started trying to explain this to Jerry, but he shook his

head, and said, "Let's talk about someone good. Afghan Whigs' *Gentlemen*. The Bible of how love, and sex, are dirty and dangerous—if you're doing them right."

He lit my cigarette, and gave me an intense stare.

"Although one of Jesus's little sunbeams, hanging with the fat sad mums in Oklahoma, would probably disagree."

Ah, if I could go back and talk to me then, I would say, "Johanna! Never trust a man who says sex and love are dirty and dangerous! Never go along with it—because to nod is to check the 'I agree to terms and conditions' box of the man who is telling you *he* is dirty and dangerous. He's telling you, right up front, what his world is like. *He's showing you the contract.*"

But I am nineteen, alone in a big city, excited to be talking to the edgy comedian, and there is a huge body of evidence to suggest he is right. Half the songs I love. Half the books I love. Last year's terrible affair with Tony Rich at *D&ME*, where he tried to inveigle me into a threesome. It does, surely, mark you out as dangerously innocent and jejune to argue against all this—to still claim, despite everything you've so far experienced, that love and sex can be . . . lovely? Jerry wants to talk to a sassy, fast-talking, streetwise broad. And so—she will appear. That's what this situation requires.

"The best nights are the ones that leave teeth marks on your soul," I say in my best dark manner.

This is the right manner: Jerry lights up.

"Show me your teeth, tiger," he says. And because I've already started doing what he asks me to, I do. I bare my teeth.

"Shall we get another drink?"

Twenty minutes later, when we get in a cab to Jerry's house—his hands all over my back—I'm thinking three things.

One: I haven't had sex for ages—almost two months—and it makes me feel kind of hungry, but in my knickers. Like my vagina is Audrey II in *Little Shop of Horrors*, shouting "FEED ME."

Two: even though I don't really fancy this comedian, Krissi will *love* the story of me having sex with him. I am going to go and make a Sex Anecdote! I am going to do this—for Krissi!

And three: as always, I wish—wish like children wish for snow—that this man I was kissing was John Kite. But he is still not available to me. So this is one of the things I will do, while I wait for him.

4

In later years, when I'm having a long lunch with some girl-friends, and we take it in turns to talk about the worst men in the world, they come up with a list of things that, if you see them in a man's flat, tip you off that you are in the presence of a Bad Man.

As they point out, whilst drinking wine and howling, Jerry's flat had the full set. A framed John Coltrane poster. A framed *Betty Blue* poster. A bookshelf filled with Hunter S. Thompson, Nietzsche, Jack Kerouac, Henry Miller, and books about the Third Reich. Several hats. A velvet frock coat. An angry-looking cat, and a litter tray full of cat shit. Some "ironic" Virgin Marys. A bodhran. The complete works of both The Fall and Frank Zappa, a pile of porn, a bottle of absinthe, and a coffee table with noticeable scratch lines—from chopping out coke.

"Any woman, when she sees those things, runs," they conclude, laughing and crying, ruefully, at the same time. "For this is the house of a man who hates women."

And they are correct.

However, I'm still only eighteen, and have yet to learn this—so I just think, "Cool! An edgy intellectual!"

"This is the Arena of My Broken Heart," Jerry says, pouring me a drink, and sitting us both down on the sofa. "This apartment seems to have been built on some kind of Hell Mouth, that attracts every fucked-up girl in Britain. Every time I think I've found some brilliant, filthy, funny sorceress back here, to enchant me, BANG! This is where she reveals herself to be some broken lunatic, with daddy issues."

His tone is conspiratorial—that he and I disdain these girls . . . that I am not like these girls.

"Are you the one to restore my faith in women?" he says, in a mocking way. "I'm just looking for that impossible thing—a brilliantly perverted woman who wants her brains fucked out, by an expert."

He looks at me intently. He's making things very clear—I just need to be a brilliantly perverted woman who wants her brains fucked out. And I can *totally* be that!

"Well, that sounds like a *lot* of fun," I say.

"Oh, it is," he says, starting to unbutton my dress, and kiss my neck.

"In terms of my qualifications as a pervert, I'm pretty sure I know my way around a penis," I say, cheerfully. "I passed my Sex Driving License with flying colors!"

He keeps kissing my neck. I am officially turned on.

"I can even—ah! Oh, that's good!—reverse one around

corners," I continue, squirming on the sofa. I am a Sassy Dame! And Jerry will love my humor! Because he is a comedian!

As it turned out, comedians don't like humor. They like blow jobs, instead. I realize this when he doesn't laugh at my joke—but lies back on the sofa, and angles his trousers at me in a way that I realize, after a moment of nonplussed staring, means, "Give me a blow job!"

Still on my noble tip, I bend over, and unzip his flies.

"What have we here?" I say, cheerfully, releasing his erection from his boxers. "An extra-long vehicle!"

I'm being polite—it's perfectly average, very white, and a bit . . . thin. Like a witch's finger. Stop describing a penis to yourself, Johanna! Concentrate!

I put the penis in my mouth, and look up, with an expression I have seen Alexis Carrington Colby use on *Dynasty*—so I know it must be of high sexual quality.

"Mmmmm," Jerry says. "Keep going."

I "do some more blow job"—I believe that's the technical term—as Jerry starts to feel around, on the coffee table, for something. His hand eventually finds the remote, and he presses a button.

"Porn?" I say, in the way I imagine a funny, filthy sorceress would. "Great! Let's make a night of it!" Because I am not like all those other girls.

I'm expecting the typical "sounds of porn"—some "ahhh," some "oooooh"—to come from the TV.

Instead, there's a click, and a hiss—and then I hear something that confuses me for a minute. A jaunty song. What *is* this?

"*Jerry—why do you do the things you do?*" a female chorus sings. "*Jerrrrrry / Why do you do the things you do?*"

It's—this is—

"*Is this your TV show?*" I ask him, disengaging my mouth from his penis.

He automatically pushes the penis back toward me—eyes glued to the TV.

"Yes," he says, shortly. "And, in a minute, you need to suck harder."

He says it so urgently that, momentarily, my mouth obediently starts heading back to the penis—before the sound of applause makes me stop. I turn around. On the screen, Jerry has just made his entrance into his sitcom flat, to audience applause. He's *watching himself* while I give him a blow job.

"Erm," I say.

"Babe, *now*," he says, pushing his crotch toward me, still staring at the TV.

I take a deep breath, sit back on my heels, and then pat his leg—consolingly, like you would a horse.

"I'm so sorry," I say, "but my Sex License doesn't cover this."

I gently put his penis back in his boxer shorts, and stand up.

"This is a specialist job. *You*, are a specialist job. I think I should get a cab," I say, looking for the telephone. "I need to leave."

"You're not *serious*?" Jerry says—staring first at me, and then his crotch, in disbelief. "You're not *seriously* leaving?"

"Afraid so," I say—delighted at how adult I am being.

Last year I turned down Tony Rich's threesome, and this year I'm turning down Jerry Sharp's TV dinner blow job. Maybe my whole "thing" will be sexually disappointing renowned men!

"Jesus. Tough crowd," Jerry says, hoiking his deflating penis back into his trousers, and zipping them up. "I take it you're not a comedy fan, then?"

"I just prefer Newman and Baddiel," I say, trying to keep the tone humorous.

"Have you fucked them, then?" Jerry asks, unpleasantly.

I've found the phone. I dial for a cab.

"Not yet!" I say cheerfully. "What's the address here?"

The ten minutes I have to wait for the cab are ten of the most awkward moments of my life.

For the first half, Jerry sits on the sofa, presses play on the video, and solidly ignores me whilst he watches himself, with the sound turned down, and drinks whisky. I sit on a chair by the door, dedicatedly smoking cigarettes.

"This was a good bit!" he says, at one point, gesturing to the TV. I laugh politely.

After six minutes, he seems to remember himself. Some notion of pride kicks in. He goes over to the bookshelf, and pulls out a notebook.

"So, I write poetry," he says.

In the future, when I tell this to girlfriends, they scream laughing, and say, "Of *course* he does! Of *course* he writes poetry!"

He then reads me a poem. I'll be honest; I'm not really focusing on it. I'm desperately listening out for the sound of a minicab outside—but the street is, sadly, silent.

The poem seems to be a furious meditation on unrequited love, dedicated to a mysterious and unkind woman who has used Jerry's heart "*like Raleigh's cloak / Beneath her feet.*"

Presumably fueled by his anger over his half-fellated penis, Jerry appears to be aiming the reading of this poem at me—taking particular delight in delivering the line, "*In bed she lies / And lies*" with side-eyed venom.

Having someone read bad poetry to you, angrily, is oddly sinister. I'm surprised people don't get more baddies to do it in horror films—it's quite chilling. Not so much from the power of the imagery. More because you really want to laugh—but know that, if you do, they will become even angrier, and maybe read you *another* one. In an *even more* furious way. And that would be the worst thing of all.

"That's intense," I say, every so often, to placate him. Or: "Oh, yeah—those are the right words."

I nod a lot. That seems to be the best thing to do, to survive the poetry.

When I hear the minicab honk outside, I've never been more glad of a honking sound. It is the honk of freedom.

"Take care, Jerry," I say, lightly, saluting at him, and running down the stairs.

The last thing I hear, as I let myself out of the front door, is his voice, floating down the hallway: "But that poem isn't about *you*, of course," he shouts. "I'm not in love with *you*."

5

Waking, the next day—sleep-deprived, and with my boots still on—I was momentarily confused about what had happened the night before. This is one of the hazards of encountering famous people—when you're used to seeing them on the TV, or in magazines, your memories of actually meeting them in real life seem vaguely surreal: did you *really* see the penis of the guy who was on the cover of *Time Out* last month?

I looked in the mirror, and saw the love bite Jerry had left there.

"Yes, Johanna," I told myself, as I swung my legs out of bed. "You did see that penis. And it saw you. But only briefly."

You must not despair, I consoled myself as I got dressed— you still have all the fun of telling Krissi about this insane encounter. He's going to be both *really* impressed when you tell him you pulled that comedian that he fancies; and then amused when you tell him how bizarrely it ended. This is going to be fun!

I bounce upstairs, and find Dadda in the kitchen.

"All right, you dirty stop-out," he says. He's already very stoned, and it's only 10:00 a.m. Dadda's trip down Memory Lane is turning into quite the Long March.

Krissi is sitting at the table, looking very hungover, and eating a huge fried breakfast. My father appears to have used every single utensil in the house to cook it—the sink is full of dirty dishes.

"Tea?" Krissi says, pushing a cup over.

I take the cup, sit down, and prepare my best "I have news" face.

"So, you'll never guess what! I did it! I pulled Jerry Sharp! Ask me any question you like!"

Krissi stares at me. There is a long, confused pause.

"Who's Jerry Sharp?"

"Jerry Sharp! That comedian you fancy! I did it for you! I pulled him! Ask me anything you want!"

"Jerry Sharp?" Krissi says, again. "I don't know who Jerry Sharp is."

"That comedian—at the gig last night! The one you were freaking out over!"

"Oh," Krissi says. "Oh dear. That was Jerry Sharp? Oh, I don't fancy *Jerry Sharp*."

He looks at me, clearly puzzled. "I saw him on *Have I Got News for You*, once . . . I thought he was a bit of a prick, to be honest," Krissi shrugs. "I thought that guy last night was *Denis Leary*. Now *him*, I fancy. Oh God, I really *was* drunk."

"Johanna, you want a sausage?" Dadda says, pushing a plate over.

I stare down at it.

All of last night suddenly seems like a very bad idea.

As it turns out, I have no idea just how bad.

STILL, LIFE GOES on, doesn't it? It really always does. It keeps bloody going on. I mean that in a good way, of course. However much you fuck things up, life just keeps going on, washing you downriver—even if you're just floating there, like a listless dead thing, making no effort, mouthing *"Oh God, oh God,"* facedown underneath the water. The current bears you on until, soon, the awful events are just tiny specks, left far behind you, and you can say, "Oh well, it was just a bad sexual tussle. I barely remember it now."

Today, I have to work; I have go into *D&ME*, to file my copy. After eating what I think of as, unfortunately, "Dad's Bad Sex Consolation Sausage," I have a bath, put on something that doesn't smell of Jerry, or fags, clap on my hat, and get the bus.

Luckily, I don't have a hangover. You don't really have hangovers when you're nineteen. Your liver and kidneys are young, and vigorous. They can process alcohol quite efficiently. You might feel a bit sleep-deprived, and more inclined to eat a whole loaf of bread, but it's not really a "hangover" as older people know them: the pain, suffering, nausea, and terror.

In many ways, our laws around the vending and consumption of alcohol are all wrong. Teenagers are the best people to be drinking it. It doesn't hurt them so much. By the time you're of legal age to drink, you've only got a few years left before it starts to destroy you. Were I in charge, I would make it illegal to drink alcohol after the age of twenty-one. Teenagers can handle it. Anyone older can't.

So, no. I'm not really physically suffering.

What I *am* experiencing is regret.

And if you have regret—which is just a thought—then, in order to feel better, all you have to do is crush the regretful thought with a *bigger, non-regretful* thought.

However, as I cast around for a thought that is bigger than my regret about Jerry Sharp, I come up against the biggest thought in my head: John Kite.

Oh, John Kite! Do you know how much I think of you? I sometimes think you do—and it's what both gives me hope, and kills me. You are the first and third thought in any sequence—the fifth and the ninth. I think about you, on average, every seven minutes. That's what love is, isn't it? When you've met someone so exciting and endless that the whole world is simply, "things that are them," and "things that are not them"?

This bus route is filled with "things that are John." It's like running through a tunnel of ghosts. Past the Good Mixer pub, where I sat and cried with him, brokenhearted, after I'd broken up with Tony Rich, and he roared "If any cunt has hurt you, he will RUE ME!"

Past the off-license where we bought cherry brandy, and walked down the street, while he showed me how to shape chords on the bottle neck.

Past the busker at the Tube station—the same one!—who John gave a twenty-pound note to, telling me, "You've got to pass it on, babe," before asking the busker one favor: "Don't play Nirvana, babe—it's too sunny for a downer."

And the trees of Regent's Park . . . Regent's Park, where I kissed John. It was definitely *me*, kissing *him*; he explained that I was too young to kiss back, but that we *would* kiss one day, as, "You're a you, and I'm a me."

And on this gentle, jokey promise—on this kind thing, said to a sad girl—I have moved down to London, because, one day, I will be old enough for him to want to kiss me back, and I want to make sure I'm standing right next to him when that happens. That's why I'm here. That's the basis of my whole life.

And this is a good, solid, sensible plan to have.

Other people might call it "unrequited love," but I call it "everything to play for." I am a grafter. I am unafraid of pain. I like just hanging out on my cross, here, for John. And, besides, it all worked out for Jesus. Pretty much.

THERE IS A problem with my plan, however—to have John realize he's in love with me, and for us to spend the rest of our lives together.

Because, in the three years that I have known him, John Kite has become very famous. His second album—which I call, in my head, *Since I Met Johanna*, but which everyone else refers to by its title, *Everyone's Wrong Except You*—has seen him unbutton his shirt and let all his songs fly out, like birds from a cage, and they have migrated across the world, and landed on radio waves, and into bedrooms. They have done the unfortunate thing of sharing John with the world.

Now, he is known by hundreds of thousands—and this is my greatest possible sorrow. It is difficult enough to be seriously, officially in love with someone who still thinks you're too young to be loved back. But it becomes whole fathoms harder when there are thousands of other young girls who are *also* in love with your love.

I hate every single one of his new fans, even as I admire their great taste. Part of the reason I fell in love with John is because no one else seemed to be in love with him; he was an unlikely heartthrob, and I applauded my rare good taste in wanting him, whilst also coldly calculating that my chances of having him were all the higher, given his bearlike shuffle, squashed face, and shabby suits.

But now, he's famous for being an unlikely heartthrob—*i-D* had him on the cover, with lipstick kisses on his face, and the headline "YOUR NEW CRUSH," and every time John appears on the cover of a magazine, I feel like angrily hovering by the newsstand, and interrogating every girl who buys it: "Did you love him back in 1992, when no one cared? Did you love him when he wore that coat that was a bit too small, and his hair was still a bit shit? Did you? Then your love is invalid. GOOD DAY TO YOU, MADAM—GOOD DAY."

The most fundamental thing about being famous—being known by hundreds of thousands of people—is that you become very busy. When John was just a cult figure, he lived the pleasingly low-key life of a dole bum. There would be whole weeks when he was doing nothing, except "writing," which seemed to be a moveable feast—we would spend days in the pub, or walking around, or going to gigs, or watching TV while it rained outside: him with the dog draped, hugely, across his lap, occasionally being startled when John shouted out "CANDIDATE!" very loudly, at the *Countdown* conundrum.

Since this album came out, however, he is always away—touring, being interviewed, in the studio recording the endless B sides singles needed, in the nineties.

At first, he treated it like a Tommy, in the First World War: "I'm a flash in the pan," he said, cheerfully, after his first *Top of the Pops* appearance. "I'll be all over by Christmas."

But as the album takes off in Italy, Australia, Sweden, the end point of the publicity campaign gets pushed further and further away. New tours are tacked onto the end of the itinerary, so he won't be finished until September, November, March.

First weeks, and then months go by where I don't see him. I watch *Countdown* on my own. I have the keys to his house—I go in, occasionally, to water his plants, stack up his post by the phone, and lie facedown on his dirty pillow for twenty minutes, breathing in his fading head-smell, sighing, "Your fading head grease is as opium to me," then letting myself out of the house again.

We are phone friends, now—it will ring at 11:00 p.m., 2:00 a.m., 3:00 a.m., and a drunken John will be on the other end, saying, "Sorry Dutch—I can't work out what time it is there. Can you talk?"

And of *course* I'm free—because I'm not with him! The only thing that would *ever* occupy me enough to not talk to him, would be *being with him*. Does he not understand that the rest of the calendar is in plain black and white—just hours, with events written in them—and that anything to do with him is illuminated like a medieval manuscript, with gold-leaf griffins and azure-blue saints scrolling into the margins, and bursting out across the room?

I lean my head on the bus's window glass—to cool my face—and think about John. I read a quote, by Carson McCullers, recently.

"The way I need you is a loneliness I can't bear."

I burst into tears when I read it. When you feel you have found your other half—the one you were meant to do everything with—every moment without them is just that: an unbearable loneliness.

The nearest I've ever got to praying is for John Kite.

"Please, world," I say, quietly, looking out of the window, at the bench where we kissed. "Please give me John. I will be so good if you do. I will work."

I notice I'm crying. Maybe I am hungover after all.

IN THE *D&ME* office, it's business as usual. The landscape: a room full of old papers, and records. The vibe: like a Wild West saloon, filled with rock cowboys.

When I first started working here, at the age of sixteen, I was a wholly innocent, pudding-faced girl—blown away at getting a job where music lived. In an office of oddballs—*D&ME* employs ex-punks, drug addicts, Goths—I was just another oddball: a sexually voracious sixteen-year-old girl in a hat, with oddly Victorian locution. I presumed we would all accept each other's oddnesses, and proceed as esteemed colleagues and equals. My Lady Sex Pirate adventures were no more to be judged than Rob's ferocious amphetamine habit, Armand's continuing habit of making up entire interviews, and Kenny being convinced that everyone is secretly gay, and making that the subtext of all his features.

But, over the last year, I've become more attuned to certain . . . currents, flowing through the place. Let me be specific: since I had a brief dalliance with the paper's star writer, Tony Rich, which ended when I declined a threesome with him, and was then sick out of the window of his parents' house, I have been the Number 1 subject of innuendo, double entendre, and outright speculation on my freewheeling sexual attitude.

I did not complete my mission. My mouth wrote a sex check my vagina eventually declined to cash—and, now, as a result, I'm devalued. I'm the kind of person who sexually betrays men. I'm a quitter. I will walk away from an erection. And this kind of girl, I have discovered, makes men angry. It makes them *bitchy*.

I only found this out when I was drunk, at an aftershow party, when I decided to tell everyone the story of me and Tony Rich. I thought they would find it . . . funny.

". . . and when he called me his 'bit of rough,'" I said, leaning on the bar of the Astoria, "I swiveled on my heel, like a Musketeer, gathered my dignity around me, like a fur coat, and I walked out of that threesome. I said 'Good day' to him, gentlemen. Good day!"

I expected all "the guys" to respond like women would: "Oh my God!" "Good on you!" "Fuck him!"

Instead, they all sniggered a bit, and then Kenny said, "I'm surprised, given your reputation, that you turned it down, darling. I believed your motto was, in tribute to John Lewis, 'Never knowingly under-hoe'd.'"

And I laughed, because everyone else was laughing, and it was a good pun, and because, at home, Krissi only ever makes jokes about me because he loves me. That's what horrible jokes are, at home. But I feel like they might not be, here.

SO I'M PART of the gang, but not part of the gang. This is a common position for girls to be in. See: Mary Magdalene and the disciples; Madame Cholet in *The Wombles*; Carol Cleveland in Monty Python. I'm not actually part of the gang at all. I'm just . . . "The Girl."

"So, scores on the doors. What have we got this week?" Kenny asks, at the Editorial Meeting.

As always, the Editorial Meeting does not look like an editorial meeting. People are smoking, drinking, telling anecdotes, coming down off pills. If someone who did not know the working methods of the *D&ME* passed by, they would presume this was a field hospital in the Rock Wars.

Rob has his head down on the desk, and is being fed dry Krackawheat from a packet "to help with the terrible burning and nausea."

Tony Rich is looking at his reflection in the window, and fiddling with his hair, whilst pouting. In advance of seeing him, I have spent weeks practicing a "noble face," in case we make eye contact. When he finally does look up, it's with a horrible, knowing grin, which 100 percent means "I can remember having sex with you whenever I want," and I reflect on how unfair it is that people get to keep their memories of you, even when you have removed them from your life. If only there were some way you could, whilst breaking up with them, flounce around their head with a bin bag, going, "And I'm going to take this image of me giving you a blow job, and this vignette in the back of a cab, and I'm absolutely reclaiming *all* footage of me losing my virginity to you." If only you had copyright on memories of yourself. If I could charge him a fiver each time he thinks about me, that would be justice. And would pay for a very good lunch.

There are the usual squabbles/agreements about work. Tony Rich is being dispatched to do his latest in a long line of eviscerations of U2 on tour. Rob's done Oasis, hence his "rock illness" this morning.

"At one point, Liam started arguing with himself," Rob marvels. "Said Oasis were the best band in the world, then said, 'Fuck anyone who thinks we're the best band in the world—we're the best band *of all time*. Fuck those nipples.' Got proper furious. Amazing."

Talk then turns to John Kite, whose latest single has just gone into the Top Ten.

"Don't bother putting your hand up, Dolly," Kenny says with a sigh, even as my hand is going up. "I think you have delighted us enough with your thoughts on the *swoon-some* Kite."

The first feature I did for *D&ME*, three years ago, was interviewing Kite. High off spending a night in Dublin talking with him, it was, essentially, a love letter, and nearly resulted in me being sacked "for being an overexcited teenage girl." For the last two years, it has been the office in-joke that I am in love with him, and that his record company have requested I remain a minimum of one hundred yards away from him, lest they have to summon security. I tried, once, to explain that we are actually friends, in real life, and that I water his plants when he's on tour, which resulted in Kenny screeching, "Mark Chapman's got the keys to Lennon's house! RUN, JOHN, RUN!" So now, I say nothing.

"Big crossover audience," Kenny was saying. "The Kids are into it. What's our take?"

"I volunteer," Tony Rich says, raising his hand languidly. "I feel like I've got some stuff I could run with."

"SOLD!" Kenny says. "We done? Pub?"

Everyone half stands, ready to leave.

"It's just . . ." I say.

Everyone turns to look at me, and then sits back down, reluctantly.

"I was thinking of doing a piece . . . about how male Britpop is?"

I would say the response around the table is "mainly irritated."

"Go on, Gloria Steinem," Kenny sighs.

"It's really noticeable how few female artists are involved in Britpop," I say, earnestly. "Basically, Louise from Sleeper is having to represent a whole gender. Do you know how many bands at last year's Reading Festival had women in? Eight. Out of sixty-six. Elastica, Echobelly, Lush, Hole, Sleeper, Transglobal Underground, Tiny Monroe, and Salad. That's it. It's all very blokey. It's all a bit 'No girls allowed in the treehouse.'"

"You know, she's got a point," Rob said. Rob was the nearest I had to a feminist ally at the paper, although he did feminism his way. Today, this was by adding, sympathetically: "There's hardly *any* flange in the paper."

He starts leafing through this week's issue, on the table, reviewing each page. "No flange; no flange; no flange; flange—oh no. That's *not* flange. That's Richey from the Manics. Get a *haircut*, love. You're confusing me."

"So, what should we do?" Kenny asks, slightly aggressively. He really wants to go to the pub.

The problem is, I don't know, exactly, what we should do—I have this thing where I don't often know what I really think until I start talking, and then my mouth suddenly says what I was subconsciously pondering. I was hoping that, when I raised the issue, everyone else would join in, and we'd have a conversation about it, and I'd work it out. But there is no conversation happening here. So I can't work it out.

I shrug.

"Important point raised, Wilde," Kenny says, impatiently. "Keep having a think about it, and let us know, yeah? And . . . off we fuck to the pub, then."

Everyone gets up to leave, and I think: I don't know if I should work here anymore. I feel . . . lonely. I feel like all those pictures of the heads of state of the world, where it's eighty-nine men in suits, and then the Queen, being a woman, on her own. I feel like the Queen, but without her backup of castles.

As I fiddle around with a broken strap on my rucksack, Kenny sidles over to me.

"Did you know Tony's seeing Camilla from Polydor now?" he says, a look of sly glee on his face.

Camilla is a very posh, very blond, very thin woman who, I believe, on her passport, under "occupation," has "coke whore." Even though *she's* awful and *he's* a bastard, and my mother would refer to such a situation with a tight-lipped, "Well, at least they're not ruining another couple," this information still makes me feel slightly nauseous. There's always a part of you that hopes, when you break up with someone, that they cry for six weeks, then get on a horse and say, "No woman will ever be your equal. I am going to join the Crusades, and die for Christ in your name, you extraordinary creature."

Banging Camilla from Polydor is the exact opposite of that.

"I wish them both great joy," I say with dignity. "If they share things equally, that's an inch of penis each—enough for a sexual feast."

Actually, Tony Rich has a perfectly average-sized penis—but it is traditional, as soon as you break up with someone, to tell everyone they have a tiny penis. The impression you have to give is that, when you broke up, you took most of their penis with you. I presume it's an ancient, witchcraft thing. I can't argue with it.

Kenny is still laughing as I leave, thinking, *it's time for me to leave this place. The Queen would not put up with this.*

6

A week later, I went to the Good Mixer, to meet Zee. Zee
was already standing at the bar, and at the center of
some fuss, as usual. Zee does not drink alcohol—something
so unusual, in the nineties, that barmen across London were
regularly put into a tailspin by his presence.

As I draw level with Zee, and hug him, the barman is saying, in a borderline angry way, "What—you mean . . . just a
black currant? With nothing *in it*?"

"Yes—just a pint of Ribena, please," Zee says, blinking
anxiously. He hates to cause fuss or disturbance of any kind—
and, knowing how regularly problematic his nondrinking is,
he regularly asks if we can not meet in a pub. I have to tell
him, sadly, that that will never be possible, for the pub is the
citadel of all joy.

"Not even . . . a vodka?" the barman continues incredulously. "Just with . . . water? I mean, I don't even know what to *charge* you."

He fiddles around with the till, disgustedly. It appears there is no "pint of Ribena" button. He sighs—the deep, heavy sigh of a man who has been tested to the limits.

"Ten pence?"

Zee slides across a ten pence piece. Even though the barman has asked for it, he looks as if picking up such a small sum will degrade him.

"Thank you, thank you," Zee says, blinking, and taking a sip of Ribena. The barman is still agitated.

"I mean, it's not even worth getting the glass wet for ten pence," he continues to complain before turning to me. "What do you want?"

"Three shots of Jack in a pint glass, topped up with Coke," I say, briskly. This is my drink, "The Wilde." You can sip it like a pint, but it kicks like spirits. I am endlessly impressed with this invention.

"A proper drink, then," the barman says, pointedly, to Zee.

I carefully take my receipt, and put it in my special purse. I can claim all drinks "on expenses." This is one of many odd things about my life. I can get drunk for free—indeed, I travel around the world for free, interviewing bands—but I cannot afford new clothes, or "stuff," or a flat bigger than a medium-sized shed. I live a life in which luxuries are essentials, but practical things unaffordable. It lends an odd perspective. I essentially lead the life of a globe-trotting, drunken, yet bankrupt playboy.

We take our glasses to an empty table, and sit. I beam at

Zee. It's lovely to see him. I take a sip of my drink, which tastes—as the first drink always does—like the beginning of adventures, and light a cigarette which tastes—as the first cigarette always does—like the beginning of the conversation.

The late-summer sunshine is slanting, copper, through the windows—the open door lets the sound of the men from Arlington House, the homeless refuge, float in; they are sitting on the doorstep outside, arguing. Behind me, two members of Blur are playing pool. I feel a swell of love for London. It's always so busy being London. Oh, this is definitely the place for me.

"So—how are you?" I ask Zee. "Snazzy jumper."

"Yeah—it's another Mum Special," Zee says. Zee's mum gets him all his clothes. He's head-to-toe in Marks & Spencer's stuff she bought him in the sales. He's the only person I know who wears ironed clothes. She comes down every month, and does his laundry: "Don't argue with Iranian mums," he sighs.

We swap life news. For the last few months, Zee has been making gnomic statements about something he's doing, referring to it as "that thing," or "you know."

For a while, I just nodded—pretending I knew what it was even though I didn't. Then I found out that he was actually starting his own record label, but was too embarrassed to talk about it. This was mainly because the *D&ME* staff found it hilarious.

The last time I was in the office, Rob Grant greeted him with an, "Awlright, Richard Branson," as Zee shuffled in to file his copy. "You parked the balloon outside? You wanna watch the wardens on the double yellows. Don't wanna get a ticket for your blimp. That'll dent your trillions."

When it came to Zee's record label, the guys at the *D&ME* had the air of leisured gentlemen, horrified that an acquaintance has betrayed them, and gone into trade.

"Why the fuck would you want to make more records?" Rob would ask, casting a hand around the *D&ME* offices.

There were records everywhere you looked, piled on shelves, scattered across desks, heaped on the floor, nailed to the wall with "FUCK OFF" scrawled across them.

As if to prove his point, the postboy arrived at that moment, with another sack full of them.

"They're replicating, like fucking Tribbles," Rob continued, despairingly.

That afternoon finished, as many afternoons at *D&ME* did: with Kenny opening the windows, and skimming records out, one at a time, into the London sky, whilst Rob Grant shot at them with a BB gun.

"Fuck you, Yoghurt Belly! African Head Charge! Land of Barbara! Mr. Ray's Wig World! Huge Baby!" Rob screamed, as he pumped pellets into them, and they exploded over the Thames.

Zee, however, has continued in his quiet, determined way.

"How is Zee Records?" I ask.

"Still not called that. Still not called anything."

We spend ten minutes spitballing names for the label: "Unisex"; "Test Pressing" . . . I like "The Vinyl Solution" but Zee vetoes it. We order more drinks.

"So, what you up to?" Zee asks.

I don't want to explain that I'm trying, desperately, not

to go back to my flat, as my father and brother are getting stoned there, so I talk about work instead.

"Do you think the *D&ME* is a bit . . . blokey?" I say. "This time last year, it was all Riot Grrrl and PJ Harvey. This week, the *only* picture of a woman—in the entire paper—is of the *Titanic*."

Zee looks confused.

"All ships are female," I explain. He winces at the fact—and then, in a rare moment of insistence, leans across the table and says:

"And *this* is why you need to come and see this band tonight. I've just discovered them. I think I'm going to sign them. I think you'd like them," Zee says. "I think you'd like . . . *her*."

MAKING AN ENTRANCE is an underrated art. We throw the phrase around too casually—we use it about someone who has simply walked through a door. Most people just . . . walk through the goddamn door. But people who can really make an entrance walk in like they've just left the Napoleonic battlefield, or the Algonquin Round Table, or a Roman orgy, and stepped into your world. That only a second ago, they put down a sword, or a cocktail, or a man—and that, soon, they will return to them. Making an entrance is their *job*.

The rest of the band were already onstage: a drummer, who was just "the drummer," an identikit man who I would imagine even the band referred to as just "the drummer." On bass was a brown girl with a massive corona of hair, wearing Wellington boots and a yellow rain mac. She had the pissed-off air of Chris Lowe from the Pet Shop Boys—I enjoyed her anti-Britpop mardiness. She looked like, at any minute, she might look at her watch, sigh, and leave the stage. Her un-rock 'n' rollness was *very* rock 'n' roll. She and the drummer held down a basic, restless backbeat whilst we waited for the lead singer to arrive.

AND THEN—THERE SHE was. Cigarette in mouth, dressed in junk-shop glam—leopard-skin fur coat, pearls, thighs, blue suede boots—striding across the stage as if she were about to start a fight. As the band reached a fraught crescendo, she threw down her cigarette, brought the guitar round with a flourish, shouted "NOW!" and struck the opening chord.

"*That* is Suzanne Banks," Zee shouted into my ear.

Most people are built around a heart, and a nervous system. Suzanne appeared to be built around a whirlwind, kept trapped in a black glass jar. She seemed never to think before she spoke, took a drink, or opened a bottle of pills. She already seemed to be living three hours in the future. She was like a bomb that kept exploding, over and over.

I could feel that my mouth was open, like in a cartoon. I went right down the front, into the mosh pit, so I could be as near to her as possible.

"Good EVENING!" she roared. "We're The Branks, and we have three cool songs, two great ones, and three flaming shits. The trick is—can you tell which is which? I can't."

And, still laughing, she started singing.

Oh man. Ten seconds in, and I think she's the most brilliant thing I've ever seen.

WHEN THE GIG finished—enlivened, at one point, by Suzanne wading into the audience and punching a man on the side of the head who kept shouting "SHOW ME YOUR TITS!"—Zee said, "Shall we go and meet her?" and I said, "Absolutely."

We walked into the dressing room. I stood there for ten seconds, wondering what to do next—before Suzanne saw me, ran across, grabbed my hand, and roared, "Oh my God! You're Dolly Wilde! Dolly Wilde from the *D&ME*! Honey! I used to be AS FAT as you! The secret is—*don't eat cheese!*"

Within seconds, I realized that talking to Suzanne was like starting to watch a movie, twenty minutes in. Somehow, you've missed the vital first bit where all the characters are introduced, and the plot is established, and you get your bearings—and, instead, you joined when someone you'd never met was driving a car, backward, down a street, screaming, "Get in! We have to get those plans before midnight! Where's Adam?"

Suzanne never, ever started a conversation with a "Hello! How you doing?" or, "I see it hasn't stopped raining yet." It was always straight into Ragnarök.

"Dolly! Dolly come here!" Suzanne was, clearly, high on something. She put her arm around me, and hugged me into her bosoms. She was much taller than me. "We have to talk. We have a common interest. I heard we're Fuck Cousins!"

I had no idea what she was on about.

"I do come from a large extended family . . ." I began. "But my uncle . . ."

"No, no!" Suzanne bawled. "Fuck Cousins. We're related not by blood—but by jizz. I don't like to talk about it in public"—voice just as loud as it was before—"but I believe you have 'knowledge' of . . ."

And here she mouthed the words *Jerry Sharp*.

I don't know how she managed to do it, but she silently mouthed these words in what I can only describe as "a loud way." Several people turned to stare.

"Isn't he a dog?" she said, furiously. "A man-dog?"

"Yes?" I said, faintly, and quietly. "I have . . . been with Jerry Sharp. How do you know this?"

"Oh, he's a leaky vessel. He tells everyone. Don't worry. Everyone's slept with Jerry, baby," she said, taking a cigarette from my packet, and opening it. "He's like the Welcoming Committee for Likely Ladies. You can't get into London without having to push through his cock, like a turnstile. He's just *there*, waiting. Do you know who else he's had? Justine. Anna-Marie. Rachel."

I had no idea who these people were.

"How was he with you?" she asked solicitously. "Any freaky . . . stuff?"

She stared at me, intently. I'd only just met her, and I was in a room full of people—including Zee, who was so gentle and asexual, I'd always presumed that, if he had a penis, it was a knitted one—like his cardigans. I was not going to share the story of Comedian Sex Shame with this room. I shook my head.

"Come here," she hissed, and pulled me underneath the table. We sat.

"When I encountered *Mr. Sharp*," Suzanne said, "he took me back to his and tried to get me to watch his sitcom—while we fucked."

"He did that to me!" I say. "Me too! Oh my God! I can't believe this! What did you do?"

"Well, it's not my first rodeo with a pervert. I've been around the block a few times. *I'm twenty-five.*"

"Plus the VAT," a dolorous voice said. I looked up. Julia—the mardy bass player—was staring under the table.

"Shut up, Julia," Suzanne said.

Suzanne pulled her under the table, too.

"Dolly—Julia. Julia—Dolly."

I nodded to her. Julia had the tired, patient air of a zoo-keeper. Suzanne, clearly, was the livestock.

"For the purposes of rock 'n' roll, I am absolutely twenty-five," Suzanne clarified, as Julia, next to her, mouthed, "*Thirty-one.*"

"So what did you *do*?" I asked.

"What any sane woman *would* have done: I stood up, and gathered my fur coat around me, like a cloak of dignity, and said, 'I'm so sorry, I've just remembered I need to absolutely fuck off,' and left. Can you *imagine*?" Suzanne boggled at me. "Shagging while watching his *own show*! It's like Picasso trying to fuck you, whilst drawing an eye on your chin."

"Do you think he does that with everyone?"

"It's always the same type of girl he hits on," Suzanne said. "They've always just moved to London, they're ambitious, maybe don't know many people . . . they're always . . . *shiny*. The ones with a bit of moxie. The ones who are going places. He fucks them up, then . . . *eats their souls*. Jerry Sharp is a vampire."

"He's just a prick, Suzanne. You don't need to over-egg it," Julia said, sensibly.

"You agreed with me when I said this!"

"I wanted you to shut up. The whole top deck of that bus thought you were insane."

"It's true," Suzanne said, earnestly, to me. "The stories about vampires are true. They walk among us. Some men are into feet. Some men are into being sat on. And some men are into . . . making girls feel small. Fucking with girls. Shrinking girls. They huff their burning confidence like crack cocaine."

I thought back to the night I spent with Jerry. It was not . . . an equal sexual exchange.

Zee's head appeared under the table.

"Is there no such thing as *privacy*?" Suzanne roared. "This under-table area is *reserved*. For *women*."

Zee looked abashed.

"I'm so sorry," he said, "but I'd like to talk to you, Suzanne, if I may?"

"Do *you* have fuck gossip?" Suzanne asked. "Do *you* know any sexual vampires?"

"No," Zee said, looking very awkward, "but I think I'd like to offer you a record deal?"

If Suzanne was enlivened by gossip, talk of a record deal engaged her booster rockets. She pulled Zee under the table, and her body language constructed a secret booth that she and Zee were in, and in which a bright key light illuminated her whole face. She looked beautiful.

"Tell me more, Mr. Zeigfield. What's your *deal*?"

Zee explained, with much stuttering, that his record label was new, but offered a 50/50 deal to bands—"It seems only fair"—and that they had complete artistic control. As he ran Suzanne through the details, it occured to me that Zee wore his knowledge about music very lightly. In all my excited conversations with him about Erasure, or Crowded House, he'd never let on, for one second, that he knew any more about music than I did. He could have steamrollered me at any minute. Instead, he just listened to all my theories, and excitement, and joined in.

Oddly, because of this, I suddenly found him ten times more impressive than I did before. I'd never met anyone with "hidden depths" before. Everyone else I knew—my dad, John Kite, me—laid out the entire buffet of their personality straightaway; as if we had pork pies and cakes stapled to our chests. Zee, it seems, only brought it out if someone actually said they were hungry.

Mulling on the novelty of this, I crawled out from under the table to leave. Suzanne grabbed my arm.

"You're going?"

I looked at Zee. He clearly had much more to say.

"Yes."

"Thursday. Come to my house on Thursday. We're going to be friends," she said, as if this was something non-debatable. "Julia—give Dolly my address. I'm going to talk to The Man."

And she exited from under the table, and walked off with Zee.

"Do I have any say in this?" I asked Julia, as she wrote out Suzanne's address on a piece of paper. "Do I get to *choose* to be her friend?"

"No," she said, simply. "You've been chosen. In the words of Princess Leia to Luke—'Good luck.'"

I was still looking at the piece of paper—noting that Suzanne lived in Kentish Town, very near to me—when I heard her roar from across the room: "Dolly—we'll list every girl he's fucked! AND REMEMBER! *NO CHEESE!*"

7

There is an unspoken understanding that the person who's in a band is the social superior—even if they're in a band no one has heard of. It's something to do with the fact that they have formed a gang, and given it a name, and decided there are things they stand for, and things they don't. Suzanne is "Suzanne Banks, from The World of The Branks." I'm just . . . me, on my own. She literally out-branks me.

So it's quite awkward when I turn up, the next day, on her doorstep, for our appointment, as arranged, and—after I've rung on the doorbell several times—Suzanne opens the door, in her toweling robe, having clearly just been woken up, and looks at me like I'm insane . . . even though this was all her idea.

"Hello?" she says.

"You said to come round today? I am wearing my best Fuck Gossip Hat," I say. I point to my top hat, which—where the Mad Hatter has a ticket that says "10/6"—I've written, helpfully, "FUCK GOSSIP."

"Today—what day is today?" she asks, vaguely.

"Thursday," I remind her, helpfully.

"Thursday . . . Thursday," she says, as if Thursday is something she's heard about, happening to other people, but which she herself has not experienced.

"I bought a Rolodex," I say, bringing it out of my bag, by way of jogging her memory. "To alphabetize all the names? Of the people Jerry's fucked?"

In the early-morning Camden sunshine, holding out a Rolodex to file away sex stories seems very wrong.

"It was seventeen pounds ninety-nine," I add, by way of further information. "I can claim it, on 'business expenses.'" Suzanne looks pained.

"I think you need to go back to sleep . . ." I say, stepping backward. "Sorry. I'll see you around."

I start to walk away, but Suzanne emits a kind of "Gnargh" sound.

"No—come back. I guess I *should* do Thursday," she says, gesturing me through the door. "Come *in*; come *round*; come *on*," she adds—more to herself than anyone else.

I come into her front room and find Julia sitting at the table, eating a Tupperware container of dhal, and reading a book.

"Oh, hi," I say, slightly discombobulated.

Julia looks up.

"Hello," she says, in return.

"I didn't know you lived together!" I say, brightly. "At the gig, Suzanne called this 'her' house."

Julia stares at me, balefully.

"Well, she would, wouldn't she?"

"Sorry about ringing on the doorbell so many times," I say. "That must have been annoying."

"Julia never answers the door. It's never for Julia," Suzanne says, breezily. "I'm just going to get ready."

She disappears. Occasionally, we hear her shout something from her room—"Make yourself tea!" "Get cigarettes from the corner shop!" "Answer the door, would you?" and "My God—all my pores have opened up. They look like the mouths of fucking *baby clams*"—whilst Julia studiedly ignores me.

I try. "Do I detect a . . . Midlands accent?" I say, brightly, after the first, silent minute, as Julia continues to eat, and turn the pages of her book. "Because—I'm from Wolverhampton!"

"I'm so sorry about that," Julia replies, which is a very Midlands thing to say. After another minute of silence, she adds, possibly out of pity, "Yes. You *are* correct in detecting a Midlands accent. I am from Kidderminster."

"Kiddy! Posh!" I say, which is the traditional Midlands thing to say about people from Kidderminster.

"Yeah—everyone says that," Julia says, still not looking up from her book. "But if you think about it, Kiddy's exactly like Wolvo, but with a river. And a river isn't *innately* posh, is it? It's just . . . nature's drain."

"I hadn't thought of rivers like that before," I concede.

As Julia makes it very clear she doesn't want to talk, I amuse myself by looking around the flat, instead—it's clearly been decorated by Suzanne.

The walls are painted teal, an unusual color in those days—"I had to get it mixed up by a guy in the theater," she told me, later—and everywhere there are piles of old *Vogues* from the 1950s and '60s, delicate silk Chinese fans, embroidered shawls, and beat-up volumes that seem to encompass Suzanne's two favorite things: Romantic poetry, and radical feminist classics. Keats and Yeats battled for space with Valerie Solanas's *SCUM Manifesto* and Andrea Dworkin. The combination has the effect of overripe lush excess—like a perfect peach, in the first hour it turns, and starts to decay.

It immediately becomes my ideal of how a grown woman's house should be. It feels like Suzanne instinctively homed in on the most pure, extreme things. There is nothing make-do, and plain, in the house—no cheap beige mugs from the market, or a normal cushion from BHS. Everything has weight, history, purpose, impact. Everything means something.

I rapidly compile a list of neat touches I will steal for my flat—the beaded rose-colored veils over the lamps; the photo of an old lady hitting a Nazi with her handbag—when Suzanne roars from her room, "JULIA! Where are my BLUE PILLS?"

"On your dressing table," Julia says at a normal volume.

"JULIA! Where are my BLUE PILLS?" Suzanne roars again. "My TRIANGULAR BLUE PILLS?"

"ON. YOUR. DRESSING. TABLE."

There's the sound of enormous crashing and bashing—as if many things are being overturned—and then Suzanne finally emerges, fully painted, in jodhpurs, riding boots, ornate Victorian blouse, and ratty sheepskin coat. She looks like Virginia Woolf, managing a football team. She's just . . . good at clothes. Clothes liked her. She can make them look funny and hot at the same time. It's an amazing trick.

"I can't *find* them. I'm taking the red ones, instead," Suzanne says, eating the pills in her hand.

"Oh, Christ," Julia sighs.

Suzanne swallows them with a flourish.

"Phase One completed. Now—Phase Two," she says, starting to make coffee in a stove-top pot, and lighting a cigarette.

I never found out exactly what all these pills were—the "blue triangular ones" were her favorite, and made her gracious, and tactile, and there were small red ones that made her "lively," and some white-and-yellow ones that seemed to have a random, lottery effect on her moods, which certainly added an extra pep to the day. When I found out that Suzanne's mother was American, it all made sense. Americans, I had noticed, love prescription pills. Suzanne had inherited her love of pills from her mother—like a chin, or a religious inclination.

"So, *you'll* get this," she says, sitting down, drinking the coffee, and dragging on her cigarette. "My whole thing is, I want to write songs for *ugly* girls."

I don't quite know how to take this. I see Julia roll her eyes, and bury herself deeper in her book.

"Have you noticed how all songs about girls are written about beautiful girls?" she says. "All of them. They're all fucking mesmerizing; they all walk into a room and light it up; they've all got fucking . . . charm. But girls like that don't need songs written about them. The whole fucking *world* is writing songs about them. Give them a break. Leave them alone. Write songs about the ugly girls—*they're* the ones who need them. And that's what *I'm* gonna do. I want to make biffers swagger. I wanna make terrible skanky whores strut. I'm gonna come and get these girls, and mind-fuck them to glory. I'm going to *lead the charge*."

It's ten past one, on a Thursday. I don't think ten past one on a Thursday expects this kind of speech. I certainly hadn't. But all the hairs are standing up on my arms.

"Look at all the women wanking themselves silly over Gerard Depardieu," Suzanne continues. "He's a fucking hog of a man! A HOG! So why's he sexy? I'll tell you why: because he's famous. Put an ugly face on a million posters and, suddenly, this ugly guy's got currency. *Awwww, Depardieu,* we go, the fiftieth time we see him. *I have become fond of your face!* Because he's famous—because we see him every day. *Men have a bigger lexicon of what is hot.* He's hot now! With a face that *literally* looks like someone drew some eyes on a cock and balls! No plastic surgery or self-loathing for men who look like Gerard Depardieu! They're beating off the fanny with a stick. So, that's what *we* have to do. Women. We have to make ugly girls famous, too. Increase *our* lexicon. We've got to make lady-trolls as hot as man-hogs. Famous is the shortcut to power. It's how you hot-wire the revolution. I'm gonna make lady-hogs *sexy*. And then—because there's more of us . . . because we've got the numbers—the ugly girls are going to *take over the world*."

I look at Suzanne. I guess you could call her "ugly"—a word I wince to think, let alone say, because it, along with the word "fat," is used so often as a weapon, it puts my nerves on edge to hear it used as a simple descriptor. But she *is* ugly—her nose looks like it should have a Roman centurion's helmet pressing down on the bridge, and her eyes are, now I look closer, quite small: it is the cunning, theatrical application of makeup and lashes that make them seem intense, and stare-y. She has wide shoulders, and huge feet, and the faint trace of a harelip operation, from nose to lipstick. In short, she's not the kind of woman a small girl would draw as a princess.

And yet, she's so fucking fizzy and delicious, I want to swim around in her innards, like a dolphin.

"How are you going to do it?" I ask.

Suzanne gives a dramatic pause—one that has all the hallmarks of having been rehearsed many times, and being even more enjoyable because of it.

"Be the change you want to see. *I am the revolution.* Make me famous, and *you fuck up the world.* I'm—*Ugly Jesus.* Do you know why we're called 'The Branks'?"

"No."

" 'The branks' was a scold's bridle they used to put on women, in Scotland. To stop them speaking," she explains. She pauses. "So it's the best fucking band name *ever.*"

Suzanne is the biggest fan of Suzanne. It's oddly endearing.

She looks up at the clock.

"Oh my God—it's two! The revolution has to go to *work.*"

"What work?"

"Publicity," Suzanne says. "Julia. Come."

She applies lipstick with her cigarette still in her mouth—something I've never seen before (nor since).

"It's my day off," Julia complains.

"The revolution doesn't have a day off!" Suzanne shouts.

"I'm not the revolution," Julia replies. "I do admin for the revolution. I was doing it until two this morning. Now, I am enjoying my leisure."

Suzanne flings the front door open, and stands dramatically in the doorway.

"JULIA!" she barks. "COME!"

Julia sighs, puts a dosa in her pocket, and follows Suzanne out of the door.

WE SPEND THE next two hours walking around Camden. The market's in full flow, and—in 1994—at the height of its freaky powers. Here is all the detritus of England's lost empire, piled high: crinolines, gramophones, army surplus, ball gowns from coming-out parties—along with its current, edgy, black-market economy: bongs, bootleg CDs, and dealers selling either hash, or Oxo cubes, depending on your guile and/or luck. And, flowing through it: boys in greatcoats; girls in petticoats and ratty fur stoles; Goths; greboes; skaters; indie kids in stripey tights; and the newly forming Britpop massive, in their Adidas, and wooden necklaces.

"What are we doing?" I ask Suzanne, who is sitting on the bridge, smoking a cigarette, and surveying them all.

"Finding my people," she says, suddenly sliding off the bridge, and approaching a girl with sea-green hair.

"Hello!" she says, brightly. "Might I say how *greatly* I appreciate your look?"

The girl smiles at her—happy, but confused.

"Thanks?" she replies.

"May I ask what you've come here to find today?" Suzanne asks.

"Well, I'm just browsing . . ." the girl starts.

"Because—you've just found it," Suzanne continues, taking the girl's hand, and pressing something onto it.

The girl is so surprised, she says nothing, and just looks down at her hand. On the back of it, there is now stamped, in ink, the legend: "This girl belongs to The Branks. 12/9/94. 9 p.m., Electric Ballroom, Camden."

"We're The Branks. You're welcome," Suzanne says, with a flourish.

The girl's still staring at her hand.

"That's our next gig. In two weeks. Come! Tell your friends! Tell your friends to come!"

Suzanne starts to walk away.

"Hey! What are The Branks?" the girl shouts after her.

"*The rest of your life!*" Suzanne shouts back, without turning round.

We spend the next hour doing this: searching for likely-looking girls—the ones with piercings; Day-Glo hair; Doc Martens; fat; eyeliner; hungry, fizzing eyes—and stamping their hands with The Branks' tattoo flyer.

Some protest—"What are you doing?"—to which Suzanne replies, variously, "You can't fight an unstoppable force!," "When I'm famous, you'll tell everyone about this!," or, tetchily, to those who protest the longest, "It's just ink, for fuck's sake—it'll wash off. Don't be such a pussy."

"It was Julia's idea," Suzanne explains at one point—as we stand by the entrance to the Stables, scanning the crowd. "Instead of paper flyers."

"I hate litter," Julia says, shortly. "It clogs up drains. Causes localized flooding."

I nod, and make a mental note of this: Julia fears localized flooding.

I'm still digesting this when I notice Suzanne is caught up in a contretemps, several yards ahead.

Julia and I jog to catch up with her, and find her surrounded by four lads—two in Oasis tops—arguing with her.

"Why are you doing *just* the women?" one's asking.

"Yeah—*we* want your stamp. What's it for?" the other chips in.

They have that always-dangerous air of young men with nothing to do, looking for reasons to get chippy. Like open-mouthed baleen whales, sieving the whole ocean for a spoonful of grief.

"It's a women-only gig, I'm afraid," Suzanne says, cheerfully. "No stamps for you."

"There shouldn't be things for just women. We're all equal. Having things just for women is *sexist*," the shorter one says, smugly. "Are you *sexist?*"

"Oh, yes—I'm *definitely* sexist," Suzanne says, beaming.

This throws the short one. "So, you hate all men, then?" he says, clearly confident Suzanne will say no.

"Well, I've not met *all* of them yet," Suzanne says, reasonably.

The taller one takes a step forward, and opens his mouth to continue the argument. Sighing, Suzanne takes a small red klaxon out of her rucksack, and presses the button. The volume makes my tongue swell, and my eyes bulge—it was a proper, honking weapon.

Camden grinds entirely to a halt—staring at her.

Eventually, she lets go of the button. The dying echoes seem to slide down the walls.

"Pub?" she says, turning on her heel, and walking toward the Mixer.

"Why did you . . . ?" I start to say.

"No conversation with cunts, baby," she says, not breaking her stride. "No conversation with cunts."

8

But sometimes there *are* conversations with cunts.

"I don't understand."

It's 3:00 a.m., and John is on the phone. From Poland, I think.

"Am I a cunt? Is John a cunt?"

John is half-drunk, and I am half-awake—so, intellectually, we're both equally poorly equipped to deal with this question.

"I mean, did I fuck this guy's wife without knowing? Have I run over his child? Have I missed my own, terrible abomination?"

Yesterday, the new *D&ME* came out, and in it was a massive interview with John, conducted by Tony Rich. As Rich had promised in the editorial meeting, he has a "few ideas" about John's recent success, and new audience. Those ideas, it turns out, are based around the opinion that John is a cunt.

The piece started with brisk hatred, and then continued in that vein for another two thousand words. "It's always interesting: finding out which 'artists' insist they are in it for the music, maaaan—here to push boundaries, blow our minds, shake things up, or just speak from the depths of their broken heart, but who will abandon it all in a second when they hear the rattle of a teenage girl's piggy bank. Two short years ago, when John Kite was the shambling, revered chronicler of the darkest part of the night, who could have guessed that, in 1994, he would be putting out singles that made R.E.M.'s 'Shiny Happy People' sound like Skin's *Shame, Humility, Revenge*, and causing teenage girls to cream their jeans when he appears on *Top of the Pops*?"

The basic premise is that John is a craven, opportunistic arsehole who has sold out.

"You were really onto something, man," Rich writes, at one point. "We all thought you were the real deal—that the prize you were jumping for was to be this decade's Tim Buckley, Nick Drake, Mark Eitzel. Instead, it turns out, you just wanted to be this decade's Herman's Hermits."

John is surprisingly hurt by all of this. I'd always thought that he was pleasingly distanced from the barroom sniping of the music press—"They're just comics for kids who can't get laid"—but then, he was always their darling before. Now they've turned on him, I can see, for the first time, how, underneath all the Hemingway-esque bluster of the cigarettes, whisky, fur coats, and signet rings, he's just an indie kid from

Wales who grew up on these magazines, and can't understand why they've suddenly rejected him.

"Do they know how hard it is to write pop songs?" he rages, at one point. "Everyone's trying to. Ask fucking Kevin Shields from My Bloody Valentine, or fucking Public Enemy. They're all just trying to write a pop song. Public Enemy are pop, anyway. Everyone can sing 'Fight the Power.' It's popular! That's a pop song! The Dewey decimal system would file it under pop!"

He sighs, and says, "I don't get it. I thought they would be— haha!—oh God. I thought they would be . . . *proud* of me."

He's clearly embarrassed he's said it, so I ask him what his room's like to change the topic.

"Booked before I sold out, honey—crappy brick thing, by a motorway, a literal whole mad sausage in the fridge. It would be better with you here."

"Not for me," I say, cheerfully, whilst filing this comment away in the treasure box in my head where I file every lovely thing John has ever said to me. My plan is that when this hits one hundred quotes, I will say them all back to John, and end it with, "Look! One hundred compliments! This means you're in love with me! Here is the inventory of all your unrealized love!"

The thing is, as soon as I read Tony's piece, I knew exactly what he was doing: he was using John as my whipping boy. Tony is exactly the kind of peevish, spiteful man who would publicly eviscerate a man's career, just to get at a woman who once sexually rejected him. I have been John's cheerleader— and so, now, in the quiet, cold war between Tony and me, John must be taken down, as a strategic stronghold. This kind of thing happens all the time in the music press—it's such a small, incestuous world that the magazines are often used by way of a dead letter box, for writers to codedly snipe at each other, in front of eighty thousand bewildered readers. Tony's not even being subtle about this effort: one paragraph talks of "a certain kind of teenage girl—the loud, attention-seeking, drunken ladette on the night bus, pock-marked with love bites, desperately name-dropping titles of books she read and did not understand, in the hope of impressing boys who are secretly horrified by her. Perhaps you know a girl like that—eh, readers?"

I can't help but feel that the unspoken last line of this Kite feature might be "Receipt for sexual rejection, issued to: Dolly Wilde. Account now closed."

John's starting to sound sleepy, so I wind up the conversation.

"Anyway, sorry to bore you, babe," he says, as we make our final good-byes, and arrange to meet when he gets back, and send each other our love, "but it's just: what if I *am* a cunt?"

And then the man who had made twenty-six hundred people that night sing, and cry, and feel better about the world, rings off.

I sit there for a while, burning with fury that my editor—Kenny—had let Tony put in that reference to a girl like me. Tried to *shame* me—*at work*.

I smoke a cigarette, and then write a fax, to Kenny.

"Surely the point of an editor is to edit out internecine hissy fits, posing as journalism?" I write. "Tony Rich has essentially used a national publication like a toilet wall, to write 'Dolly Wilde is a slag.' Am I now supposed to reply with a two-thousand-word feature on Pulp—half of which is a covert rebuttal, accusing him of being a dirty old man who shags teenage girls? Is this how it works?"

In the morning, the reply has scrolled through: "Personally, I would find that deeply amusing."

I know the exact smirk he would have worn when he wrote that. I ring him.

"Kenny!" I say, when he answers. "I want to work somewhere where I'm not being semi-harassed in print. Is that possible?"

"I'm afraid we are as we are, Wilde. This is the way of my people. If you can't take the heat, get out of the bitching."

"Are you asking me to resign?"

"Are you offering to?"

And I was so angry, I replied, "Yes."

9

So that was early Friday morning. On Saturday morning, I realized something quite important.

I was on the phone to Krissi, who'd gone back to Manchester. We were doing our usual thing of watching *Live & Kicking* together, whilst eating cereal. This was our Saturday morning routine.

We'd just been analyzing Trev and Simon doing "The Singing Corner" again—it was a particularly good one—when a thought struck me:

"Kriss?" I say, chewing on cornflakes and chopped-up banana. "I think Dad's . . . moved in with me."

I looked out of the window. Dad was in the garden, digging a vegetable patch.

"You wanna get your broad beans in now," he'd said, going out there at 8:00 a.m. "It always pays to be self-sufficient, babe. The breakdown of civilization is always around the corner, heh heh heh. And who will survive? The working-man, who knows how to graft for himself. Peasant skills. That's what you need. Get your veg in."

I enjoyed that this ode to working-class self-sufficiency was delivered whilst he held a spade he'd stolen from my posh next-door neighbors.

When Krissi left, four days ago, my father notably declined to go with him. He said he wanted to hang around to "do a couple of little things around the house. Help out my lovely daughter!"

He'd fitted a huge bolt to the front door, "for security," but used screws that were too long, so they jutted out and kept snagging my tights. He'd noticed the rug in the hallway kept rucking up, and nailed it down—thus almost certainly invalidating my tenant's agreement; run an illegal secondary phone line to my bedroom, "So you don't have to get out of bed to tell people to fuck off, heh heh heh"; and made a "coffee table" for the front room by stealing an empty wooden cable reel out of a skip, knocking most of the spiders off it, and rolling it into place, in front of the sofa.

It was now very difficult to reach the sofa. You had to kind of climb over the cable reel to get to it. Also, the surviving spiders have now taken up residence in the top left-hand corner of the room, in a terrifyingly large complex of webs. It means I have to keep them in awkward visual contact at all times when I'm over there, turning the TV on—in case they want to do that spider thing of jumping onto me, and burrowing into my hair. This is why I'm generally not going in the front room, anymore. That, and the fact my dad's sleeping on the sofa, naked.

This is a sad return to a persistent trope of my childhood—being haunted by my dad's knackers. One of the main things I was looking forward to, about leaving home, was never again seeing my father's genitals, resting in his lap like a sad, furless Bagpuss. But here they are again. Will I ever be free of them? My father's balls are the albatross around my neck. Why must I always be confronted with the place from which I sprang? Can I never leave my roots? Is this a gigantic metaphor for being working class?

When I asked him if he could, maybe, borrow and wear one of my nighties—they're roomy!—he replied, "Nah, kid—I sweat a lot"—an unnecessary comment, as the room reeked of his Guinness sweats.

On hot mornings, there was a palpable miasma. Like the kind of mist you get in rain forests. It made you feel drunk, to walk into it. It left a Turin Shroud–like imprint of his body, on the sofa.

"It's just occurred to me," I say to Krissi now, watching Dadda lean on his spade, and smoke a fag. "He's not actually leaving . . . he's starting to *cultivate*. That's not a man who's leaving, is it? A cultivator? He's planning a spring harvest."

"This is his midlife crisis, Johanna," Krissi says, spitefully. "He's left Mum for a younger woman. You."

"Shut up."

"Not in a sexual way—he just wants you to look after him."

"SHUT UP!"

"You're his . . . Sugar Baby."

"KRISSI STOP IT."

"Johanna, I know you're not going to like this—"

"No!"

"—but you know what you have to do—"

"No!"

"You're going to have to talk to Mum."

TEN MINUTES LATER—AFTER bracing myself by listening to the Pixies' "Debaser" three times in a row—I ring my mother, from the illegal phone in the bedroom, so my dad can't hear.

"Oh, Johanna. To what do I owe the honor?" she says, in her usual, needling way. It's a weird thing she has—always wanting you to ring her, but then making you feel bad when you do. I don't understand it. When people I like call me, I scream "HELLO HELLO HELLO HELLO!" at the top of my voice. I like the start of a phone call to feel like the start of a party—not the start of a landmark case at the European Court of Guilt.

"How are you?" I ask, deciding to get all the heavy work out of the way at the beginning of the conversation.

She tells me that she still feels depressed; Lupin's being "a pain"; the twins have moved on from the "terrible twos" and are now in the "feral fives"; her feet hurt "all the time," even with her new special sandals; the washing machine is "erratic"; and that she's still angry about Sue Lawley presenting *Desert Island Discs*: "She's too severe, Johanna. It's like she's put them on that island on purpose."

"Did you get my last check?" I ask. I am sending Mum a check for £50 a month, to help out. It means I can't afford to buy any new clothes, but, as my mother once pointed out, "You might as well save the money for when you've lost weight, and can buy something nice."

The first time she said that to me—when I was thirteen—I decided to get anorexia, to make her feel bad. I lasted until 6:00 p.m. It was baked potatoes for tea. I love baked potatoes.

"Yes," she says, and doesn't mention it again. I cut to the chase.

"So . . . Dad. How are you and . . . him?"

"Well, as you know, Johanna, things have been changing," she says, sounding aggrieved.

"Yes," I say. "Changing. Yes. Changing. I couldn't help but notice that . . . he's still here, with me."

"Hmmm," she says. Nothing else. She waits for me to say something.

"And, uh, I didn't . . . know? He was going to stay here?"

"It's just your dad. Why wouldn't you want your dad there? He's helping, isn't he?"

She knows! She knows about this! This was a plan!

"The thing is . . ."

The thing is, I don't want him here. I went to the entire trouble of getting a whole other building I could live in so I could finally do what I want, when I want, with who I want, without anyone else being around. Last night I came back from a gig around midnight and turned on the shower, to shower off all the fag smells—in the nineties, everyone smokes at gigs: going to one is like moshing for two hours inside a blazing humidor—and he poked his head out into the hallway, hair all sticking up, and said, "I've got the boiler right next to my head, Johanna, and it's making a racket. You want to save it till morning?"

And I did! I just sprayed myself with Chanel No. 5—John Kite's Christmas gift to me; which I pretend is his love, in a bottle—in order to be halfway palatable to myself, and went to bed, all rancid.

Nick Kent did not throw himself under all that heroin so that music journalists would live like this.

"This is what families do, Johanna," my mother says, firmly.

"I literally don't know a family that has done this," I reply. "None."

"Well, that's a judgment on them, isn't it?" my mother says, tartly. "It's good to know we're better than everyone else."

I realize now I've made a fundamental error—I should have taken a pad and pencil, and spent an hour preplanning this phone call: trying to guess every single thing my mother would say, and preparing for it. I should have been like Bobby Fischer, researching the playing technique of Boris Spassky for months, before ever entering this contest. I've been outplayed, in under a minute, and on my phone bill. I am a fool.

"Do you know how . . . long . . . I will have to be better than everyone else?" I ask, knowing these are already the dying throes of a match my mother has won.

"Well, that's down to how good you are at talking to your father," my mother says, before lobbing in a few more complaints about the next-door neighbors ("Their garden gives me hay fever"), and ringing off.

AFTER ANOTHER TEN days of living with my father, I did myself the favor of telling him I was off to review The Shamen in Belgium, and I was taking the dog with me.

"You can take dogs on planes?" he asked.

"It's Belgium," I replied, airily. He seemed to accept this.

I packed a rucksack, whistled for the dog, and walked to John's house, in Hampstead.

It was the middle of October, and nearly 70 degrees—one of those warm autumn days where the golden roar of the trees makes you feel like your planet has a sun that's dying with great aplomb. Really going out gloriously—like an old theatrical legend, descending the staircase, in red taffeta and tiger's-eye rings, holding a glass of claret, and singing "*Non, je ne regrette rien*" so sweetly, dying seemed magnificent.

I have three reasons for coming here. The first is, obviously, to get away from my father, as he's driving me absolutely insane. On the very first day he was here, he came into the front room, said, "And now it's over to Kelly with the weather!," lifted his leg, and farted. I wouldn't have minded, but I was doing a phone interview with Tori Amos at the time, and she was crying about her sexual assault, so it was entirely inappropriate.

The second—a not inconsiderable reason—is to go around John's flat, reverently picking up and putting down his things; memorizing what books he has on his shelves, so I can read them, too, and have the same memories as him, and sniffing anything that might smell of him: a combination of Rive Gauche, cigarettes, whisky, junk-shop coats, and sex.

This isn't sinister—although I do appreciate that any sentence that starts with "This isn't sinister" does, immediately, sound quite sinister. But he's actually, formally, legally asked me to "keep an eye" on the house, and surely the third job of a house sitter—after watering the plants, and piling up the post—is to keep the house feeling "lived-in," and homely. And what could make a house feel more lived-in than someone trailing around the house, full of unrequited love, and leaving a faint, greasy aura of adoration on the house owner's cups, jumpers, books, and records? I'm simply being a good friend.

The third is the biggest: to begin a new career. Having now resigned from the *D&ME*, I must move fast. My £200 overdraft limit is purely theoretical, and the unopened letters on the doormat are looking evermore unpleasant. I must now, quickly, be amazing. For cash.

Obviously, "be amazing" has broadly been my own, self-imposed remit for the last two years—but I've decided I need to do something specifically, pointedly, targetedly amazing now. Something big. I need to go up a level—because that is what John has done, and you always judge what is normal, or possible, in your own life by the lives of your peers. You want to stay on a vaguely even pegging with them—or else get left behind. That's what all the artistic movements are, really: a group of people, all egging each other on. Going, "Blimey. I didn't know you could get away with painting a melted clock. I now see I could totally paint an apple wearing a bowler hat. I'm on it. Let's *all* be the Surrealists!"

So—my plan. I've been thinking about John being famous, and how I've spent two years, now, observing the general serried ranks of the en-famed. I've noticed that fame appears to be a metaphysical world laid onto the corporeal world, in which all the rules are different, and which makes the famous the same, but not the same as everyone else. And what seems the most extraordinary thing, is that I've never read anything about this process. We all know about fame, and yet we do not: no one has ever written a simple guide to how you get famous, why you would get famous, the practical day-to-day consequences of belonging to this other category—a celebrity—and, most importantly, how simultaneously heartbreaking, yet funny, it is. Famous people are treated like gods—but gods that must regularly hide in cupboards, to escape fans. They are deities that must appear on childrens' TV shows, talking to puppets, or else pose on magazine covers, pretending a banana is a phone. At any one time, a thousand people could be in the pub, discussing why they hate a celebrity; whilst another thousand shake, or cry, just thinking about them. If you invented modern fame from scratch, now, and told people what it would consist of, they would think you were crackers.

But here we are now, at the end of the twentieth century, with thousands of famous people in the world, going around, famousing, and no one is picking it apart, and boggling at it, or trying to work out how it works. There is no fame dictionary, encyclopedia, or Haynes Manual. And I think the person who could write those things could be . . . me.

And the killer thing about this idea, which I already love, is that it would, tangentially, be about John. He has entered the world of fame, and what I will write will be by way of letters to him, in his loneliness and confusion—making him feel as if he has someone on his side, making sense of things. I will Paul his Corinthians. I'll Jiminy his Pinocchio. I'll be his candle on the water, like in *Pete's Dragon*. *This* is how I'm going to court him. I'm going to be a Fame Doctor.

In this world, by and large, men don't love girls for what

they do. They just love them because they're gentle, and beautiful.

Well, I am going to have to reinvent falling in love. I am not going to get John by being gentle, and beautiful—because I am not. Instead, I am going to *win* him through endeavor: I am going to invent the thing of "girls winning boys." I am going to write a series of pieces so funny, insightful, wise, and somehow hot that he will fall in love with me—just as his songs made me fall in love with him. This, now, is an *art battle*. He is my prose victim. I am going to use my talent to prove I am old enough, and wise enough to be with him. Suzanne might believe that art is all about revenge, but I believe art is about making someone fall in love with you. This is the big difference between us.

I sit at John's kitchen table, the dog curled up at my feet, take out my most treasured possession—my laptop; a whole month's wages, but it's the computer Douglas Adams uses, so I was compelled to buy it—light a cigarette, and start writing what is basically a letter to John, wherever he is. A cheerful missive, full of silent messages that only he will pick up on.

10

Ten Things I Have Noticed in Two Years of Interacting with Famous People

BY DOLLY WILDE

Since 1992, I have been meeting famous people. On average, I would say I meet two or three famouses a week. Some, I'm interviewing them—a surreal hour in a hotel, where you ask questions they don't want to answer, and you often get more excited about using their bathroom and seeing what products they have scattered on the sideboard (acne cream! and Valium! interesting!) than anything you bring back on your tape.

Other times, I'm just seeing famouses in the pub, or at parties—living in London means you are surrounded by famouses. They are like sheep, in Wales—just part of the ecology. This week alone, I saw Alan Bennett chaining his bicycle up outside Marks & Spencer, Graham from Blur banging a defunct hand dryer in the toilets of the Good Mixer, and *Men Behaving Badly* star Neil Morrissey standing in the rain outside an estate agent's window, smoking a fag and looking at a studio flat for sale in Belsize Park.

I hereby offer up all that I have noticed about famouses, in the last two years.

1.   Famous people don't have coats. No coats! Here's how the Hot Young Star from *EastEnders* explained it to me: "You get into a car to go to the premiere, so you don't need a coat. Then you do the red carpet, where a coat would obscure your outfit. And then you go into the venue, where you don't need a coat. At the end of the evening, another car drives you home. We don't wear coats. We wear cars." Famous people don't have coats. Don't buy them a duffel for Christmas. It won't get much use.

2.   Famous people are very short. Even the big action heroes. Arnold Schwarzenegger is actually 4'10". In person, he looks like a child made out of cricket balls. Walking into an A-list party, you will feel like some mad, spade-handed giant, apt to knock over tiny, famous Oompa Loompas. Most big premieres could be held in a playhouse, or shoebox. How many famous people can you fit in a Mini? Over a million. That's not even a joke. It's a fact.

3.   Famous people know all the other famous people. They might not have met them—but they all know each other. On entering a party, or gathering, and spotting another Famous they have no previous encounters with, they do "The Nod," which means, "I, A Famous, acknowledge you, another A Famous. We currently live in a shared reality different to that of everyone else in the room." Don't, as a non-Famous, try to "The Nod" A Famous. They will un-Nod you, jerking their head upward, and away, like a horse rejecting a snaffle: "Take your The Nod back." Only a Nod-er can become a Nod-ee.

4.   Despite being short, as discussed in (1), Famouses have huge heads. HUGE. This is not a metaphor— they genuinely have bigger heads. Often, on meeting A Famous, one has to repress an initial exclamation of "My God, you look just like Frank Sidebottom!" I have long pondered why this might be. I've decided it's because we live in a predominantly visual age—TV, movies, photo shoots—and natural selection genetically favors those with large, expressive heads, and bodies that generally don't "get in the way." If you, as a proud parent, have just given birth to a child that looks like an Easter Island statue, then congratulations! There's every chance that, in twenty-two years' time, they will be on the cover of a magazine!

5.   Famouses don't use names. They dispensed with them years ago. "Babe," "Man," "Darling," "Dude," "Boss" . . . they address everyone they know by some universal descriptor. This is because they meet so

many people, remembering names became impossible some years ago. If A Famous had to draw the Earth, in space, it would have an arrow pointing at it, with "7b babes live here." The only exception to this is when they refer to other Famouses, whom they invariably reference by their first names: "Bob," "Joni," "Bruce." This is confusing for you, and when you listen back to your interview, you hear yourself going, "Do you mean . . . Forsyth?" and them replying, "No— Springsteen." To which you say, "Oh yeah—that does make more sense. Because Bruce Forsyth did not record *Nebraska*. I knew that."

6. If you make a joke, they won't laugh. Ever. They merely reply, "That's funny," sometimes wonderingly, sometimes firmly. But never laughingly. This is particularly true of Americans. Comedians might reply, "Good bit," briskly. But none of them ever laugh. Don't bother trying to be funny. They don't have time for it. Their minds are elsewhere. Laughing at your joke would take up valuable time, plus upset the power balance.

7. They're all "working on a really exciting project!" they can't talk to you about yet. For the first two years, I presumed this was because of the parlous nature of creative collaborations, an unwillingness to put the cart before the horses, contractual wrangles, etc. Then, one night, I got a famous actor very drunk, and asked him again what his secret project was. "I'm getting a roof garden! It's going to be covered in jasmine! It's going to be amazing!"

8. If you unexpectedly get on with A Famous—an interview that turns into a drinking session, which turns into hailing a cab, then dancing, then ending back at their house, being confessional until 2:00 a.m.—you will go back, and write a piece about how you've found one of the few, real, unaffected, normal, grounded famous people. Someone who is a shining exemplar to all the rest; the watermark by which "remaining true to yourself" should be judged, in future. Two weeks later, the tabloids will be full of how this celebrity has just entered rehab, after realizing their drinking is out of control, and they are in the throes of a nervous breakdown. "Oh," you think. "That's why they were being fun. They were insane." Then you realize that how they acted on that night is how you act all the time. "Am I insane, too?" you wonder. "Do I need to go into rehab?" To which the answer is, "No. Because you're too poor to afford it. You must just do what Blanche from *Coronation Street* suggested, in the event of a nervous breakdown: stay at home, get drunk, and bite down on a shoe."

9. They're all terrified. Something happened in their childhood, or adolescence, that they're running from—that made them want to not be normal anymore; to defy fate; to supersede gravity—and they fear that, any minute, they'll run out of road, and be dumped back where they came from. When they lie down at night, they remember their tiny childhood beds—the sweat, the mildew, the fear—and the feeling of being trapped in a small town, and they can't

sleep. They know if they have to return there, it will be an admission of failure; they rejected and betrayed their families, and their hometowns, but now have to return, broken, with their tails between their legs. A former Famous. A failed Famous. Sad Icarus in the pub, aging, paunchy, bitter, and covered in wax. That is why they work, and work, and work.

10. Almost every time you meet A Famous, you walk away feeling sorry for them. You did not expect this. But you find you are not a jealous Salieri. You are relieved their life is not yours. You are glad you are not A Famous.

I read it through, when I finish it. I feel like I have written a letter to John that will both amuse him, and make him see I understand what his life is like now. I press save, treat myself to five minutes of looking at all of John's mugs, and trying to work out which one is his favorite—I think it's the biggest one: that seems very "him"—kiss the mug, and take the dog for a walk on the Heath.

11

"Why do you want to work for *The Face*?" the editor asks me.

It's a month later, and I've sent *The Face* my "What I've Learned About Famouses" piece, plus two other pieces, entitled, "In Defense of the Groupie: Why It's Actually Quite Sensible to Want to Fuck Famous People" and "Why I Would Not Like to Be Famous." These are the first three columns for what I hope will be a regular, monthly slot in the magazine. I have formulated a full plan, for the next part of my life, and am now dedicated to carrying it out. In order to get my new career, I have simply copied the tactics of a fellow, working-class writer, Keith Waterhouse, author of *Billy Liar*. I once read that, when he was a teenage journalist, he decided which newspaper he wanted to work for, and sent them a column, every day, in the post, with a covering note, that read, "This is what I would have filed for you today, if I worked for you." After six days, and six columns, they gave him the job.

As I can think of no better role model than Keith Waterhouse, this is what I have done, too. Except I've only written three columns, because I am more impatient than Keith Waterhouse. He was sixteen when he carried out his plan. I'm eighteen. Time's running out.

The editor is looking at the columns now, printed out, in his hands.

"Why do I want to work for *The Face*?" I repeat, leaning on his desk, casually. "Well, I'll level with you."

I've decided that, today, I am going to be channeling Brunhilde Esterhazy—the sexually confident, upfront lady cabdriver from *On the Town*. The one who keeps trying to get Frank Sinatra, as a sailor, into bed. She gets things done.

"I'm eighteen. I'm too old to work for *D&ME* anymore."

He is surprised—he laughs. It's a good laugh.

"Also, I slept with someone there, which was an error. Then I noticed how sexist they were, which was a bummer. On top of the error and the bummer, they slagged off a friend of mine, and so I had to resign in a spectacular manner. Ordinarily, one would then simply live off one's parents for a while, but it currently costs *me* fifty quid every time I speak to my mother, and my father appears to be in the eye of some mental storm, and has just moved in with me in order to smoke weed, and breed spiders. As you can see, these are all excellent motivators to seek employment at the best magazine in the world."

This is true—that *The Face is* the best magazine in the

world. In the nineties, it simply means "Everything that is cool this month." Everything that is not in *The Face* is, however hard it tries, not quite as cool as something that *is* in *The Face*.

Because of this, I was excited to be in the office—and, also, intimidated. I am used to the *D&ME*, which basically felt like a pub, full of people in jeans and band T-shirts, mooching around.

This, by way of contrast, actually *is* an office, and everyone in it is much better dressed than at *D&ME*. They are wearing trainers I can tell are rare—mainly because, every so often, someone comments on someone else's trainers— "Nice. Where from?" "New York"—and sporty, zip-up jackets, and . . . colorful things. There are *women* here—*five* of them. And they're all a lot younger than the staff of the *D&ME*, and have actual "haircuts," rather than "just some hair."

This has been my one big worry about potentially working for *The Face*—that I don't look like the kind of person who works for *The Face*. I still have no money to buy clothes— which is a moot point, as the shops don't sell things that would fit me anyway. Dorothy Perkins—the unofficial National Outfitters of Teenage Girls—only goes up to a size 14. I don't know what size I am, but it's not a 14. I've never even tried to put on something in Dorothy Perkins, as they have communal dressing rooms, which work by way of a booth into which you can enter, in order to give yourself intense and immediate suicidal feelings.

Recently I have adopted the motto, "If you can't fit in, fit OUT." This means wearing things that make it very, very clear I'm not even trying to look like everyone else. As a consequence, today I am wearing a floor-length, red-and-gold-sequinned sari skirt, bought at a jumble sale in Wolverhampton for 50p, a black polo-neck jumper, a leopard-skin fake-fur jacket, and my forehead is covered in stick-on bindis, as sported by Björk on the cover of *Debut*. I look like the drag queen Divine, trying to get cast in a Bollywood movie.

"So—what's it been like, at the *D&ME*?" the editor asks, conversationally. "Had any good trips?"

This throws me. At *D&ME*, the drugs of choice are beer, very cheap speed, spliff, and, if there's a generous press officer around, cocaine. Most conversations the men have are about hangovers, or how much their teeth hurt, from taking speed. But this is, clearly, a place where the Big Drugs are used. I feel like I need to explain myself.

"My father always said I had exactly the wrong personality for acid," I say, truthfully. "He used to be a dealer, and when I was eleven, he told me I must never, ever touch it. 'You think you're taking acid—but the acid takes you,' he said. 'You get caught in a silent scream.' So I've never had a trip, no. But I think if you've got a very vivid imagination, you don't need to? I can *imagine* anything. Like, policemen on horses—they're basically centaurs, aren't they? When you think about it. Protests are policed by heroes from Narnia. I think I'd like Ecstasy, though. That seems to have a favorable reputation."

There's a pause.

"I meant, have you gone on any trips, *abroad*?" the editor says, faintly. "Tokyo? New York? To interview someone?"

"Oh, no," I say, cheerfully. "I've been to Dublin—that was

nice. And I like Manchester. All journeys north and west are exciting, aren't they? But the farther east you go, the more boring it gets. Norfolk is just . . . a sugar beet farm."

I decide I should stop talking at this point, mainly because the editor looks completely confused, if amused.

"Dolly, if I may, I'm just going to have a quick chat, with some colleagues," the editor says, standing up.

"Before you do, can I do my one-minute pitch?" I say, sensing that a decision is close to being made, and I might have fatally confused things with my drug chat. "I work hard, and I work fast, and promise you that, if you take me on, I will file, early, every month, and every piece will make you laugh at least three times—or you can fire me. And, ah, I won't sleep with anyone here. Unless it seems like a very good idea. That's a thing I've learned. I'm very . . . learned."

"Right," the editor says. "I'll bear that in mind. Back in a minute."

He goes over to a colleague at a far desk, and starts having an intense conversation with him. I see the colleague look over at me, and so I quickly arrange my face into an expression which I hope conveys that I am full of great words. I am later told that, at that moment, I looked as if I was suddenly very hungry. To be fair, I was. Dadda had eaten the last of the cereal that morning. When I got to the packet, there was only cornflakes dust left, which turned to gummy corn paste when I added milk. And the milk was off, anyway. So it was all for the best, really.

The colleague starts reading the columns the editor has given him, and I cross all my fingers, and toes, and legs, and say "white rabbit, white rabbit" to myself, over and over—

because if the first thing you say, on the first day of each month, is "white rabbit," you get to make a wish, and I have been saving up all my white rabbits since July. I have a rabbit farm of wishes.

After thirty seconds of reading, he laughs, and looks up at me again, and smiles, and gives a tiny nod, and I sigh, and uncross my legs, and quietly think to myself, "I think you might be able to buy some cornflakes on the way home—to celebrate. Maybe even Crunchy Nut!"

"Let's go to the Groucho," the editor says, when he comes back. "Knock a few ideas around. We're intrigued. I want to hear more about you."

12

On an already amazing day, this is the exploding cherry on the cake. I know about the Groucho Club. I had read a piece about it in *The Sunday Times Magazine*, when I was thirteen—it was a ground plan of the club, like a map, showing all the tables, and who sits where: the table by the bar is Stephen Fry's; Emma Thompson likes the one in the middle; Melvyn Bragg prefers the corner banquette. If London is the center of Britain, then the Groucho Club is the center of London. The shiny brass hub. The pivot. It's where "everyone" goes. I had that map on my wall for years—planning which table *I* would sit at, if I went. *When* I went. For you had still not arrived in London until you went there. And now, finally, I am here.

It's 4:00 p.m. on a Tuesday afternoon. Quiet, but buzzy.

The bar gleams like the bar on the *Titanic*. There's a piano, where a man is playing "Life on Mars," gently. Another man is propped up on the piano, singing along. It's Keith Allen. I save this up, in my head, to tell Krissi. We have watched all the *Comic Strip* films. Keith Allen!

A small, dark man in a zebra-print suit greets the editor.

"Bernie!" the editor says.

"Darling, all the usual cunts are here," Bernie says, by way of greeting. "I've kept the scratters out of *your* place, though."

He seats us by the window, and I try to look legendary while he gets the drinks. The editor seems to know half the people here. I think how wonderful it would be if *I* knew people here—walking in, like Norm from *Cheers*, and being all like, "Evening, everyone," to which the bar would reply, "Norm!"

"So, let me run you through a couple of things," the editor says, "about working for *The Face*. I've heard what it's like at *D&ME*, and things are a little . . . *different* with us."

"Okay," I say, taking a pen out of my bag, and assuming an air of diligence. "I am ready for instruction."

"Well, I don't know how to put this, but you can't just . . . make stuff up. You have to do your research. Like, in this piece on 'Why I Would Not Like to Be Famous,' you've referred to an ELO song called 'Bruce.' There is no ELO song called 'Bruce.'"

"There is!" I say, indignantly. "You know! 'Don't bring me down, Bruce!'"

"That's called 'Don't Bring Me Down,' Dolly," the editor says. "Do you not fact-check your pieces?"

I laugh. "How would someone do that?" I ask, like he's asked me to write it in pieces of fruit.

"In the reference library?" he says, astonished. "You would check your facts in the reference library of the magazine?"

"Reference library of the magazine?" I repeat, confused. Some dim memory stirs in my head. Actually, I think we *did* have a reference library at *D&ME*, but it was a badge of honor to never go in there. It's where Rob kept all the spare booze.

"I think I have been brought up in a journalistic environment where facts are . . . malleable," I confess. "Kenny says he never tapes an interview—he just 'remembers the good bits.'"

The editor winces, hard. In 1992, *The Face* published a feature on pop star Jason Donovan, which insinuated, incorrectly, that he was gay. The subsequent libel case nearly closed the magazine. Facts have been painful at *The Face*.

"But I'm totally on board with facts now!" I say, cheerfully. "I will fact you! I will be absolutely factual at all times!"

It's just as I have made this unbending vow of journalistic integrity when I hear someone say, "Well, that's an offer no man can refuse."

I turn around, and see Jerry Sharp. The editor stands, and shakes hands with him. I stand too.

"Jerry!" the editor says. "Hello, fella!"

Everyone called everyone "fella" in 1994.

"Long time no see! Jerry—this is Dolly Wilde. She's generously considering becoming our new columnist," the editor says, charmingly.

"I know Dolly," Jerry says, kissing my cheek. "I've had that pleasure. So glad to hear she will fact *you*."

I can't help myself—I go red when he says it. Looking

around, I can see Jerry's presence has caused a small stir here. Several people are curiously checking out the fat, hat-wearing teenage girl he is talking to. That fat, hat-wearing teenage girl is me.

"Well, we're both young roister-doisterers, out on the town, loving the rock music!" I whirlwind, aware we are being observed. "No sleep until dawn."

"No—no sleep until dawn," Jerry says, slowly, staring at me intently. And I blush again. This is odd. He is flirting with me, in front of the audience of this whole bar.

He looks more . . . *together* than last time I saw him. Sober, and shaved, and wearing a suit with a T-shirt. He looks more like that famous guy off TV—and less like that drunk guy on the sofa, angling his crotch at me in a flat full of tat.

I can see a couple of people at the bar are now discussing Jerry and me. "Jerry and me." I have someone here who knows me.

"So—seen anything good on TV recently?" I parry, with a knowing look.

And *he* blushes. I have power over him! I guess that night *does* have the potential to be a funny anecdote, after all.

"Good callback," he says with a nod. "Establishes a narrative. Good."

And he smiles at me—a warm smile.

Suddenly, I feel like I *get it*. Men and women—it's just a word battle. So long as you keep being sassy, and wisecracking, they will respect you, in the end. You just have to show you're strong enough. This thought makes me feel incredibly powerful. *I* am in charge of this! I can win! Words are *what I do!*

I sip my whisky through a straw in what I believe is a minxish way. Jerry stares at me, intently.

The editor is looking at us both—he can see there's something going on.

"It's always good to see writers swapping tips!" he says, to break the slightly charged silence. "Want a drink, Jerry? Care to join us?"

Despite all my reservations about Jerry, my heart leaps a little. A man who can be that funny and lovable on TV can *surely* be that funny and lovable in real life, too, if you find the right conversation to have with him? If you just . . . become a little bit magic? But Jerry shakes his head.

"Sorry guys—would love to. But I can't leave Michael Stipe."

He lets that hang, as the editor and I go, "The *fuck* are you here with Michael Stipe," and, "Yes, because that's a thing that's really happening."

Jerry smiles, and gestures to a table on the other side of the room. And there, indeed—wearing the beanie hat that famous people wear when they don't want to be recognized, but which totally makes them recognizable, because the only people who wear beanie hats somewhere posh are famous people, so it might as well be a helmet with FAMOUS written on it—is Michael Stipe.

"You're with *him*?" I say. Then: "I thought you thought he'd sold out?"

"No," Jerry says, blankly. "He's a fan of the show. *He* likes watching it."

And he shoots me another challenging look.

"That's you in the corner," I say, because Stipe's table is in the corner, and that is a reference to an R.E.M. lyric.

"Nice," Jerry says, amused. Or as amused as comedians get at other people's jokes.

He shakes the editor's hand again, and kisses me good-bye, saying, "Good luck with your . . . *job*. Don't *blow* it," in a saucy manner.

When I sit down, I don't quite know what to think.

"You know him, then?" the editor says.

"We met at a gig," I say. And then, in an attempt to look worldly wise, and like I know what I'm doing, "He's quite a troubled character. But then, all the best people are, aren't they?"

I feel so knowing.

I have just turned nineteen.

The editor gets more drinks in, and asks me about myself: "You're quite . . . *unusual*." So I tell him about being brought up on benefits, and worrying they'd be taken away, and making a pact with Jesus that I wouldn't masturbate if he kept us safe, but being unable to keep that promise to Jesus for more than twenty-four hours, "because it was summer, and hot," and so deciding I'd better *earn* money, and become a writer, and sending stuff off to the *D&ME*.

The editor keeps ordering more drinks, and laughing at my jokes—because I'm making the whole story as funny as possible—and I'm feeling so happy. This is a warm and twinkly bar, and it looks like I have a new job, and the editor is so nice, and, every so often, Jerry darts a look at me from the other side of the room, and I feel like everyone else can see it, and so know that I truly belong here. If London is a game, tonight I am winning it. I have a line of cherries. The machine is full of gold.

When I go to the toilet—gently bumping off things; I've had a *lot* of whisky—I'm humming to myself, with joy. And on the way back, I bump into Jerry, by the bar, settling up his bill.

"Dolly, may I be honest?" he says, drawing me close to him. "I can't stop thinking about you. I am mortified. Last time, you did not see me on my best day, and I apologize. I'd just got out of a bad relationship, and I think I may have been . . . *ungentlemanly.*"

"You were bestial," I confirm, cheerfully. The sassier you are, the more they respect you.

"Life seems so fucking shitty and hopeless—but you seem to have some knack of seeing the world as innately wonderful. How do you *do* that?"

There is something very powerful about someone making an observation about you, and then wishing they could be like you.

"Oh, I have my dark side," I say, because that seems to be the appropriate thing for Sassy Dolly to say, and I want Jerry to feel okay about his dark side. Everyone should feel . . . understood.

"Do you?" he says, getting closer.

At that point, Michael Stipe comes over to say good-bye to Jerry.

"Early start tomorrow," he explains, from under his FA-MOUS FAMOUS FAMOUS beanie hat.

"Michael, this is Dolly," Jerry says, introducing me to Stipe, and putting his arm around me. Stipe looks at us.

"You make a lovely couple," he says, nodding to us both. He then leaves.

There is a pause.

"Did we just get . . . married by Michael Stipe?" I ask.

"It felt quite official," Jerry says, and kisses my hand. "And I feel, now we're married, that I should know about my wife's 'dark side.'"

I think. Do I have a dark side? Everyone does, I guess. I've just not found mine yet, because I'm nineteen. But I don't want him thinking I'm . . . *vanilla*. Sassy Dolly isn't vanilla. And Sassy Dolly's doing very well tonight, so far.

"Well," I say, slowly, "I just feel like I think too much. And the only time I stop thinking is when I'm . . . fucking."

Jerry kisses my hand again, more slowly.

"Honey," he says. "I feel bad—because last time, I promised to fuck your brains out, and I didn't. But I'd like to do that now, very, very much. If that's something you're interested in."

He stares at me. I think. I really am perfectly divided, 50/50, on whether to go or not. Last time was, undoubtedly, awful. I thought he revealed himself to be a bad man.

But in the end, the optimist in me wins out. You should always give everyone a second chance! Maybe he was just having a bad day! Maybe I will make him have a good day! And sex is more exciting than going back to my house, where my father is chopping up seed potatoes, ready for planting.

So when he says, "Shall we go?" I pause, then say, "Yes."

HERE IS THE full list of reasons you will have sex again with someone you did not enjoy attempting sex with the first time—on top of generally being an optimist. (1) You're not a quitter! (2) Maybe you just needed to get to know each other better—and that first, unfond shit shag was your "meet cute," from which something *amazing* will grow. (3) You have nothing else to do. (4) You know no one else here. (5) You should always be up for adventure! (6) You like being kissed. (7) Girls just do, don't they? I mean, we all have stories like this.

I went back to Jerry's house, to have my brains fucked out. At 10:37 p.m., I had realized he was not, after all, fucking my brains out—I was lying there, thinking, sadly, "He still can't kiss properly. And there is no good sex without good kissing."

And then at 10:47 p.m., he crawled across the bed and turned the video camera on, saying, "So, jolly Dolly Wilde. Let's see your dark side, then."

PART II

13

I don't think I'm going to tell this sex anecdote to Krissi. That's what I'm thinking, in Dadda's car, driving back to Wolverhampton for Christmas. Although I'm sure that, in time, this story will mature into something amusing, that I will tell at parties, to raucous laughter, right now, I don't quite know what to make of it. I don't know what my *angle* is. Every way I think about it at the moment, it feels like my "angle" is that I went and had really awful sex that was videoed by a man who has now *twice* been a bad night out—but that's an unhappy thought, and I don't like where it leads.

So my current policy is to not tell Krissi about it, and, indeed, not to think about it. I am locking this memory up in a box—like something radioactive. I am going to wait until the isotopes die down a bit, before I open it again. I feel—again, in a similar way to radioactive waste—that the technology has not yet been invented to deal with it, and so I'm going to entomb it in concrete, and wait until humanity has found a new and effective way to deal with shameful sexual memories. Whenever I have flashbacks—awful, sweaty, nightmarish flashbacks—I suspect this may take centuries. So I am not thinking about it at all.

In this endeavor, my father is being an inadvertently useful distraction, as he will not shut up.

"The thing about your mother is," he says, rolling a ciggie with one hand, like a trucker, whilst overtaking a caravan, "is that she can't have it both ways, yeah? You can't shack up with the Cosmic Joker, then get huffy when he lets his freak flag fly."

I say, mildly, "I think she was just a bit upset you bought this—admittedly very lovely—sports car," and fiddle with the radio, to indicate I don't care about his reply.

John's song comes on—as it so often does, these days—halfway through the bit where he's singing, *Well I survived this / Well I survived us!*," and the choir and orchestra come in, and drowns out my father's reply. I have the same adrenalized stab I get whenever I unexpectedly hear him—a feeling that his ghost is in the room, and that, if I could finesse the tuning on the radio, he would suddenly manifest, wholly, next to me, roaring, "DUCHESS!," and we would simply jump out of this moving car, and run away somewhere better.

I have not seen him for so long. The success of this song is what is getting between us. With each play, he is galloping a little farther away from me: if something doesn't happen soon, in my career, to let me draw equal with him, I might never catch him up. I can't wait until my first column appears in *The Face*. I am counting down the days. January 8th. That's when my plan activates. Oh, wait for me! Don't forget me! I am made of the same stuff as you! Soon, I will prove it!

I'm so bored of my father now. By "bored," I mean "in a state of annoyance so extreme, I've had to crush all my emotions." Honestly, it's like living with a teenager. Two weeks ago, he went out to "revisit some old stomping grounds," and just . . . didn't come back. I didn't really notice until 1:00 a.m., and then I was up until 6:00, envisioning him having been set upon by footpads, or finally being recruited into the IRA, which apparently happens every time he visits an Irish pub, and they clock the name, and the Guinness he's inhaling.

"I always let them buy me a couple of pints before I say no," he would say, returning home, shit-faced. "Good expenses, the IRA are on. Great hospitality. Good lads."

This time, he finally comes home at midday, stinking of booze and weed, and owlishly explains he met a "cracking little dolly bird" and ended up going back to her flat.

"And you didn't think to ring? To call?" I say, going full Maureen Lipman in the BT ads. "I've been up all night worrying about you!"

"Why would you worry about me, my love?" he asks, swaying from side to side, with his eyes pointing in different directions, like Nookie Bear.

I tell him to have a bath and get straight into bed, and I'm just about to tell him to give me his dirty clothes, so I can stick a darks wash on, before I realize that I am being a nineteen-year-old mother to a forty-five-year-old man who once confessed he'd beaten a man to death with a pool cue in a carpark—"Well, I presume he was dead. He wasn't making any other wise-arse remarks about my hair. 'Killer Hippy.' That's what they called me, heh heh heh"—and did what I increasingly did, in those days: left him to sleep on the sofa, in his own horrible miasma, whilst I went round to John's house to comfort myself by folding up all his trousers, and putting them in a color-coded pile: darkest at the bottom, palest on the top. Sometimes, I kiss the fly buttons—but I want you to forget I just told you that.

WHEN DAD AND I arrive back at Mum's for Christmas, Krissi's already there—sitting glumly up the tree in the garden, with five-year-old David on his lap, trying to smoke "secretly" behind him.

"He's driving me fucking mental," I say, gesturing to the house, and Dad. "There's no way he's coming back with me to London. I've done my bit. We've got to get him to stay here."

"That ain't gonna fly, dog," Krissi said ruefully, taking another deep drag on his fag. "Mum's made him up a bed in the shed—by which I mean she's just thrown a sleeping bag on the lawn mower—and she hasn't bought a gammon."

"She hasn't bought a gammon?"

"She hasn't bought a gammon."

This is big, big news—a seismic event. For reasons that have never been made clear, for my father, Christmas is essentially a festival in celebration of gammon. Mum will buy a gammon joint, and Dad will spend days lovingly marinating it, boiling it, coating it in honey and spices, and then roasting it. It's the one bit of cooking he does all year—the revering of the gammon. He will dote on it as one would dote on a child. Indeed, as my mother would always point out, with cheeringly festive hatred, "He's spent more time pampering that gammon that he's ever spent on any of you lot."

This led to Krissi and me confessing to each other that, when she said that, we imagined her giving birth to five little gammons—all in knitted hats and booties—and that this is one of the many, many reasons we do not eat Dadda's gammon: it would be like eating a sibling.

The main reason we do not eat the gammon is because our father will not let us eat the gammon. "It's too orangey for crows," he would say, lovingly wrapping it in tinfoil, and putting it in the fridge, before shouting, "No one touch my frigging gammon!"

Over the course of the festive period, my father would live almost solely on the gammon—accompanied by a variety of chutneys—and to walk into the kitchen at any point would be to find him hunched over it, carving off a slice, and looking like a dragon crouched on its pig-based horde. Given that the other mainstay of my father's diet was a fry-up—bacon, sausage, and black pudding—we could only conclude that, in the world of pigs, he was essentially Hitler: responsible for a swine Holocaust over decades of a dedicated mono diet of pork. Oh, and pork scratchings. He loved pork scratchings, too. To him, *The Three Little Pigs* was not a fairy tale, but a menu. God, my father loved pork. The year I forgot to feed the dog her dinner, and she got into the kitchen and stole his gammon off the sideboard, was a brutal year indeed.

"ME GAMMON! IT'S HAD ME PIGGING GAM-MON!" my father shouted, so angry, tears welled in his eyes, as he beat the dog with a broom. As it was Boxing Day, and the shops were closed, he had to drive over to my Uncle Steve's house, and borrow some of his Christmas gammon. All the Morrigan men had Christmas gammons. That was their thing.

AS YOU MIGHT imagine, Christmas was a desultory affair. With Mum and Dad still not talking to each other, the atmosphere is strained, and Dad is a particular liability, as he has nothing to do. Mum has requisitioned the TV—"As I'm the one who lives here, it's my TV now"—and is watching *Jules et Jim*, thus preventing Dad from his usual festive watching of *Das Boot* with the sound right up. And with no gammon to tend, either, he is entirely without occupation. I suggest to him that he take Lupin out and teach him to ride his bike, at which point he stands up, and goes to the pub.

Krissi and I try as hard as we can to make it magical for the kids—we invent a game where you have to climb out of the bedroom window, onto the porch roof, and then jump down onto the lawn, which fills a good hour or two—but the Christmas dinner is undeniably poor: my mother has over-cooked the turkey by a good two hours, and it's as tough as string—and by Boxing Day, the effort of trying to cover up the seething hatred between my mother and my father is so exhausting, we decide to bunk off down the pub, too.

"After all," as Krissi says, sipping on his first pint, "it's a traditional part of Christmas, as a kid—your parents rowing with each other."

"We shouldn't disrupt that tradition," I agree, clinking my pint against his.

It feels exciting—being able to leave the house at Christmas, and go to the pub.

"This is a definite developmental landmark," I say to Krissi, after our third—around the time I'm starting to think that, next time "Fairytale of New York" comes on the jukebox, I will give the room the benefit of my Kirsty MacColl. "Being able to run away from a miserable house, and go to the pub."

"You can kind of see why the old man does it," Krissi says.

"Except he's the one making the house miserable in the first place," I point out. We both think about this for a while.

"Do you think we should reverse the polarity—invite *Mum* to the pub?" Krissi says. We consider this.

"The first thing she'd say is, 'Oooooh, well aren't I the lucky one—being invited to the pub by the cool kids,'" Krissi points out.

"She'd have a go at me eating these crisps, as well," I say, pointing to the split-open packet on the table. "'Laying down a fat reserve for winter, like a little bear?'"

We both shudder.

"Fuck Mum, then," Krissi says, raising his glass, in toast.

"Yeah. Fuck Mum," I say. "Fuck this Christmas. No fun. It's been meager."

"Just crackers and an old, dry bird," Krissi sighs. "Which, incidentally, is the perfect description of Mum and Dad."

THE NEXT DAY, with a slight hangover, I wake up to find Lupin squatting over my sleeping bag, on the floor, staring at me.

"How long have you been there?" I ask, lying as still and flat as can be, like a run-over badger.

"Hours," he says. "There's nothing else to do."

I remember these levels of boredom from when I was young—before I could go out and have sex, smoke cigarettes and listen to hot loud bands. Krissi and I used to have a game called "Staring," where we would lie on the floor. On the count of "Three!" we would open our eyes, and stare out of the window, at the telegraph wires going into the house, un-blinkingly, for as long as possible, until we cried. The point of it was to stare so long, you cried. That was the fun bit. We enjoyed the crying. It was the most exciting option available to us.

"Can I talk to you?" Lupin said, assuming a businesslike air. He was eleven now—grown so much in the time since I'd left that I started to get the first intimations of what it was like to be one of those aunts, or uncles, who comes over to your house, and can only say, "Oh my God! You're so big now! How did that happen? Where's the little babba I knew?" over and over again. I'm not quite at that stage. But I can almost see it, from here.

"Absolutely," I say, continuing to lie very still. I hope that, whatever this conversation is, it doesn't involve me having to move, at any point. The rest of the house is so cold, and I have finally built up enough body heat in this sleeping bag to make the idea of leaving it very, very unappealing.

"I don't have any stuff," he says, continuing to stare at me.

"What do you mean—any stuff?"

"Any. Stuff," he says. "All the things I put on my Christmas list—I didn't get them."

"What did you put on your Christmas list, honey?" I ask. "Action Man? A gun?"

"A coat," Lupin says, blankly. "I need a coat. And shoes. And a bed."

"What do you mean—a bed?" I say. I'm lying on the floor next to his bed. He has a bed.

"It's not a bed. Look," he says. He takes off the duvet, and mattress—and reveals four bales of Thomson Local directories, bundled in polythene wrap, on which three planks are balanced. These are what the mattress has been laid upon.

"They keep going apart," Lupin said, illustrating this by putting the mattress down and sitting on it. He wriggles a little, and there's a thud, and the mattress falls between the planks, and Lupin disappears.

"What happened to your other bed?" I ask.

"It broke," he said, flatly. "Mum said you'd get me a new one."

I see the news of my possible job at *The Face* has reached my mother, and she has made some calculations. It seems there is no such thing as something that is just "good news for Johanna."

"She said you've got a new job now, and you're rolling in it. She's got a new job, too."

"What's that?"

"Delivering those," Lupin says, pointing at the undelivered Thomson directories. We stare at them for a minute. They are very much not distributed across the local area.

"It was raining," Lupin explains. He pauses. "Are you rolling in it?"

I consider this, for a moment. The short answer is no—I

am overdrawn by £158.97—but my first *Face* column runs in two weeks, and that will be £250.

One of my favorite bits in any book, ever, is in *A Little Princess*, when sad orphan Sara wakes up in her freezing garret and finds that, overnight, it has been transformed by an anonymous benefactor, and that she is lying under a luxurious quilt, with a fire burning in the fireplace, and a new coat lies on a new chair. I vaguely remember she gets given a parrot, or a monkey, as a pet, too. It's quite the lifestyle makeover.

Imagine being able to make it true!

"Come on," I say, getting out of my sleeping bag, and crushing Lupin's fat little face with my hand lovingly. "Let's go rolling."

THREE HOURS LATER, Lupin and I return to the house in a taxi. A taxi! I didn't even know they existed in Wolverhampton, but the man in the junk shop suggested we order one, just after we bought a single pine bed frame there, for £25.

Lupin is wearing a huge Puffa jacket—"THAT ONE!" he shrieked, when he saw it in C&A—and new trainers, which we had argued over immensely. He wanted white ones, and I—with all the wisdom of my nineteen years—told him they'd get all dirty cuffy immediately, but then he looked brave, and pretended he didn't mind getting the sensible black ones I had picked out for him, and I suddenly became overwhelmed with joy at the idea of just fucking everything, and getting him the ones he dreamed of.

I never had the shoes I dreamed of when I was eleven.

Mum and Dad insisted on buying me "boy shoes"—sensible brown lace-ups, that looked like horrible pasties—which I feel were the primary source of my belief that I was an ugly girl who could never have beautiful shiny shoes, such as the ones Leanne Parry had, and very possibly contributed to the fact that, eight years later, I had such low self-esteem that I thought it was okay to have bad sex with Jerry Sharp. If you don't think you deserve pretty shoes, you don't think you deserve pretty boys. The world, with its ugly shoes, has marked you as "generally accepting of disappointment."

As I looked at Lupin's sad face, I felt like Mr. Blunden in *The Amazing Mr. Blunden*: suddenly able to right a terrible historic wrong. In *The Amazing Mr. Blunden*, the plot is that he travels in time to stop two orphans burning to death. In this day, the plot is that I bought Lupin the impractical shoes he loved. I felt the two stories to be pretty much equal.

"You will never have sex with someone who makes you feel unworthy," I whispered to Lupin's back, as he danced up the path, into the house, buoyant with New Shoe Joy. "I have seen to that, with your Magic Shoes. You will always think you are beautiful."

Krissi and I assembled Lupin's new bed whilst listening to Massive Attack, and drinking some whisky Krissi had bought, "for emergencies." "And there's no greater emergency than furniture assembly," as Krissi pointed out.

Halfway through—at the sweatiest stage, when all the wing nuts were insisting on jamming at awkward angles, and I was having trouble singing the high notes quite as well as Shara Nelson—our mother came in, and leant against the door frame, and said, "Oh! I see Lady Bounty has been busy!," and then moaned about how her bed was very un-comfortable, too.

"But that's the thing about being a mother," she concluded, with a sigh. "No one sees you as someone with needs."

It was around that point that I ran out of nobleness, fin-ished assembling Lupin's bed, packed my rucksack, and got the bus to the train station, to go back to London. Krissi came with me—"I'm not staying here without you. If it ever comes to a court case with Mum, I want reliable witnesses as to how I killed her"—in order to get the train back to Manchester.

"My friend Suzanne says that our parents don't have any boundaries," I tell Krissi, as we wait on the freezing train platform, for our trains.

"That's because you haven't bought them any," Krissi says. "Jo, if you haven't bought it, it's not in this family. It's entirely your fault."

14

The best thing about going home early, I reflect, later, on the train, is that I've left Dad behind. He was in the pub when I left. I've stranded him. Yes!

"He'll have to stand on his own two feet," I tell the dog, who's sitting at my feet, chewing on an empty crisp packet.

The timing is perfect, because I really need my flat for a while—John Kite is back off his European tour, to play a one-off London gig, and so I can't go and hide at his house anymore in order to escape my father.

Just thinking about how John is back in London makes my heart puff up and fill my whole body—until my head feels like a joyful red enamel ventricle. This train is bulleting toward a city that has, in the center of it, the source of all happiness: John. John. That word is the best word in the world. Science can prove that the letter "J" is the most beautiful letter; it shames the rest of the alphabet, because it is the letter of "John." All Johns in history are more fascinating, because they are the precursors of this one. All men who smoke Marlboros and have messy hair are more glorious, because they must be a little like my John. If he is back in London, then London is like Narnia when Aslan returns: great merriment will occur! Dawns will be observed from balconies, as we talk! Roads will light up, and glow, as we walk down them! We will own whole days together. We will talk, knee to knee, with the jukebox playing our songs, and a bottle between us, like a Maypole, and we will weave in and out of each other's sentences, until the twined ribbons of our thoughts run short, and the music stops, and we stand, facing each other, and bow.

I spend the rest of the train ride imagining what the best outfit would be to wear, the first time he properly kisses me. I settle, in the end, for green velvet. I want to look like wet river moss when he kisses me. I want to look like something from a legend.

WHEN I GET back, it takes me four hours to rinse the flat clean of every trace of Dadda. I scrub the toilet, and throw away all his greening bacon in the fridge, and try to remove his sweaty Turin Shroud outline from the pleather sofa. When this fails—his body fog is more powerful than Flash—I just cover the whole sofa with a rug, and light a joss stick.

I then wander around the flat, trying to remember what I used to do when Dadda wasn't here. He's been cramping my style for so long, I can't remember. In the end, I have a hot bath, because that's always a good thing to do, and try to masturbate with the showerhead, because I keep reading in dirty airport novels that that's a thing, and I've had it on my "To Do to Me" list for a while, but I don't think any of the women in dirty airport novels can have the kind of dodgy Camden plumbing I do. The water keeps running suddenly hot, then cold, in bursts—which alarms my vagina into curling up like a panicked hedgehog does, on spotting a speeding truck. Also, some of the jet goes up my bum, which I don't find erotic at all: it just makes me want to do a poo.

In the end, I get out of the bath, and masturbate the old-fashioned way: with my trusty two fingers, on the bed. I love that it's these two fingers that makes girls come—when people do the "gun fingers" sign, using the same two, I pretend they are not using an imaginary gun, but suggesting a wank, instead. This amuses me roughly fifty times a year.

I'm having a wank because it's important to come when you return home after time away—it lets both the house, and your body, know you're back. Besides, I haven't been able to come for nearly a week, because I am fat, and the sleeping bag in Lupin's room was very tight, and after I'd waited patiently, for hours, for him to go to sleep, I found I couldn't form the necessary angle with my hand, because the bag was too tight, and it would get tired in the new position, and so, in the end, I just gave up, after whispering "sorry" to my frustrated libido.

Here, in the freedom of my own bed, I can position my hand wherever I please, and so I have a leisurely wank thinking about John's hands on the guitar when he plays the really fast chords in "Count to Ten." I make sure I say his name when I come—"John!"—because that is like saying "white rabbit" on the first day of each month. Coming is powerful—it basically borders on magic—and so when you say someone's name, it's like a little, lucky spell that binds them to you. I believe that, wherever that person is, it makes them think about you—just for a second—when it happens.

One day, when we are together, I will tell John about this, and we will spend exciting, erotic hours comparing notes on all the times he suddenly and mysteriously thought about me, over the years, as I crow "That's because I was calling your name as I had a fiddle!"

As I muse on this—lying on the bed, feeling very relaxed—I realize I have probably based this belief on the bit in *Jane Eyre* where Mr. Rochester calls out Jane's name, and she—hundreds of miles away, being bored to death by the drippy St. John—hears him, and comes running to him.

I like to think this was Charlotte Brontë's codified way of referring to how she, too, called out people's names when she came. I bet all the Brontë sisters wanked a lot. Their books are dead sexy, and, let's face it, there was nothing else to do in that parsonage, except tut at Branwell. All the Brontës go on about secret mossy pools, and hard rain on their skin, and the stroking of frightened rabbits/horses, which gradually calm to their touch. I'm sure this is their secret way of trying to write about masturbation. I am sure there are secret messages in all books, if you look hard enough. Generations of girls trying to tell other girls secrets, without getting found out.

I am dwelling on this thought because—I am putting

secret messages in my columns to John. I am becoming obsessed with the whole idea of secret messages in art. I recently read both *Moby-Dick*, and *The Complete Works of Oscar Wilde*—the first because Courtney Love recommended it, in an interview, and the second because Morrissey always bangs on about Wilde, and if I ever bump into him in the Europa mini-market round the corner, I want to make sure I get any Wilde references he drops whilst we're queuing together in the Five Items or Less line—in between him inevitably fretting that the proper grammar is Five Items or Fewer.

Moby-Dick makes me sad that I haven't read it earlier in my life—I'd always thought it was basically some dull, Hemingway-esque novel about fishing, and eschewed it on that basis. Turns out, it's the gayest book ever—the first fifty pages are basically Melville crushing on the hotness of Queequeg, and trying to lie as close as possible to him in bed, and the rest of it reads like someone trapped in another century, trying to communicate with those in a future he imagines to be freer, and more glorious. Those long, bright pages are bursting with everything he knows—all that he has observed about waves, and wind, and men, and whale oil, and knives, and boats, and love, and fear. A burning desire to chronicle everything that he is, and knows, on the page, just to prove he existed. Just to prove you could be someone like Herman Melville, when everyone else in the world was not. A letter to a reader he can never know.

I look at the picture of Melville, on the back cover—a bearded clerk, who died without glory—and instantly burst into tears. I am so sure we would be friends, if we met now! I am sure we would go to a bar with Queequeg, and drink cocktails, and dance, and talk of great theories of humanity whilst lying on our backs in the park, crushing lavender in our hands, and they would kiss whilst I sang "Astral Weeks" to them, which they would never have heard, and would think of as magic.

And how Melville would have loved Wilde—also trapped in a smaller, tighter, more loveless century, trying to find ways to talk about the boys he loves, and the worlds he dreams of, without getting found out. Trying to tell the truth whilst disguising the noisy talk of his heart with art—using the goldenest curlicues and sharpest phrases, by way of camouflage and weapons—trying to smuggle the truth out into the future, and still being caught, and brought down, and broken. I would find them both, and invite them out to dinner together, and they would talk to each other so hard their faces would burn up like lanterns, and they would plan a dozen—a hundred—a million—new books, even before the waiter brought the bill.

Herman Melville! Oscar Wilde! You would love this world so much! I think. *You would have felt so at home here! And all you could do was imagine it, and write it in your books, and then hide inside those books, and come talk to me, a hundred years later. That is where you live. A book is a beautiful, paper mausoleum, or tomb, in which to store ideas . . . to keep the bones of your thoughts in one place, for all time. I just want to say—"Hello. We can hear you. The words survived."*

Thinking things like this makes me cry, so I have another wank—a more sorrowful, reflective one, in honor of the dead geniuses—and fall asleep.

15

It's January 8th. Suzanne is over at my flat, sitting in a chair by the window, smoking a cigarette, and picking at a spot on her chin. My first column in *The Face* was published today, and Suzanne rang me at 1:00 p.m., saying, "I'm coming over to talk about this now," and then put the phone down.

She is currently twenty minutes into her first thought about it.

"I have five main reactions to this," she'd said, coming into the flat, and slapping the magazine down on the table. "The third is quite long, so bear with me."

The headline is "IN DEFENSE OF GROUPIES," and it's my explanation of why I don't understand why groupies are so looked down upon and pitied, as I think it's actually a good, healthy thing that teenage girls want to hang around stage doors, and try to have sex with pretty, famous, talented men. I've never seen anyone write about this before.

"So, you're a teenage girl, and you're hot to trot," the piece begins. "You're supposed to be revising your geography homework, and all those sedimentary layers—but your knickers are screaming 'TAKE ME OUT AND PARTY!' and you just can't stop looking at the picture of Jeff Buckley's arms that you've got Blu-Tack'd to the wall. You want to have sex with someone, and you're bored of that someone being you. You want to bring a second person into this relationship.

"At this point, you only really have two options. The first is to bite the bullet, and have sex with some guy you know at school, which is what you are supposed to do. That's the normal, 'good' thing to do. But why? Why is it the good option for me to have sex with some inexperienced, nervy, trigger-happy, warty-fingered Herbert I've known since I was eleven, and who is statistically very likely to turn up at school the next day and act like bragging Danny Zuko in the opening act of *Grease*—'She got friendly / Down in the sand'—and make me the subject of gossip for the next six months?

"This is why I think option two—having sex with rock stars—is a far more useful option. Say what you want about Robert Plant and his teenage groupies, but (a) I've never seen a picture of him with warts, (b) he was almost certainly better in the sack than anyone currently living in the Whitmore Reans area of Wolverhampton, and (c) he was far too busy singing 'Immigrant Song' to subsequently write 'Dolly is a slag' on the toilets of Highfields School, and go around the canteen saying, 'Smell my fingers. Guess who it is?' whilst people are trying to eat sponge, and weird pink custard.

"Why can't a teenage girl be ambitious with whom she wishes to sex with? Why can't she shoot, literally, for the stars? I instinctively like a girl who wants to have sex with rock stars. It suggests she has a healthy level of confidence, is culturally engaged, wants to seek out the best for her knickers, would prefer to have sex in a nice hotel suite rather than at the top of the 'big slide' in the playground, and wants to learn about humping from someone with a bit of experience. Those are all good things! That's likely to be a positive experiment! After all, what are the other options for 'having sex with someone with a bit of experience'? Shagging one of the weird blokes who hangs around outside the school, or one of your dad's mates. When it comes down to it, when I finish a one-night stand, I'd far prefer a lover who cynically said, 'Babe, thanks for all the teenage poon, but you've got to go now. I've got another three groupies lined up outside, and a seven a.m. flight to Denver,' over someone likely to say, 'Next time you see your dad, tell him I've got him that gravel he wanted from Wickes.'"

"I LOVE THIS!" Suzanne roars, pointing at the paragraph. "YES! YES! I mean, obviously, there's tons of creepy, rape-y pop stars taking advantage of young women, but that's true of any profession you work in. The most I ever got propositioned was when I worked in the DVLA. You've just got to figure that, wherever you are, twenty percent of men are dog rapists. Twenty percent of all conversations are basically a man saying, 'If this was 1642 and we were alone in a field, I would be fucking you right now.'"

Although this seems dubious to me, Suzanne seems very confident about this statistic, so I let it pass. She starts reading the next part of the column out loud.

"Most rock stars are men, and most people writing about rock stars are men. Of course they wouldn't think it was good for teenage girls to want to fuck rock stars. That's not what they see when they look at them. I guess it's kind of upsetting, that their heroes have a whole other life that doesn't include them . . . that is only for their girl fans. Something they're totally excluded from, and unwanted in. Something they can't have. Something they're missing out on. The sex. That's just between the rock stars and the girls. Seen from a male point of view, those girls might well look as if they're being 'used' by the be-leathered yodelers. Those men want to protect the young women. What they can't see in this scenario—the information that isn't appearing on the graph; that is invisible to them; that is so obvious I'm screaming as I type it—is that the young women WANT to fuck the rock stars. They are simply making a decision—'I want that thing'—and then going and getting the thing. And the thing wants them back.

" 'Protecting' women from rock stars is basically preventing women trying to do something, which is one of man's most prevalent and tedious pursuits. It's just one of a million daily instances of young women being told what to do—being told that their thoughts and their desires are wrong—and which happens so constantly, and on such a wide scale ('You don't want to: be a firefighter/get a tattoo/get drunk/study physics/cut your hair/eat that cake/wear those trousers/fuck a rock star') that it's little wonder modern women's most frequent refrain is 'I don't know who I am, or what I want! I don't know who I am!'

"Young women do know who they are—OF COURSE THEY DO!—it's just they're told they're not allowed to be it so often, and told to suppress their feelings so continually, that they gradually lose their entire instinct for happiness and self-realization, and turn into those panicking creatures you meet at parties who dance madly when 'I Am What I Am' comes on the stereo, then spend the rest of the evening crying.

"And this is, surely, one of the big purposes of culture—of heroes. Of famous people. They're supposed to be desirable things—the things we want . . . the things we want to be. To deny half of their purpose is to be blind to fifty percent of all art, and it leaves people emotionally broken. And all of this could be avoided if, at the age of sixteen, when girls say, 'I'm off for the evening—I'm going to hang around the stage door at the Civic Hall in Wolverhampton and see if I can bang that dreamy bass player from Teenage Fanclub,' their parents said, 'That sounds very healthy, dear. Give him one for me.'"

Suzanne is snorting with laughter over her favorite bits.

"This is so the theme I'm working on at the moment," she says, picking up her guitar, and starting to tune it. Suzanne is terrible at tuning her guitar. She always makes it sound worse than when she's started, then says "Punk rock!" and plays it anyway. "The idea that women's desires are dangerous to them, and have to be constantly chivvied, and nursed. Have you read Nancy Friday's *My Secret Garden*?"

"I've read Frances Hodgson Burnett's *The Secret Garden*?" I say. "Poor, pale Colin," I add, sympathetically.

"Nancy Friday's secret garden is a very different garden, Dolly. It's a collection of women's secret sexual fantasies," Suzanne says, strumming away, tunelessly. "They're filth. They turn into huge robots, and crush men under their robot feet, or squirt their breast milk all over them. It's really fierce. Like, scary, and disgusting, and therefore amazing. Women *are* scary, and disgusting. That's one of our biggest secrets. What's the most disgusting sexual fantasy *you've* ever had?"

"Covering Keanu Reeves in melted-down Cadbury's Caramel," I say, automatically.

"Balls," Suzanne says. "That's no one's actual sexual fantasy. That's just what they say on the letters page of *More*. Who really wants a man covered in chocolate? Think about it."

I think about it. She's right. I actually don't want Keanu Reeves covered in chocolate. He'd be all sticky and brown, and I'd feel sick after about thirty seconds of eating his sexy crust. Plus, it would take a minimum of five minutes to cover Reeves in chocolate, and what would we talk about whilst I industriously emptied pans of Cadbury's Caramel all over some of the more boring bits—like knees, and toes? "I can't wait to lick all this chocolate off you—thus solving the problem I am currently busily creating—and get down to some actual pumping"? Why don't I just cut to the chase, and pump him? But only in *Bill & Ted's Excellent Adventure*. Not *Point Break*. He's too serious in that.

"I dream I get fucked by wolves," Suzanne says, conversationally, interrupting my thought process. "And dogs. Really desperate dogs. Under the table in a cafeteria, with everyone watching. If I'm really good at fucking the wolves, I get to fuck the men."

She looks up.

"Your turn. For instance: have you ever wanted to fuck a woman?"

"That's . . . random."

"Not really, baby. It's 1995. Everyone's bisexual after eleven p.m."

"I don't think I am," I say, sadly. "I once made a list of all the women I fancy—Brunhilde Esterhazy, Elizabeth Taylor, Ava Gardner, Doris from *Fame*—but then I noticed they were all women I think are a bit like me. I just fancy me. I'm not a lesbian. I'm a me-bian."

Suzanne laughs.

"Well, get ready to talk about it. You're a woman writing about sex in a public arena now. People are going to want to talk about it. People are going to ask you weird questions. Girls aren't supposed to talk about sex. You're just supposed to do it, and shut up. You're going to make a *lot* of people very uncomfortable."

16

Suzanne was right—that people wanted to talk about it. That afternoon, I got three calls from *The Face*, who'd had people on radio shows who wanted me to come on and talk about being a teenage groupie.

"They do understand I'm not a teenage groupie?" I said, three times in a row. "And that I'm just defending the general idea, not opening my sexual journal? I've only had sex with one actual famous person, and he'd read my stuff, so that felt like more of a—fuck between colleagues?"

That's how I'm thinking about Jerry Sharp now. A fuck between colleagues.

"I'm sure they'd love you to explain the difference," the editor said, wryly. "Although without the word 'fuck.' This is daytime LBC. You'll need to use a euphemism—preferably nineteenth century."

"I could say, 'esteemed peer who troubled my petticoats'? Or 'respectful mutual tumbling'? Or maybe 'courteous reciprocal fiddlement'?"

"You'll have a ball," he said.

"Can I be honest with you?" I asked, staring at my byline picture in the magazine.

It was taken by a *Face* photographer in the editor's office, when I popped by a few weeks ago. In it, the flash is so bright you almost can't see my nose—I'm just two huge eyes, and a mouth I have concentrated very hard on making pouty. "Having a flash so bright you almost can't see someone's nose" is the fashionable thing in photographs in the mid-nineties. The singer-songwriter Cathy Dennis hasn't had a nose on the cover of her last five singles. Björk's comes and goes, seemingly at will.

I felt conflicted about this photograph. On the one hand, I didn't like how sexy, sassy, and cool I look in it. I have an instinctive worry that having a picture so kind of . . . arrogant . . . will make people hate me. I'd far rather be pulling a silly face. I feel, instinctively, that's what my soul looks like. A bit silly.

On the other hand, I loved the nose-less-ness, as I believe I have inherited my mother's nose, and every time I look at a picture of it, I imagine it sitting reproachfully in the middle of my face, saying, "Johanna," in a guilt-inducing way. It's hard, inheriting your parents' body parts. I often wondered if that's why Michael Jackson has had so much surgery. It's not so much being in denial of his blackness, as just not wanting to look at his infamously unkind dad's nose every morning. I could see how that would be an immediate bummer, every morning. Having a face which, when you look in the mirror, looks as though it's about to start shouting "Dance! Do it again, Michael! BETTER! HURRY UP AND RECORD *THRILLER!*"

Anyway, I digress.

"Fire away," the editor said.

"I am scared of going on the radio," I said.

I told him about how, when I was fourteen, I appeared on local TV, reading out a poem about my dog, and got over-nervous, and went temporarily mental, and ended up howling "Scooby dooby doooooo!" as the presenter desperately cut me off, and I subsequently became a laughingstock at school.

"I'm worried I might have another . . . conversational accident like that," I finished.

The editor was laughing so hard, it took him a minute to gather his breath.

"It's not funny!" I said, also laughing. "It's traumatized me for life. I can't watch live interviews on TV now without getting very tense that one of the people taking part in it might have some kind of nervo, and do something similar."

"You have to write a column about this, at some point," the editor said.

"Another column?" I said. "So, you're going to keep me?"

My heart raced.

"Magazines love columnists who appear on radio, talking about their controversial columns," the editor said.

"Even if they end up howling 'Scooby dooby dooo'?"

"Speaking for myself, personally, particularly if they do that," the editor said.

I thought about this for a second.

"Okay. I'll do it," I said.

"Congratulations on your new job," the editor said. "I think I'm going to enjoy this," and rang off.

THE RADIO INTERVIEWS went okay, I think. I am referred to, variously, in my introductions, as "the new enfant terrible of Fleet Street," "the new Julie Burchill," and "self-confessed teenage groupie Dolly Wilde," but I have plenty of time to correct them.

"I would prefer '*enfant lovely*' I think—no one wants to be 'terrible,'" I told one DJ; whilst the one who called me a "self-confessed teenage groupie" had it explained to him that I've had more sex with people called "Russell" (two) than I have with famous people (one), and so I'm technically not so much "a groupie," more "a member of the Russell Group."

But he didn't get this reference to the slightly obscure organization that represents the UK's seventeen leading universities—and so, yet again, I observed my humor to go without honor in its time. I had long intended to get a notebook, to keep a record of all the jokes I made that no one got—so that future, more humorously advanced generations would still be able to appreciate them, when their evolution kicked in. I knew John would get all these jokes. It was another reason I knew I must marry him. There were so many jokes I was making for him, still waiting to be laughed at.

All the interviewers missed the point. To a greater or lesser extent all said, "So, you're suggesting teenage schoolgirls should down their textbooks, and go off to have sex with rock stars?" whilst I patiently explained that I was not telling them to do this, merely acknowledging that quite a few already wanted to, and that it was a perfectly sensible desire, inasmuch as desire can be sensible.

One of them went full Bill Grundy, and asked me which famous people I'd had sex with, and it was only when I was halfway through a list that included "all of The Goodies except Graeme Garden, but including the big kitten" that he realized I was taking the piss, and got quite arsey.

Before each interview, I felt a kind of anxiety I'd never felt in any other situation—as if my belly was a cradle of filthy nerves, all of which are fizzing, and shorting out—but afterward, I felt so high and triumphant that they went okay—I pulled it off! I didn't fuck up! I was actually funny on a few occasions! It was easy! I could do it again! It's just *talking*!—that I arranged to meet Zee in the pub, because his new record company offices were just around the corner from the BBC, and I hadn't seen him in a while, and I wanted to drink a celebratory drink to me in his presence.

"You're famous!" he said, clinking his pint of milk against my whisky and Coke. "You're everywhere right now!"

He showed me a piece in today's *Evening Standard*, in which Martin Amis had railed against me "Talking like a bloke" about sex. I read it in disbelief.

"He thinks only men talk about sex?" I said. "That just makes him look weird. He's basically saying no woman he knows has ever talked to him about sex. That's embarrassing for Martin Amis."

"Famous," Zee said again. "You used to talk about Martin Amis. Now Martin Amis is talking about you."

"I'm not famous," I said. "I'm just . . . not not famous.

I'm . . . point zero zero one percent famous. Like, a homeo-pathic amount."

"*The Face* must be delighted," he said. "You are a creditable employee."

"Talking of creditable employees," I said, lighting a ciga-rette, "how's The Branks' album going?"

Suzanne has been signed to Zee's label—now called Jubilee—for five months, and their debut album is scheduled to come out at the beginning of spring. However, when I mentioned this, Zee looked a bit worried.

"She's got so many great ideas," he said. "She comes into the office, and tells us about what she wants to do, and how it's going to change the world—but she's not let us actually listen to anything yet."

"I'm sure it will be amazing," I said. "I've got a massive girl-crush on her. She's the revolution. She makes me excited."

"Sometimes I can't tell if I'm excited, or scared," Zee said. "My parents have remortgaged their house for this label. So far, the time she's spent in the studio amounts to their front room, and half of their porch. If this tanks, they're going to have to live in their kitchen."

"I think she's the safest bet you could have," I said, sooth-ingly. "I don't know anyone who wants more to be famous than Suzanne. She is a star."

"Yes," Zee said, unwillingly. "But I'm not sure if she's realized yet that stars have to do something to be famous. Anyway, talking of which, shall we make a move?"

John Kite is playing his first UK date in eight months to-night, finishing off his world tour with a night at the Astoria. It sold out the day tickets went on sale—it's the month's big gig. He is the homecoming hero: "all" of London is going tonight, by which I mean "some other people in bands, some comedians, and me." It has given me an absolute thrill to be able to ring John, and suggest we meet up, beforehand, and then go into the gig together. We agreed on the bar over the road from the Astoria, a little bar underneath the Phoenix Theatre, which for some reason we all refer to as "Shuttle-worth's."

I will admit, imagining this for the last two months has been my main motivating dream. The outfit I'm wearing— a moss-green silk blouse, tights, shorts, and boots, with an Afghan coat—has been designed to be the perfect "Of course I'm with the hero!" outfit. I am going to bank this memory hard. I'm seeing John!

"Come on," Zee says. "We can walk it in ten minutes."

17

When I got to the bar, John was already there, and already quite drunk, and already with other people. This is the worst thing about knowing someone famous—aside from the fact that they are always busy, they are never alone. They are always surrounded by people. You can always tell where a famous person is in a room—they will be at the epicenter of the cluster of oddly overanimated people, all essentially queuing to talk to them.

I didn't like the look of the people he was with—there is an immediately identifiable aura to people who take a lot of cocaine. For ages, I struggled to put my finger on it—until I realized that they all basically remind me of the Child Catcher in *Chitty Chitty Bang Bang*. Black leather, silly John Lennon glasses, greasy hair, twitchy noses.

I felt an emotion I had never had before, when looking at John: disappointment. Who *were* these new people? They weren't his usual friends—the sleepy-eyed librarian; the man in the jumper called Rob; the roadie who can balance 10p on a lemon floating in a pint glass; me.

"I'm going to the bar. Drink?" Zee said.

"Whisky," I replied.

I waved at John, in a kind of "I'm here, but not going to bother you" way, but he stood up—slightly unsteadily—and roared, "DUCHESS! DUCHESS! I DID NOT KNOW YOU COULD GET HEAVEN BIKED TO HELL!" I did not know if that was a reference to me—or to all the drugs he'd clearly had delivered here.

I pushed through the crowd toward him, and—as there were no spare chairs—he pulled me onto his knee, where I observed how he was vibrating on a different frequency to the one I was accustomed to, and which I didn't like; but he still smelled like John as I kissed his greasy, sweaty, dear forehead. And there—there came the rush. The same jolt, the same flood of love. It was beyond reason, these days. I am a dog, and he is the bell.

"Dutch, Dutch—you've got to meet Mike. Mike—Dutch. Dutch—Mike."

A ratty man looked at me, and his thought receipt was, clearly, "Here is a fat child I have absolutely no interest in. This is not crumpet."

"Mike's got some pretty punchy theories about the murder of JFK," John said. "Hit her, Mike!"

Mike looked like the kind of man who, a few drinks down the line, might take that command literally, and so I said,

"Mike! Hello! Tell me the story of Mike, with your voice!," just to clarify things.

"Well," Mike said. He had a very unlovable voice. Like a rat trying to sound like an undercover cop. "Think about this, right? We've had all these claims, over the years, about who killed JFK. CIA, right-wing conspiracy, lone nutter. But who had the most to gain from him dying? Whose lives were changed instantly the moment he got his head blown off? You gotta follow the money. Who? WHO?"

"I don't know, Mike!" I said, pleasantly. John handed me his whisky. I sipped it.

"The fucking Beatles," Mike said, looking triumphant. "JFK dies, America has a vacuum for a new hero and, four weeks later, the Mop-Tops turn up—and they fucking coin it. Think about it! They've even got a 'tell'! All that shaking their heads— what does that look like? Someone having their brains blown out. Like their victim. And what are they saying when they do that? 'Yeah yeah yeah.' It's a confession! They fucking did it!"

This sounds like a theory Mike came up with as a joke at some point—but which the years of retelling, mixed in with the drugs, have seen calcify into something Mike now pretty much believes. Because he's very dim.

"It's an intriguing proposition," I said, as positively as possible, whilst John shifted me slightly on his knee, to a more comfortable position.

"Alley-oop!" he said, jovially.

On seeing this, Mike's face became a little shinier and more rat-like.

"You almost in?" he asked John, ignoring me as if I were a deaf-mute child, or a ventriloquist's puppet.

"What?" John asked, drunkenly befuddled.

"*You* know. You almost there?"

John and I both realized at exactly the same time that what Mike was asking him, is if he'd managed to get his cock into me, whilst I was sitting on his knee.

I hadn't even had time to start having an emotion about this when John stood up, put his arm around me, and said, to the crowd, "Gotta go!"—herding me toward the door.

"Yeah—alleyway's the best place!" Mike shouted after him, conspiratorially. "Keep her warm for me!"

John said, evenly, "Excuse me, Dutch," went over to Mike, placed his face very close to Mike's—which was still beaming, brattishly—and said, "Friend. Friend. If I hear you say something like that again, about this, or any other woman, you'll spend the rest of your life pissing through a straw." Then he came back to me, and ushered me out of the bar.

The sudden cold dark air, combined with the rapidity of the mood switch, meant that, for a minute, I didn't know what to say.

"I'm so sorry," I said, eventually, because that's what girls automatically say when something bad happens to them.

John grabbed me by the arms, and looked me right in the eye.

"No one talks to you like that, honey," he said, firmly. "If anyone ever talks to you like that again, take their name. I will end them."

"I don't know if you would ever have time. The world is full of evenings like this," I said. I mean it to sound jaunty, but it comes out unexpectedly sad. John tilts my head up.

"You okay, babe?" he said, concerned.

"Yes, yes," I said. Why have I sadded this moment? This moment should be amazing! I shake my head, and re-amazen it.

"My first column in *The Face* came out this week! I am now a national columnist!"

"Ah, you fucking *maven*!" he said, picking me up, and whirling me around, and then dumping me back on the pavement with a kiss. "Oh, we must celebrate this! With *champagne*!"

He turned to the cashpoint next to us, and punched in his PIN. "No! *Not* champagne! Dolly—have you ever had a martini? Here is their mechanism: they set fire to tomorrow, to make tonight glorious. They send away the watchmen of the mind. They are, without doubt, the fastest route to prison. I recommend them highly."

And then he stopped, staring at the screen.

"What? What?" I asked, as he'd gone quite pale.

"Look," he said, quietly.

I came round, right behind him, and looked at the screen. It said, in little green letters on black, "Available balance: £1,203,833.00."

18

If John was drunk before—and he really was very drunk—in the hour that followed he essentially became vapor. When Zee—slightly confused—came out of the bar to see where we'd got to, he found John carrying me down the street on his back, screaming "I'M FILTHY FUCKING RICH! LET'S SPEND IT! QUICK!" and desperately trying to find somewhere to buy something on Charing Cross Road at 7:00 p.m.—not a place overburdened with shops that are not antiquarian-book shops.

"But what do you want to buy?" I was asking him, clinging onto his back.

"ANYTHING! EVERYTHING! I AM MIDAS!" he replied, going into the WHSmith's and picking up a gigantic Toblerone, a calculator ("To work out HOW FILTHY

STINKING FUCKING WEALTHY I AM NOW!!!!"), a VHS box set of *Seinfeld*, and a two-liter bottle of Fanta.

"The millionaire must have stuff," he said, paying for it, before pinballing back out of the shop, and to the back entrance of the Astoria.

In the dressing room, downing a shot before he even took his coat off, he went for a piss with the door of the toilet open, shouting "Behold—the sound of my millionaire's urination!"

"Don't forget to wash your hands," I said, primly, and he stuck each of his hands under the two available dryers, and stood, legs apart, like Henry VIII having his hands blow-dried, shouting "BEHOLD! I AM AS A GOD!"

I was just in the middle of pouring John a drink, as requested—well, not quite as requested. He'd told me to serve it in my shoe. I had gone for the more prosaic option of "a glass"—and cheerfully punching John's arm when John's new PR, Andy Wolf, entered the room.

"Quick word in your shell-like," Wolf said, beckoning me into the corridor. He had an eternally peevish air. Like a man who has, in his time, sent back a lot of soup.

"Yes?" I said, as I closed the dressing room door behind me. The "click" sound seemed to instantly activate some latent "Enraged Fucker" mode in Andy.

"What the *fuck* are you doing, getting my artist this drunk?" he hissed.

"What?"

"He's onstage in half an hour, and he's so drunk he can barely stand up."

I was so surprised, I couldn't think of anything to say.

"I'm going to give you some advice, sweetheart. If you want to stay in this industry, don't hang around in an artist's dressing room getting drunk, punching him, and acting like a fucking competition winner, okay?"

"But . . . we're friends. We're just joking. It's what we do."

"Well I'm sure—as his friend—you won't want to make his evening more difficult," Andy said. "He's at work. If you want to have an attention-seeking pretend argument with him, I'm sure you can have it in the cab, going home with him."

Oh, there was so much spite in the sentence—the presumption I will not be in a cab with John, as I don't really know him that well; the slight inference of whorishness. My face went red. I felt like a messy child, making things difficult for the grown-ups.

John poked his head out of the door, banging it on the frame.

"Shit!" he said. "This door needs to slow down."

"I'm just going to make you a big, black coffee, John," Andy said, going into the dressing room, and shooting a hateful look at me.

"And I'd best be going, too," I said, dutifully.

John came out into the corridor, and closed the door behind him.

"You're going?" he said, beaming but confused.

I considered telling him about Andy, but nobly decided, in the end, to suck it up. John is, after all, just about to go to work. And at nineteen, I already have the sense that it is the job of women to simply absorb the unpleasantness that bad men dole out to us. If we stopped doing this—revealing all the awfulness sloshing around—then all the good men would become sad, and anxious, on our behalves, and the world would consist only of bad men, and sad men, and be no fun at all. It's the work of mere seconds to simply cut the unhappiness, and keep the world more joyful. It's no effort at all!

"I just want to get down the front . . . get a good spot," I said.

"But I'll see you later, yes?" Kite said, urgently, grabbing my hands. "We have to celebrate my becoming richer than God."

"I'm always up for a party," I said.

"No. Not a party. Bored of parties. Just you. Let's fuck off somewhere, quiet, and talk balls all night."

He looked at me—pissed, and warm.

"I've missed you," he said, urgently. "Really missed you."

"I've missed you," I said.

And he leant forward, and for the second time in my life, kissed me on the mouth—a good-bye kiss, but a more-than-good-bye kiss; mouth closed, heart open; a kiss that changed the whole corridor, and made it the most important place in the world—better than the Taj Mahal, or . . . or other places that were built out of love, that I can't think of right now.

"I'm just going to play fourteen smash hits in a row, and then I'm all yours," he said.

THE GIG STARTED well. I bumped into Suzanne in the toilets—she came out of a cubicle, drunk, and laughing so hard I presumed she was in there with a friend.

"No," she said, when I looked inside, and found it empty. "I was just remembering how funny Ian Astbury's hat is."

We got drinks, and flashed our AAA passes at the guy on the sound desk, so we could climb up onto his little stage and see the whole gig. John came onstage to an escalating "WhooooOOOOO!," and everyone stood a little taller, to see how he looked: expansive, in his usual shabby suit, with his hair already stuck to his forehead with sweat. He threw his arms open wide, like a loving bear, miming how much he'd had to drink: "Good evening! I appear to have accidentally got drunk—has anyone else done that tonight?"

The crowd cheered. Suzanne and I raised our glasses.

He started putting on his guitar. "But luckily, I've noticed, over the years, that my hands are like the hero's horse, in a film—they always seem to know the way home. Let's see if they still do tonight. Giddy-up, hands!"

He started playing the opening chords to "Count to Ten"— the audience cheered, and John looked at his hands with joy.

"Good boys!" he shouted, before starting to sing. "Good boys!"

The first half of the show was a joy—John rattling through the new album, whilst basically doing stand-up in between each song, as was his wont.

"Ah, look at him," I say to Suzanne, at one point, just after he'd made the whole audience do a Mexican wave in time to his first verse. "He's just the best thing."

She swiveled to look at me.

"Do you fancy him?"

"No," I said, my face like a lantern. I could feel her side-eyeing me, with a knowing look on her face.

The song ended.

"Give yourselves a round of applause for your superlative Mexican waving," John said. "We always have problems trying to do the Mexican wave in Mexico—because we don't know what to call it. They all just end up waving at us. Which is quite nice, really. Hands across the water, and all that. Anyway, time for a bit of an emotional handbrake-turn," he continued, tuning up his guitar. "This song is about my mother dying."

Because John's mood had been so jocular all evening, and because it was such an unexpected thing for him to say, a group of teenage girls down the front laughed. Instantly, a group of older, disapproving men booed them.

"Hey, hey, now," John said now, looking down the front. "No booing. Some people don't know the older songs, and my tragic backstory, and that's fine. It's good to make new friends. Everyone is welcome here. Hello, girls. You were probably only, like, ten when that song came out. You don't know about my classically troubled past. You are blissfully ignorant of my formative tumult."

John took a swig of his whisky, tentatively played another chord, looked at the girls at the front, and then stopped.

"Hmmm. Maybe the dead mum song *would* be a bit of a downer," he mused. "Shall we leave the ghost of Old Ma Kite off the stage, for now, and play a hit, instead? A new song? A Number Five smash hit—as seen on *Top of the Pops*? Do you want to *boogie*, girls?"

The girls whooped. John gave them the thumbs-up. But, from the back, one man shouted, loudly, "JUDAS!"

This threw the crowd into confusion. Some people booed

the "JUDAS!" man, some laughed at the reference, and all the naturally appeasing Neville Chamberlains in the audience started applauding, to try and smooth everything over. The girls down the front, meanwhile, waited for a pause, then screamed "WE LOVE YOU, JOHN!"

In reply, the "Judas" man shouted "WE LOVE YOU—WHEN YOU PLAY SOMETHING GOOD!"

Now the atmosphere began to splinter—between the new fans, and the old. Between the old indie men, and the new teenage girls.

In his drunken state—and unable to see who was shouting what, and why—John was thrown.

"Well, now," he said, looking down at his guitar. "It seems the audience is divided in what it wants tonight. What do you want to play, hands?"

His hands were still for a moment—thinking—then played the intro to his first single, "Wine Teeth." As the older fans in the audience roared, John looked up, beamed, and then stomped on the FX pedal that switched everything to furious feedback.

I could see what he was doing—he was too pissed to think, and so had fallen back on noise: like a Snow Queen conjuring up a blizzard, to bring a battle to a halt. He played the long version, and then slid straight into another, old, loud song—"Castling"—head down, hands a blur.

When the song finished—with its queasy, looping feedback sounding like the still-turning engine of a plane that was nose-down, and sinking fast in the sea—he lit a fag, took another swig of whisky, and began, conversationally, "I don't know if any of you saw the *D&ME* a couple of weeks ago."

"Oh no. No no no. Don't do this," Suzanne murmured.

The audience booed at the mention of the *D&ME*.

"*They* discussed the matter of my new audience," he continued, rubbing his forehead, as if trying to get blood to it. "They presented a rather . . . *acidulous* view of my career, suggesting I've 'sold out.' Do you—ignoring the inconvenient fact that this gig has *literally* sold out—think I've sold out?" he asked the crowd.

"NO!" they shouted.

"Ah, Tony Rich. You should be here tonight. I'm playing all your favorite songs. All the *old* ones," John continued, still smoking his fag. "Old songs, and young girls. That's what you like, I'm led to believe. This set list and the front row of this audience would be your idea of heaven."

"He means *me*!" I told Suzanne, excitedly. "He's referring to *my* inappropriate and possibly abusive sexual relationship there!"

"I'm proud of you, kid," Suzanne said, bemused.

"Truth be told, this has been a rum evening," John continued, leaning against the mic. "We're all friends here, so I can share with you this odd fact: tonight, I put my card into the hole-in-the-wall, checked my balance—found out that I am, apparently, now, a millionaire. A MILLIONAIRE! I think that calls for a celebratory drink. I'm buying *all* the front row a drink."

He got his whisky bottle, went to the front of the stage, knelt, and started splashing whisky into people's glasses. This got a round of applause. One very young girl held up her glass.

"Sorry—I'm going to have to ask you for ID," John said. Laughter. Then: "Fuck it. Underage drinking at gigs was the making of me," and topped up her glass. More cheers.

"I have to admit now, I'm pretty fucked-up tonight," he said, still on his knees, and lighting a fag. "Do you want to get fucked-up with me?"

"YES!"

"Then—LET'S GO, MOTHERFUCKERS!"

He played the first four chords of "Everyone's Wrong—Except You," to delighted cheers—the hit!—and then slid into an old B side. This was exactly what most of the room did not want. There was a restlessness—and then the slow, noticeable drift to the bar, and toilets. This gig had struggled, and now this gig was over. The vibe had died.

"Oh my God—he's fucking it," Suzanne said, with horrified delight. "What's he doing? He's losing them. He's playing all the not-hits. He's . . . playing this set at Tony Rich. What a fucking pointless thing to do."

I looked at John, staggering around the stage, head down, seemingly oblivious to the fact half his audience had disappeared, and that he was snatching defeat from the jaws of victory.

"Man, he needs an intervention," Suzanne says.

John finished the song, and looked up at the audience. There was applause, but it had an odd sound to it. I don't know how "clapping hands" can sound so different, when it's just hands, clapping, but this applause felt . . . sympathetic. Pitying.

"I can't watch this anymore," Suzanne said, getting down from the sound mixer. "It's like someone committing career suicide. In a bad way." I followed her.

"I'll talk to him, after," I said, as we went to the toilets. "He's just had a weird night."

I felt very protective of him. "I think he just needs a bit of time—to process it all."

"For fuck's sake, I could process it all in less than a minute," Suzanne said, briskly, eyes shining. "'Oh, I've got loads of hot new fans, and now I'm a millionaire. Great!' Bang. Done. I'm all over it."

"It's different for him," I said. "You want to be famous. He never has."

"Balls," Suzanne said. "Everyone wants to be famous."

"I really don't think John does," I said. "For him, it's just . . . a by-product of his job."

"*Exactly!*" Suzanne said, furiously. "It's a *job*—so *treat* it like one. Come on, make an effort, and fuck off again."

I was surprised she was this angry about it.

"It's just . . . sloppy," Suzanne continued, firmly. "It's ungrateful. I would never waste an opportunity like this. Never."

I thought of Zee—fretting over Suzanne not turning up to recording sessions, re-mortgaging his parents' house—but said nothing.

19

We stayed in the toilets until the gig ended, and then went to the aftershow. John clearly needed someone to talk to, but I wasn't going to go back to his dressing room, and have Andy Wolf tutting at me again. I would wait, at this party, until he arrived. What could go wrong? Except me getting very drunk. But that is one of the things about being friends with someone famous. They have so many people they have to talk to before they get to you . . . you are often very drunk by the time they finally materialize.

Suzanne and I were attending to all the business of an aftershow—smoking cigarettes, chatting balls, waiting for John to rock up—when I looked over to the bar, and nudged her.

"Look!" I said. "It's me, but a month ago!"

Waiting to be served—looking, as always, quite peevish—was Jerry Sharp. I had no idea he was a fan of John Kite! He was with a round-faced girl with a nose piercing, and a short skirt. She couldn't be any more than seventeen.

Jerry was looming over her, in a possessive way, and she was staring up at him in a way that said, "It looks like I will end the evening having sex with this famous comedian! Wow!"

"He chatted *me* up at an aftershow! This is exactly what happened to *me*! It's like *Crimewatch* is re-creating the incident!" I said to Suzanne. "What a blast from the past! I wonder if Nick Ross will say, at the end of it, 'Sleep well—don't have nightmares.'"

"Let's observe his seduction technique from a distance, and critique it," Suzanne said, cheerfully sipping her vodka and cranberry.

We watched for a while—the ping-pong match of seduction. He said something—she lobbed it back. He moved closer.

"The predator has locked onto its prey now," Suzanne said, in a David Attenborough voice, as Jerry lit a cigarette, and blew the smoke above the girl's head.

It was weird, watching someone who once chatted you up, chatting up someone else. When it was happening to me—when Jerry was looking into *my* eyes, and talking to *me*, at a party just like this—it felt we were improvising some unique sexual magic, like lubricous jazz geniuses. That we were the first people to be quite this sexy and amazing.

However, the same scenario, viewed from fifteen feet away, and without the benefit of dialogue, all seemed so much . . . thinner. More obvious. Jerry and his girl were just two drunk horny people, playing out a scene that had been staged a million times before. From a distance, the shimmering sheen of golden lust had turned to tin.

Still, it was all quite entertaining, and we were happily providing an alternate voice-over, until Jerry said something to the girl, and she suddenly looked uncomfortable, and tried to pull her skirt back down her thighs. Jerry laughed, and then—as she still looked flustered—leant over, and touched her face. She looked confused.

This tiny moment made me very unhappy. I remembered something.

"I bet he just said something about how fat her thighs are," I said. "He said that to me. 'I love a sturdy girl who wears clothes she really shouldn't.'"

"Ugh," Suzanne said.

"Then he said, 'The great thing is, that uncomfortable skirt will be on the floor soon. The only question is—your floor, or mine?'"

"Do you think, now he's tactically belittled her, he'll use her dented confidence as an opportunity to try and have anal sex?" Suzanne asked, amusedly.

"Is that what he did to you?"

"Yeah. I told him to stop. I said, 'If my clitoris is there, I'll give you the money myself.' He withdrew. What did he do to you?"

"Ha! You'll never guess what *I* did!" I said eagerly. I was now so drunk, I was suddenly darkly excited to tell her my news. It seemed like the best joke I could ever tell. Suzanne was going to *love* this!

"Wo, you know how awful he was the first time?" I started.

"Well, I bumped into him again, last month—*and I had sex with him!*"

I did jazz hands—to amplify the entrance of this appalling fact.

"WHAT?" Suzanne wailed.

"I know! Ludicrous! But Michael Stipe thought we were a couple." I shrugged. "I didn't want to let Michael Stipe down."

"*And?*" Suzanne asked, meaning: "Give me the whole encyclopedia entry on this surely doomed fuck."

I'm prepared to say the words. For the first time.

"Well, we kissed for a bit, and then—he started to film it."

I had hoped saying it would magically turn it into an amusing anecdote.

"He *filmed* you? Having *sex?*"

I nodded.

Suzanne's face made it clear that this was *not* an amusing anecdote.

"Oh, no. That's *horrible,*" Suzanne said. "He *porned* you. Did you *want* him to?"

I was surprised to find that I was, suddenly, out of nowhere, feeling a bit wobbly-lipped. Saying the words out loud made it all sound a far, far darker, and colder, event than I had pretended it was, for months, in my head. It made me sound very . . . small. A small, crushed thing. Suzanne put her arm around me.

"I don't think I was a particularly talented first-time performer," I said, attempting cheer. "My filmic debut will not be considered the moment a star is born, such as was the case with e.g.: Debbie Reynolds's cameo in *Three Little Words*."

Suzanne sighed.

"I think, at one point—startled by a penis-angle—I mooed. He filmed me having moo-sex, Suzanne."

"You couldn't tell him to turn the camera off?"

"I didn't want to crush his creativity! And, besides—how do you know whether or not you're into being filmed, unless you give it a try? I'm not a natural naysayer, Suzanne. I say nay to naysayers. That's my thing."

We watched Jerry and the girl, for a while.

"I guess, in the future, we will be friends with that girl," I said, finally, looking at Jerry's new inamorata with pity. "Next time we bump into her, we'll end up bitching with her, in the toilets, about him. Comparing notes on bad sex."

"Oh—she's not having bad sex," Suzanne said, decisively.

Jerry had gone to the toilet—leaving the girl standing alone—and Suzanne grabbed my hand, and walked over to the girl.

"What are you *doing*?" I asked, panicked.

"I'm just going to go and . . . give her some relevant information," Suzanne said, dragging me behind her.

"Suzanne, no! Let's not. I'm too drunk, I don't want to make a fuss. It's none of our business. And I've probably remembered it all wrong, anyway."

I didn't like this at all—I had the cold, panicky feeling you had as a kid in a playground fight, when the teachers suddenly appeared, and you knew you were about to get into serious trouble.

Despite my writhing to get free, Suzanne literally pulled me to the girl.

"Hiya!" Suzanne said to the girl, who looked at us cautiously. "Can we just have a quick word with you?"

"I'm here against my will. I'm just here to say 'Hello!'" I clarified.

"Hello?" the girl said back. Suzanne extended her hand, for a handshake. The girl shook it, still looking confused.

"I'm Suzanne, and this is Dolly, and we're from the Feminist Avenging League Against Sexual Predators," Suzanne said. "We are a new service—we're here to give fellow women information about bad men," she continued, conversationally. "And you are currently being chatted up by the Number One bad guy on our Most Not-Wanted list. Jerry Sharp is a bad man, sexually."

"Personally, I still believe in total freedom of choice! You shag who you want!" I said, still wriggling in the opposite direction.

"We have both had sexual experience of Mr. Sharp, and so we are simply passing on the fruits of our research to you, in the name of sisterly solidarity," Suzanne said. "We seriously advise you *not* to have sex with this man."

I could see Jerry was returning to the bar, and I was so desperate to escape this situation that I kicked Suzanne in the shin. Unfortunately, she was wearing knee-high biker boots, and didn't feel anything.

"He tried to watch his sitcom whilst I gave him a blow job, and videoed my unwilling colleague here, during coitus," Suzanne continued, pleasantly, as Jerry joined us.

He looked at us both, confused, for a minute, and then recognized us both—me still thrashing around, trying to leave.

"Well, hello, Dolly," he said. "Whoah. Wait. That would make a *great* title for a film."

I gave in, and stopped trying to escape. It was happening.

"What are you two girls doing here?" Jerry asked—still very pleasantly.

"They said you're a bad man," the girl said. "I don't really understand."

"Word gets around, Jerry," Suzanne said, slurring slightly, but still firm. "We're just letting this girl know what your whole *deal* is."

Jerry looked at us both, and the penny dropped.

He turned to the girl. "I'm so sorry," he said. "You've seen *Fatal Attraction*?"

This was the worst thing he could do.

"Don't fucking Glenn Close *us*!" Suzanne shouted. "Don't fucking Glenn Close this situation, you Michael Douglas cunt. I could give an interview next week and tell this whole fucking story."

"And what story would you tell?" Jerry said, still being flippant. "That you and your friend both had totally consensual, amazing, dirty sex with me? Great exclusive. I don't think I'm going to look bad in that situation. Tell away."

"Did you consent to being filmed, Dolly?" Suzanne asked. Her grip on my wrist was iron.

"Uh, I don't—I don't think so. I mean, I've never wanted to be filmed. But it doesn't matter. My motto is, you know . . . let's let bygones be bygones!"

"I seem to remember Dolly was very keen to have sex with me," Jerry said. "She galloped into that taxi, didn't you, darling?"

"But she didn't *ask* you to film her?" Suzanne persisted.

"She was too busy saying 'Do it harder,' as I recall," Jerry said, still pleasantly. "She said it a lot. So I felt it was implied."

I recoiled.

There was a pause.

"You enjoying that drink?" Suzanne said, gesturing to Jerry's glass, in his hand.

"I was enjoying it more a moment ago, to be honest," Jerry replied, smoothly.

Suzanne nodded—then threw her drink into his face.

Cranberry juice dripped from his hair. The people around us stopped talking, and stared. Everything went quiet.

"What the fuck are you doing?" he asked, momentarily stunned.

"Well, you're already drinking," Suzanne replied. "So I presume you'd enjoy having one in the face, as well. I don't need to ask you. *It's implied.*"

Jerry stood there for one second more—and then went berserk.

"You fucking crazy bitch," he roared. "What the fuck do you think you're playing at? What the *fuck* are you doing?"

A bouncer appeared beside us.

"This is a metaphor for consent, Jerry—a fucking living metaphor for consent!" Suzanne screamed, as the bouncer put his hand on her arm.

"Let's go," I said to Suzanne.

"That's a good idea, love," the bouncer said, moving us toward the exit. "Out."

I panicked. I didn't want to miss John. I had a date with John! "No—I don't want to leave," I cried. "We have passes! We're here for the aftershow!" I showed the bouncer my AAA pass.

He pushed us toward the door.

"You can't throw us out! I'm friends with the band!" I said, wriggling to get free.

"No alcohol for people who are already intoxicated," he said, taking my pass off. "And that's you. Licensing laws."

"I don't want to stay at this crappy party anyway," Suzanne sniffed, starting to leave.

"I do!" I said, thinking of John. "I really do!"

"You bitches are dead. You are fucking dead," Jerry said, before realizing everyone was staring at him and regaining his composure.

"Haha—mad exes," he said, shrugging. "You don't have one for ages—then two come along at once."

There was nervous laughter.

He looked at the girl—but she wasn't looking at him. She was looking at me. She suddenly realized something.

"Hang on—aren't you Dolly Wilde?" she said. "You wrote that thing in *The Face*—about how teenage girls *should* have sex with famous people."

She looked at Jerry, and then to me again, confused.

"Yes, teenage girls should have sex with famous people," I said, as the bouncers ushered us away. "Just not *him*."

I was being pushed through the doorway, in a tangle with Suzanne.

"It's quite a complex issue, really!" I offered, finally, as we were ejected into the stairway. "I may have to write another thousand words about it! Check next month's edition for further clarification!"

The last thing I saw was the girl standing there, looking very alone, as Jerry put his arm around her, and glared after us.

"Got you taped," he mouthed—and then smiled. It was not a kind smile.

IT TOOK A very long time to find a cab—as I was being sick into a bin, from the horror, and cabdrivers tend not to favor those potential customers.

By the time I got home, after dropping Suzanne off— "Wasn't that brilliant?" Me: "Um"—there were three answer-phone messages from John.

The first—with the roar of a party in the background— was, "Where are you, honey? I'm at the aftershow—I can't find you. I thought we were going to piss off together, and chat beautiful balls? I need to download."

The second was far more slurring: "Babe, I don't know where you are. I'm too pissed to go home yet. We're going on to the Groucho now—I hate all these cunts. Why aren't you here?"

The third was just the sound of people laughing, and John breathing, then sighing, "Dutch? Dutch?" in a puzzled voice, before hanging up.

PART III

20

The next morning, I wake up very anxious.

It's all very well for Suzanne to noisily confront Jerry in a public bar, in front of the entire music industry, but my problem is that I don't know enough about having sex to be able to say, with confidence, "What Jerry did was one hundred percent wrong."

Sex is so mysterious—I mean, half of it happens *inside* you. How crazy is that?—that I just don't know if "a man filming your shit shag" is wrong. I've only ever had six sexes, and I've never read a definitive checklist of what "normal" sex is. There are *no* official guidelines on it. You *cannot* look it up at the library, as with literally everything else in my life. Maybe people are having "Jerry sex" all the time—and I am simply revealing my terrible inexperience if I wail, "Actually, I didn't want you to do that!"

I don't want to say, outright, that I hated the sex with Jerry, because it might well be that *this* kind of sex is like olives: at first, you gag, and can't understand why people go on about it; but if you keep trying then, eventually, you *get* it. You are rewarded for your persistence, and start to love the video-sex with Jerry/Olives! You are a sexually sophisticated grown-up now, that smells of olives and sexual daring!

I really want to be a sexually sophisticated grown-up that smells of olives and sexual daring.

However, I *also* only want to have sex that I actually like. And I *did* not like that sex.

The ultimate problem with Jerry is that I can't work out which of the two available truths about our shag would upset me more:

1. That I have been sexually naive and shocked about something that, actually, is perfectly normal; or
2. That I have actually been badly abused by a massive sex case.

Both of those are things I don't want. But they're my only options. Which is why I have been resolutely trying to forget the whole thing.

And now, in the midst of all this confusion, Suzanne has waded into war, and turned my vagina into a feminist battleground. That was not what I had planned for my vagina at all. I'd always been gunning for something more like "a well-loved public space, with limited parking," instead.

This whole thing is making me very anxious. I decide to ring Suzanne, and tell her we need to apologize. Just to calm everything down. That's the right thing to do. You should never instigate a full-blown nuclear Gender War when you're feeling a bit wobbly.

However, when I dial her number, it rings for ages, before she finally picks up the phone, drops it—and, before I can say anything, shouts, "Whoever you are, fuck off until midday" in a very croaky voice, before slamming the phone down again.

Although this is a very Suzanne thing to do—it is only 10:00 a.m.—it doesn't help my anxiety, or paranoia, so I ring Zee, for reassurance. Talking to Zee is always like eating a lovely baked potato. He is the human carbohydrate.

"How you doing?" I ask, sitting in bed, feeling pale.

"Bit stressed," Zee says, mildly. "Suzanne's supposed to be in the studio right now, doing vocals. Whenever I ring her up, she says 'Fuck off until midday' and puts the phone down. So far, the sound of her silence has cost me two hundred seventy quid. There goes my mum's sofa."

"Can I ask your advice?" I say.

I fill him in on last night—on Jerry, and the girl, and basically calling him a sexual pervert. "And now I feel like there's a load of bad vibes, and that I should apologize to Jerry—make everything better again."

"And what, exactly, would you apologize for?" Zee says, slightly confused. "Giving some friendly advice to a potential sexual victim?"

"When you say it like that, it sounds so reasonable!" I say.

"Well, it *is* reasonable. You're allowed to *tell* people things," Zee says, simply. "You can say how you feel. You can share your knowledge. That's a thing humans do."

"But it's causing such a *fuss*," I wail. "I don't like it."

"Sometimes, just by being alive, you cause a fuss," he says.

"Life is fussy. Look, I've got to go—got my alarm call to put into Suzanne. Take care. Call me later if you're worried. But do *not* apologize to Jerry."

I wander around the flat for a while, wondering what to do. Everything seems a bit . . . *wrong*. John, Suzanne, Zee, me—no one's in a great place. We are all stuck. Life has become weighty. The fruit machine of London seems jammed. What would make all of this better?

I run a bath, to soak my hangover, and stare at my breasts, floating on top of the water.

"What shall I do, tits?" I ask.

They carry on floating there, looking a bit confused. I guess most of the time, they can't see anything—they are essentially blindfolded, inside my bra, like birds of prey. They must be *so surprised* every time they come out! They're either in a bath, or being pawed by a random. Surprise!

"One day, I'll fill you in on all the stuff that happens in between," I promise them. "Mostly, it's just me typing."

It is, as I idly wobble my breasts, and promise them a better life, that I realize what might just make everything better, for everyone: a party! A "We're All Fucked" party! For surely, by bringing together a collection of troubled people—all loosely interconnected and/or already at odds with each other—and filling them with alcohol, things will immediately improve! If the fruit machine is jammed, just . . . *knock* it a little. Give it a bang on the side, to get things going again. That's what a party is. A bang on the side of the machine. I'm going to bang the machine.

21

Two weeks later, and I am cleaning the flat from top to bottom. I have to admit, the place has become a bit of a tip.

This morning, I hauled six, bursting, rotting bags out of the kitchen, to the bins outside. I noticed that some of them had leaked bin juice all over the floor, and that when I picked them up, there were gangs of maggots thrashing around and swimming around in the goo, like some hellish vermin swimming pool. I am disappointed in myself.

"Your destiny was not to become a maggot farmer, Johanna," I say, as I scoop them up with a J Cloth, and flick them into the garden. "You can do better than this."

Intent on improving myself, I wait until there's no one walking down the street, and then steal some tulips from next-door's garden, and put them in a milk bottle on the table.

"You lift the soul, and delight the eye!" I tell them, as I start hoovering up the roughly six tons of molted dog hair from the carpet.

In my invitation to my follow partygoers, I have explained that I would provide the venue, and, in exchange, they must bring the booze (John), food (Suzanne), and soft drinks (Zee). This is because of the spirit of the collective, and also because I'm broke: *The Face* still haven't paid me, and, last week, the electricity got cut off, and I had to go to an office on Bond Street, with cash, and pay to have it reconnected.

I took the dog with me, but she panicked on the underground, and tried to run down an up escalator, and then whined constantly while I was queuing to pay. I'm surprised major facilities such as electricity don't fast-track people who have dogs with them. Judging by how annoyed everyone looked, it would benefit everyone, and it would certainly be kinder to dogs.

Having the electricity turned back on was a mixed blessing, however. While it was off, I'd lit the flat with candles—several of them on top of the TV. When the electricity came back on, I realized that the wax from the candles had dripped down the back of the TV, and into its innards. I realized this because the TV then exploded, quite dramatically.

Today—as part of my salon preparation—I hump the dead TV out to the next-door neighbor's skip, but the skip is too full for me to fit it in. I can't believe they're so lazy about this. Sort your skip out, guys!

I leave it on the pavement next to the skip, instead. I'm getting things done.

ZEE WAS THE first to turn up. Of course he was. He had a bottle of Ribena, a bottle of Dandelion & Burdock, and a bottle of cream soda.

"All the best ones!" I said. "Quick—before Suzanne gets here: how's the album going?"

"Oh my word," Zee said. "She's killing me. She says she's scrapped everything, and started again. The stress is giving me gingivitis. It's all gone to my gums."

He looked more unhappy than I'd ever seen him.

"I'm going to pour you a bracing measure," I said, splashing the Dandelion & Burdock into a mug. "You need it. Would you like to take up smoking? I find it helps."

"Lung cancer would actually be more relaxing than this," Zee said, sadly. "She's driving me crazy. She just doesn't seem to understand deadlines. Or money. Suzanne just doesn't seem . . . scared. Of anything. She never worries."

"I guess that's the good thing about her, too," I said, dubiously.

The doorbell rang.

On the doorstep was Julia. She was wearing her Wellington boots and her yellow mac, and was looking slightly put out at being here.

"Suzanne told me to come," she said, observing my confusion.

"Oh!" I replied.

"I'm to stop her drinking more than five drinks, and I'm to put her in a taxi by midnight," Julia recited, looking sour. "She's being 'professional.'"

"It's a pleasure to have you here," I said, gallantly.

"She's really getting on my tits at the moment," Julia continued. "Really, fuck all this. I trained as an architect. I could jack this in any time."

She came in, and looked around for a drink.

"I'm so sorry—the drink hasn't arrived yet," I said, gesturing to a chair for her to sit down. "It should be arriving shortly."

Julia clocked Zee.

"Oh, right," she says. "Now I get it. 'Professional.' In a taxi by midnight. Hello, Boss."

"Hello, Julia," Zee replied.

Julia sighed.

"Shall we be honest?" she said, pouring herself a cream soda. "Now we're all here? She is a cunt, isn't she?"

The doorbell rang again.

"Is that Suzanne?" Zee asked.

Julia laughed.

"You're kidding, right?" she said, taking a drag of her fag. "Suzanne's always late. You know that. Technically, I'm still waiting for her to turn up to a lunch I invited her to. Two months ago."

It was John—in a huge, ratty fur coat, signet rings glinting. He'd put on weight in the last two weeks—his face was puffy, and he looked as fat and golden as a bottle of Ruinart champagne. I knew this, because he promptly brought six bottles of Ruinart out of his bag, and put them on the table. They looked grand—like a crowd of small kings. He was already drunk, of course. And, I thought—looking at him— high. There was the cold frost of cocaine in his eyes.

"Do you know how easy it is to start spending a million pounds?" he said, gesturing to the collection. "Fabulously easy. It's the easiest thing I've ever done. The money just *sails* out—it really is quite incredible."

Bottles deposited on the table, he caught me around the

waist, and spun me round. "It's so good to see you, honey. I will sit next to you, as is my right," he added, before taking off his coat, sitting down, lighting up a cigarette, and then extending his hand across the table, to Julia, and Zee.

"I am John," he said, beaming at them. "I have taken drugs. I shall now open champagne."

It was a measure of how delicious champagne is, and what easy company Zee and John—and, after a drink, Julia—were, that we completely forgot Suzanne was coming until we heard a kerfuffle in the hallway, an hour later. A semi-ring on the bell, followed by a thump.

"The . . . man! The man . . . needs a . . . thing," Suzanne's voice came through the letter box.

Outside, Suzanne was doubled over, still talking through the letter box, and there was a taxi, with a rather annoyed-looking driver.

"He needs . . . money," Suzanne said grandly, as Julia ran out past me to pay him.

Suzanne grabbed me, and whispered in my ear, "I'm not getting drunk in front of the boss, right? Good tactic. Clever Suzanne. But I've preloaded," and tapped her nose.

She looked wired. I couldn't work out what she had taken—my guess was that it was some random collection from her pill bowl. Still, she was dressed magnificently—red, curly-toed Moroccan slippers, a black silk jumpsuit unbuttoned to show a denim bra, and dark purple eyelids. As always, she looked as if the clothes had run toward her, going, "We wish to live nowhere else but upon you! You will make us glorious!"

If she could play guitar as well as she could wear trousers, she would be Number 1 across the world.

"So here we are, for inappropriateness, and shenanigans!" she cried out, entering the living room, depositing her battered guitar case on the sofa, and throwing her arms out wide. "I have done the catering, as requested!"

She proffered a very thin, blue carrier bag, clearly from an off-license, or petrol station. I took it from her, and put the contents on the table.

"A packet of six sausages, and eighty Marlboro Lights," I said, looking at them. Even with my lackluster housekeeping skills, I was shocked. "How is this 'the catering'?"

"There are four people here, so one and a half sausages each: that's four hundred and fifty calories. The recommended meal size. But I don't think," Suzanne said, opening the Marlboros and pausing to light one, "people are going to get that hungry. We're smoking. It's a happening! It's a party! We'll be too busy talking to use our mouths for *eating*."

She swivels to John. "And you—you are John Kite!" she said, going over, gathering his hands and kissing them, before curtsying.

"Almost constantly," John replied, equably.

"I love you, man," Suzanne said, straightening up. "But on the other hand—I fucking hate you! I *hate* you! You've had a Number One record before me, and that kills me. You're winning! You're *beating* me!"

"Well, I have the advantage of being a very, very old man," John said, calmly. "I'm twenty-seven. And you must be—?"

"Twenty-five," Suzanne said, slightly too fast.

"Yeah—in dog years," Julia said quietly, coming into the room, having put the sausages on to fry.

I was quickly learning the first thing about convening

a party of performers. Performers are semi-nomadic, and semi-feral. They don't really know how to be in a domestic environment.

FOR THE FIRST hour, we just concentrated on drinking the champagne—Suzanne very pointedly counting out "That's drink Number One—only four left!" "Drink Number Two there—only three more for me! I'm working in the morning!" in front of Zee.

I could see how painful this was for Zee—being cast as Suzanne's jailer, when the reality was he was someone who'd just given her £50,000—simply because he believed in her.

Before now, I'd never really realized that was what record companies—little indie record companies—were: transactors of love, and belief. What an amazing invention. What an amazing invention Suzanne is shitting all over.

Still, this was not my biggest problem. Since I had known them, I had harbored the fond belief that, when I got Suzanne and John together, they would become the best of friends. They were the two most alive, vital, funny, not-fuck-giving people I knew—it seemed obvious that, when we all finally gathered in one place, we would form a gang. I have never been in a gang before—ever—and the idea of finally being in one seems like the solution to all unhappiness and doubt. I'm pretty sure that I will never be sad again once I am flanked by my Friar Tuck, Potsy, and Goose.

In the event, this belief turned out to be a wrong belief.

After spending just ten minutes in Suzanne's company, John took me into the kitchen, on the pretext of finding an ashtray, knocked back two shots of whisky in one go, and said, "Is she an *actual* fucking madwoman? Has she escaped from a ward, or prison? Or suffered a recent blow to the head?"

I looked out into the living room, where Suzanne was wearing John's fur coat, and matter-of-factly crushing pills on the table with the heel of her shoe, then sprinkling them into a spliff, whilst continuing a long, unbroken monologue on how, as a teenage girl, she used to sporadically throw herself down the main staircase of her local WHSmith: "They'd think I fainted. They'd take me into their back room and give me cups of tea, and fags, and free copies of *Vogue*. It was amazing."

"Why did you do that?" Zee asked, concerned.

"To get cups of tea, and fags, and free copies of *Vogue*," Suzanne replied patiently.

When I planned this party of fuck-ups, two weeks ago, I had decided I would theme it like an informal nineteenth-century salon—beginning the evening by introducing intriguing conversational topics which would spark effervescent debate, to the edification of all. I presumed this would be a fairly normal thing to do.

As I said before, I had never thrown a party before.

As I could see that Suzanne was about to launch into another anecdote—"Therapy? Oh God, let me tell you about therapy. My first-ever therapy session, for Narcissistic Personality Disorder, I was half an hour late. I got distracted, doing a *Cosmo* quiz on 'How Self-Obsessed Are You?'"—I decided that this was the ideal time to start the intellectual part of the evening.

Again, that was a wrong decision.

Banging on the side of a mug with a spoon—"Attention, please! Hem-hem!"—I posed the first question: "An easy starter for ten: What, ultimately, is your biggest ambition?"

Julia's answer was "To leave the Branks," and John's was the purposely facetious, "The ambition in the heart of every man, darling—to make art that changes the whole world, and to lose two stone."

Zee had just started explaining why he found the idea of running a record label so moving—"It's like a union. You pay your dues—a pound ninety-nine for a single—so kids like you, can make songs about kids like you"—when Suzanne, who was personifying the belief that, really, there was no such thing as "conversation," just people waiting for other people to stop talking, so they can say something, interrupted, banging her palms on the table.

"If you're gonna ask me, I think, as an artist, your job is to fall on your *arse*," she said, restless as a wasp jar. "You have to *dare*. You have to not be *scared*. You should believe you are a blueprint of the future. 'This life is but the draft of a draft.' That's *Moby-Dick*," she added, to the table at large.

"I know it's *Moby-Dick*," John replied, tetchily.

"'Adverse winds are holding mad Christmas in me,'" Suzanne continued. "Those are words to live by. That's *Moby-Dick*, too."

"I am happy for you that you have read that book," John said. "I, too, have read that book. I am thinking about it, quietly, in my head, now."

"'It is the easiest thing in the world for a man to look as if he had a great secret in him,'" Suzanne sniped.

I didn't know much about drugs, but she seems to have

taken the drugs that make you quote *Moby-Dick* all the time. I've not come across them before today.

Is she like this all the time? John mouthed at me. I nodded.

"By the way," Suzanne said, leaning across the table, and tapping John on the arm. She beamed at him, like the news she was about to impart was tremendous. "By the way, I've made a big decision: I'm *not* going to fall in love with you."

"That's—very kind of you?" John said. It was the first time I'd ever really seen him disconcerted in a conversation.

"It would be too obvious," she continued. "You and me? Too Taylor and Burton. I mean, you are hot, there's no doubt about that. And the sex would be, of course, amazing. But we'd fight all the time—twin layers of lightning, man. And I just want some peace. So I wish you well. But—*no*."

Suzanne's air was as if John has just formally proposed to her, and she was having to regretfully crush his long-harbored dreams.

"Thank you for letting me down gently," John said. Under the table, he took hold of my hand. "Tell me, Suzanne—have you ever considered going to 'me-hab'? So you can get treatment for talking about yourself all day long?"

Suzanne ignored this completely. "John, I'm glad we have this chance to talk," she replied. Her posture changed—to that of the maverick CEO of a multinational company, about to fire the entire board. "Because, I will be honest—I accepted the invitation to this party for a reason."

Oh dear. I had a feeling this wasn't going to end well.

"I came here with a *mission*," Suzanne continued. "And I'm telling you now, because none of these other assholes will—because they don't want to be assholes . . ."

"I'm fine with being an arsehole," Julia said. "I really am."

"But John. Kite. You need to *snap out of it*, man."

Suzanne banged her fist on the table. Julia—with a practiced air—removed the drinks nearest Suzanne, and put them at the other end of the table.

"I'm so sorry," John said, with an icy formality. "But I thought I heard someone wearing Mr. Claypole's shoes telling me to 'snap out of it'?"

We all looked at Suzanne's shoes. They were a bit *Rentaghost*. I could see that now. Suzanne ignored him.

"That last gig," Suzanne said, going up a gear. "What was that? You emotionally machine-gunned the first twenty rows of that gig. You made all those teenage girls feel like *idiots* for being there. You know what? If you don't want those fans—*give them to me*. Give me those girls. Don't waste those girls! Don't treat them like that! *I* will have them. *I* have something for them."

"Is it a hat, with bells on?" John slurred, pleasantly; but his eyes were tight, and hard.

"Allow me to utter the catchphrase of all hearts: *Let me show you what I've got*," Suzanne said, getting her guitar case. She had an ability—which served her well in life—to completely ignore people taking the piss out of her. As she took the guitar out of its case, I tensed: Suzanne was an incredible person in many ways, but "playing a guitar whilst sober" was not one of her strengths, and I shuddered to imagine what she would be like in this state.

"Remember—strings at the *front*," Julia murmured.

John, sighing, reached across the table and poured himself a mug of whisky. His expression, in the face of an incoming song, was that of a baby spying its second spoonful of mashed carrots: his mouth was tightly closed.

However, when Suzanne started playing, it was unlike anything she'd played before. Her voice still sounded like a roof-cat yowl—but there was a new, true soreness that flew straight to the heart. It made me think of something I'd read about Japanese pottery—back in the library, years ago: I'd read everything else, and Japanese pottery was the only thing left—about how broken cups, and bowls, are deliberately mended with precious metals, so that the cracks look beautiful. Suzanne's voice was now like this—something broken, but threaded with platinum. A net of gold scars.

"And if God is a girl / She would not send me you / She would not let you do the things you do," Suzanne sang, sadly, and Zee suddenly looked alert—hopeful, eager—whilst John nodded, grudgingly.

Suzanne only sang the first verse and chorus before her fingers fumbled on a chord, and she hit the guitar abruptly, and stopped, with a laugh.

"It's called 'God Is a Girl,'" she said, putting the guitar down again. "We were thinking, we could put cellos on it?"

Zee calculated in his head, winced, then nodded.

"Like 'She's Leaving Home'?" he asked.

"Like 'She's Leaving Home,'" Suzanne said.

John stood up and steadied himself by putting his hands on the table.

"Suzanne," he said, swaying from side to side. "You may—you may *have* my girls. Have *all* my teenage girls. The whole fucking zoo. They're *yours*. Do with them as you will."

Suzanne did a neat bow, and John sat down again—

heavily, almost missing the chair. He was really sweating now—he looked like Henry VIII trying to get the lid off a jam jar. Some jam he *really* wanted.

"I'll . . . round them up into a fucking truck, and send them to you tomorrow," he continued. "A truck of moon-calves. With my blessing."

"Pudding, anyone?" I said, brightly. I have a Viennetta in the freezer. I though John might need food, to sober him up.

"John shall not get fatter!" he said, outraged. "John shall have his meal substitute!" He put a wrap of coke on the table, and started chopping out lines. "Just one instead of break-fast, and another at lunch, and then a healthy meal in the evening. You'll see the pounds *falling off*!"

John had always been a drinker—a joyous, Viking drinker—but this was the second time I'd seen him in this state: the kind of drunk that starts early, and explosive—then feels like a slow slide down, into darkness. Before, he seemed to drink to make the world bigger, the night longer, the stories brighter. He drank to fly.

Now, he seemed to be drinking to drown.

When he came up from snorting his line, he was gasping a little, as he thumbed his nose. The expression on people's faces the second after they take coke had always intrigued me—they always look a little surprised they've actually done it. As if, up until the last second, they thought they might think better of it—but have just realized that, actually, no: they really do just want to get fucked-up.

"My darling?" he said—offering me the rolled note, and the line on the table.

"No, thank you," I said, cheerfully.

"Waste not want not," Suzanne said—suddenly appearing beside me, and hoovering up the line expertly. She thumbed her nose, and sat back down again.

"You know, *good for you* that you don't do cocaine. Good for *you*," she said, lighting a cigarette. "It's one of the most unethical products on Earth."

"Yeah." John nodded his head. "There's no point in boycotting Nestlé, if you're then up all night railing gak. There's no *organic* cocaine. There's no friendly cooperatives of lesbians growing some mellow shit. Every single person involved in the production is a *murderer*."

As he gave this fast, sniffing speech, he chopped out another two lines.

"Colombia is fucked for *starters*," he said, bending over the table, inhaling, then sitting back in his chair, as Suzanne came in for her line.

"And now, I am high on cocaine and hypocrisy," he said, eyes slightly out of focus, lighting a cigarette.

I looked around my first ever party. Zee and Julia were by the record player, chatting over a pile of records. Suzanne and John were yabbering at each other in cocaine fast-forward, looking like some weird Eastern European cartoon.

I realized something: I was tired of my party, now. Sadness makes you tired and, tonight, John had made me sad. It wasn't really the drunkenness, or the cocaine—pretty much all of London was drunk and on cocaine. If I were to make moral judgments about everyone who was drunk and on cocaine—even something brief, like, "Oh! That's quite disappointing behavior!"—I would barely have enough time left to be disappointed in myself.

No. It's what he said earlier—about his teenage fans. That he is so careless about their love that he offered to "give" them all to Suzanne. As if their love were a commodity which he could box, and give away—rather than being the souls of actual people, who had been filled with magic by his songs. As if their love wasn't theirs at all, anymore—but *his*. Separate from the person who made it.

When John looked out at a crowd, he clearly saw just a single, solid mass, and not thousands of young women, who had waited months to be there; whose walls were covered in pictures of him; who quietly sang his lyrics to themselves when they were scared, walking down dark roads at night. Young women like me.

And this is why I was sad. Because I knew I might be an unusual teenage girl—loving music; meeting my heroes; writing about it—but I was, ultimately and undeniably, still a teenage girl. And if my best friend, and the man I loved, was so careless and disregarding of teenage girl-fans, then he was ignorant and disrespecting of my *kind*, and I could not let that stand. They are my people. My ultimate loyalty lies with girls like me.

Tonight was the night I did, for the first time, what I am destined to do at a hundred more parties in my life: I lay on the sofa, and pretended to have fallen asleep, as the party continued around me. And, as I lay there—eyes closed, listening to everyone—I thought: "I can write. I am *good* at writing. I am going to write something about teenage fans so good, it will make John a better person. I am going to *upgrade* him—with prose."

22

Of course, it takes a while to write a piece that's good enough to spark spontaneous moral evolution in the drunken, coke-blown pop star you love.

Six days later, I am up early, still working away on the piece, when I get a phone call from Krissi. It's 7:00 a.m. Seven a.m. is a very unusual time to get a phone call from Krissi. Seven in the morning is a very unusual time to get a phone call from anyone.

"I think Dad's living with me," Krissi says, before I can even say "Hello."

"What?"

"I think Dad's living with me," Krissi says, again. "He came down 'for a visit' two weeks ago, and he's still not left. Can you ask him to come down and visit you? Pretend you've got some problem you need him to help with. Putting up a shelf, or . . . explaining jazz to you."

"But what if he then just moves in with me again?"

"You've got more room there than me, so it wouldn't be so bad. I mean, that would be the best place for him, really."

"You're asking me to . . . *adopt* Dad?"

"Come on, Johanna, give me a break—it's a communal house, and it's not fair on the others."

"What do they make of him?"

"That's the worst part," Krissi says, miserably. "He gives them lifts in the MG, and gets them weed, and tells them stories about being in the toilet with Jimi Hendrix. They think he's awesome."

I can see how, if you weren't related to him, you might think that.

"Say you need him back with you, Johanna. I'm begging you," Krissi says. "I can't take it much longer. Yesterday, he said he might 'pop along' to one of my lectures, and 'give it a bang.' It's multivariate calculus and mathematical models. I'm at university with my dad."

I feel bad for Krissi—I really do. But there's no way I'm letting Dad come back here. I've only just started being able to sit naked on the sofa again without feeling inappropriate.

"He sounds very settled there," I say. "Like when a stray cat decides to move in with you. Do you want to upset the cat?"

"The cat's upsetting me, Johanna. I didn't smash my balls through GCSEs and A levels to still be living with my dad. He keeps watching the Grand Prix with the sound right up, and taking really long baths. He was in there for an hour last night. I had to pee into a jug, and throw it out of the window. I'm starting to live the life of a medieval city-dweller. I want to ring a bell at him."

"Krissi, I would love to help you," I say, staring at my laptop screen, "but first, I can't, and secondly, it's just very funny. And thirdly, at least it's not Mum."

"That is my only comfort," Krissi says, ringing off.

THAT WAS THE 30th of January. On February 6th, Zee asks if we can meet in the pub, and even though I am tits deep in writing the piece for John that will explain everything to him, and make him a better person, Zee sounds so stressed that, half an hour later, I am sitting in the Mixer, with the dog, watching Zee try to get a pint of milk off the tetchy barman without causing some kind of international incident.

"I'm going to come straight to the point," Zee says, sitting down, and looking awkward. "The Branks are still behind on their album. The lease comes up on my flat next week, and if I don't renew I get my deposit back. If I give the deposit to the studio, I can keep them in there until they finish, and hire a cellist. But that would mean I'm homeless."

"Can't you sleep in the office?" I ask.

"Dolly, I had to give up the office when Suzanne burned the first demo tapes."

"Oh." I feel ashamed I've not kept up with Zee's comings and goings. But then, he really needs to start coming into rooms, shouting, "GUESS WHAT JUST HAPPENED!," like normal people do. People who wait to be asked if their lives are collapsing are just asking for trouble, really.

I say "Oh" again—and then realize the obvious solution to all this.

"Stay at mine!" I say. "It's only the sofa, and the dog will lie on you, but I promise to open a window when I smoke, and the mice are very friendly."

"I feel terrible for asking," Zee says, looking both awkward, and relieved. "But it's only until the album comes out. And I can do you a proper deal—I could give you shares in the label?"

I would have let him stay for free anyway. The idea of having shares in something is so excitingly grown-up, I make a squeaking sound.

"Don't tell Suzanne, though," Zee says. "I don't want her to feel under any more pressure than she is. The first single is out next month—I want her all guns blazing."

"Does she have any other mode?" I ask. "I don't think she has a 'standby' function."

ON THE DAY Zee moves in, the dog stupidly barking as he carries in boxes and boxes of records—"I'm so sorry. I promise I'll be gone the moment some money comes in"—a terrible thing happens: *Melody Maker* publishes the story of me, Suzanne, and Jerry fighting on its gossip page.

I know this, because Suzanne rings me up, and after the first three minutes of her going "The bastard! The bastard! The bastard!," starts to tell me, even as I go, "No! Don't tell me! I don't want to know! I can't handle it!" and singing over her.

Even though I try to blot her out, I gather that the gossip columnist had approached Jerry for a quote about the incident, and Jerry's quote—which made my heart stop—was, "The truth always comes out, in the end. And, to both quote Jack Nicholson in *A Few Good Men*, and shag as many women as he has, a lot of people can't actually handle the truth."

"Is that him . . . threatening me?" I ask Suzanne, in a tiny voice. "Is he threatening to tell everyone we had sex and filmed it?"

"YES!" she says. "YES!"

I don't like the idea of Jerry talking about us having sex. I fear I will not come out of it well. It makes me feel incredibly anxious. He might describe my vagina to the public, and then I would have to die.

"That is blackmail, pure and simple," Suzanne continued. "He's trying to silence you. Us talking to his new birds has rattled him."

"Oh, man," I say, sitting down. In books, people always feel sick when they get bad news. I don't get that. I go kind of deaf, instead—a ringing in my ears, like I've just been hit. I can't really make out what Suzanne's saying. When my hearing comes, Suzanne's gleefully saying, "Karma's a bitch. A bitch that will bite you," and Zee is sitting next to me, patting my knee and looking concerned.

You okay? he mouths.

Yes? I mouth back.

"What should I do?" I ask Suzanne hopelessly.

"If there's one thing I know about the world, it's that it will pay him back for this," Suzanne says, grimly. "He'll get his. Anyway, I've got to go—I've got to do my solo now."

"Remember—the strings go at the front," I say, automatically, and Suzanne laughs, and rings off.

23

Friday is the last day of Kite's UK tour. The reviews have come in for the first half, and they were not good: "messy," "incoherent," "drunk." I had figured on leaving him alone, while he was on tour, but at 11:00 a.m. on Friday morning, I get a call: "Please come," he says. "It's just Eastbourne. I need to end this tour on a high, and I've no one here except that cunt Andy Wolf."

"He is a cunt," I said, cheerfully.

"I'm glad you agree!" John said.

Then I could hear something in the background.

"Andy says I'm not allowed to call him a cunt, and that you're a cunt for calling him a cunt," John said.

So I could tell John was probably already drunk.

The gig was mortifying—John played the hits at twice

their proper speed, as if horrified by them, and rambled so long between numbers that the audience became restless. Once or twice, he did something beautiful—the song about his mother, "St. Angelus Window," was sung so delicately it was as if he was that scared teenage boy again, looking through the hospital window, and realizing she was going to die, and leave him in charge of his siblings. And not even John could fuck up singing the gleeful "Misericord," yelping, *"Well I survived this / Well I survived us!,"* and then howling— although the way he sang it tonight made me think that the "us" he was singing about was the audience, who looked like patient, disappointed lovers who had had enough, and wanted to leave.

After the show, I wait in the bar at the hotel John is staying at—a huge, run-down Victorian redbrick thing, with massive windows, overlooking the sea.

John arrives with Andy Wolf, who looks like a man in a comedy film who has inherited a spirited chimpanzee from an eccentric aunt, but has yet to learn the lighthearted lesson having such chaos in his life could teach him.

"Andy, I feel you have delighted me enough with your presence," Kite says, sitting down heavily at my table, and squeezing my hand. "The duchess here can look after me now."

"Well, yes—we do have guidelines at the record company about leaving priority artists with children," Andy says, giving me a hateful smile.

"Fetch me my medicine," John says, waving his arm at the bar.

"And I'll have a whisky and coke, please, Andy," I say, smiling at him. "You're a pal."

As Andy goes to the bar, I look at John. He is a mess. The puffiness has worsened—he looks waterlogged, like Henry VIII in his final phase. His eyes are bloodshot, and his usual hand tremor is now a permanent shake, as if there are small earthquakes inside him.

"I'm so fucked, Dutch," he says, with a painfully bright smile. "I've got the morbs."

"The morbs" is John's phrase for "feeling morbid."

"Is there anything in particular?" I ask.

"I think I might be allergic to success," he says, and laughs, then looks like he might cry. "I'm *so* tired. Last week, someone suggested I try smack—they said it was like having a holiday, without disrupting your schedule. People are trying to give me heroin for *practical* reasons, Dutch."

I feel very brisk. Zee and I have spent the last few weeks talking about John, and what is happening across London. Britpop has now turned into a Faustian gold rush; a cocaine Klondyke. There are now dozens of musicians in the same position as John. The Good Mixer is full of the wired, jangling, bleary, and chaotic. And you only make a jangling sound when things are working loose, inside.

"I don't think you're allergic to success at all," I say. "You're just exhausted. You've been touring this album for almost a year now. The B sides, the videos, the photo shoots. Your brain and face are knackered."

"My face *is* knackered," John says, ruefully, pawing at it.

"And you've had a few drinks, here and there?" I say, tactfully.

"I have drunk every day since last July, except one," John replies, cheerfully. "The next morning, I woke and automatically took painkillers—before I remembered, I hadn't drunk last night. That I was actually well. I have stopped expecting wellness. I am permanently ill."

He puts his head in his heads, and says, sadly, "Maybe I do just need some relaxing heroin."

"Here's something I read," I say. "It takes you five years to understand something big that's happened in your life. Five. For you to truly see the edges of it; make sense of it. And you—you have something big happening every ten days. Most people *never* stand in front of two thousand people, and talk to them, while they scream. That would be the biggest and weirdest thing that *ever* happened to them. You do it every night. You're just suffering from cognitive overload."

I enjoy the fact that I'm saying "cognitive overload" as Andy comes back to the table with the drinks. It's the least teenage groupie thing I could be saying.

"Anyway, we should be celebrating!" John says, straightening up in front of Andy. "Look! I have been gifted! Fan booze!"

He pulls a massive bottle of champagne out of his bag, and opens it.

"I've just bought you a Jack and coke, John," Andy says, in a pained voice.

"Double fist them!" John says, taking the whisky in one hand, and the champagne in the other, and swigging from both. "Come on! Last day of the tour! John's last stand!"

He looks at us both. We both try to smile at him, but we're both clearly concerned.

"I'm just going to put something on the jukebox," he says, and disappears.

Andy and I look at each other, warily, across the table—like a divorcing couple who are still nonetheless worried about their child.

"Interesting week?" I say, diplomatically.

"Interesting week," he says back. He pushes a key across the table. "He told me to get you a room."

"Thank you," I say, very politely. "I will need somewhere to sleep."

I might as well have said, "Thank you. I am not a groupie."

Andy looks like he's about to say something in reply, when he looks out of the window, and stands up.

"Jesus Christ!" he shouts, and runs out of the bar.

I look out. There, on the beach—orange in the street-lights—is John, taking off his clothes. The bottle of champagne is rammed upright into the sand.

"Oh, fuck," I say, following Andy.

By the time we get to the beach, running across the road and through the traffic, John is twenty feet out, in the sea; the orange glow of the fag in his mouth marking where he is, like a fisherman's float. He appears to be swimming toward France.

"JOHN!" Andy bellows. "JOHN! JOHN! Christ—is that cunt doing a Reggie Perrin?"

John carries on swimming, oblivious.

"Christ alive, I'm not being paid enough for this," Andy says, starting to take off his shoes. "I'm a primarily desk-based PR."

As Andy wades into the water, shouting "JOHN! JOHN! COME BACK HERE, YOU STUPID BALLS!," John begins to circle back round to the shore—fag still glowing.

By the time Andy's up to his waist, John's wading back out again—still smoking—in nothing but his pants.

"What the fuck are you doing?" Andy says, staggering out of the water.

"Just enjoying the pursuits of the seaside," John says, cheerfully, picking up his champagne bottle and walking back to his clothes. "Taking a break, as advised. Clearing my head."

On the way back to the hotel, Andy bollocks John severely, whilst John continues to stroll, unperturbed, almost naked, and smoking in an almost postcoital manner.

"I need you to assure me you're just going to bed now," Andy says, repeatedly, as John walks across the street, swigging his champagne. "This is enough, now. ENOUGH."

"I will go to bed now," John says, sweetly. "I have had my holiday. Come, Dutch. Let's go see if we can find a quiz on TV," and we get into the lift—John still dripping—as Andy stares at us, balefully, until the doors close.

IN THE BEDROOM, John runs a bath while I put the TV on. I try to find a quiz, but there are no quizzes on, this late at night. In the end, I just put Ceefax on, take my boots off, and lie on the bed.

John has left the bathroom door ajar, as he takes his bath. On the floor is his fur coat, his trousers, his brogues. From the bed, I can see his back, in the bath—a broad, ursine expanse, like the side of a Welsh mountain. The steam from the bath is curling around him, just like the dawn mist, in the valleys. Oh! He is a whole land!

I've never seen this world before—so I lie there, just luxuriating in it. This view is my sweet reward, for being a good person. God has given it to me. Thank you, God, for putting this hot, big boy in my eyes tonight. There's something so insanely hot about the fat on his hips—that would be the bit I would have my hands on, while we were fucking; to pull him in. Why does no one ever go on about how sexy a big man is—on top of you, gently crushing you, like a bear? I have a crush on him crushing me.

He nudges the door closed with his hand, to get out of the bath, and I pretend I'm watching Ceefax. Mmm, Blue Suede Views.

He comes into the room glowing from the hot water, in a clean shirt and pants, holding the bottle of champagne, and sits on the end of the bed, weakly.

"Head rush!" he says, collapsing backward on the bed. "Nature's amyl nitrate!"

He hands me the champagne, still looking at me. "Alone, finally."

I take a swig, and shuffle down the bed, so my head is near his. I kiss his shiny, sweet forehead.

"Are you very drunk?" I say.

"Oh, yes," he replies, still looking at me. "Singingly drunk. The drunkest."

I look down at him—this drunk, shiny boy, puffy from recent unhappiness, still smarting from being booed and jeered, who has just walked out of the sea.

He looks up at me. Here we are, on a bed. I don't want to be egotistical, or boastful, but I'm pretty certain that, if I had kissed him at this moment, he would have kissed back. He was drunk, and there was nothing on TV—that is how

80 percent of kissing starts in Britain. He would absolutely have joined in in any kissing I innovated, or invented.

But . . . I didn't. Not with him messy, and sore. To have kissed him then would be like kissing something that was melting, or fragmenting. When you kiss someone, it should be the biggest, and most transforming, thing that happens in their life that year. It should be the turning point in the plot—the spike on the graph.

At this point, John's life was like a zoo on fire. Animals running everywhere. If I kissed him here, then, that kiss would just be one more confused penguin, lost in a crowd of panicking zebras, and lions trying to eat eagles. I didn't want to be a sidelined penguin. I wanted to be the whole Ark.

So because I was clever, and noble, and very good at metaphors, I did not kiss John Kite that night. This was an important moment—as it was the first ever available kiss I had not kissed. That bed, in March 1995, marked the first time I practiced sexual restraint. That it was *love* making me do it would have blown my *mind* two years previously. The idea that love, sometimes, *stopped* you kissing someone, was a lesson I had never known was there to be learned.

"Tell me," I say, laying my head on the pillow, next to him. Lying away from the kissing. "Tell me about . . . writing songs. What's it like?"

"Writing a song?" he says, slightly confused. He, too, felt that there might have been kissing, and does not know where the kissing has suddenly gone.

"Yes," I say, swigging from the champagne bottle, and handing it back to him. "I want to know what it feels like. You are amazing, you know. I want to know how you do the amazingness. What's it like, having a song inside you? I've never had a song in me. What does it feel like? How do they come?"

He thinks, for a while. I think, too—I play my favorite song of his, in my head. "Misericord," which starts in the middle of what sounds like a long night of crying—the point where you long, long ago lost any last shred of dignity, or pride—when you are on your knees, crushed, and appealing to an empty sky. "*I just don't feel like a man / Anymore,*" John sings, in his most ragged vocal.

And then, the turnaround, in the chorus—the sudden lift, to the uplands: "*But if you just stay alive / Tomorrow's tomorrow / Is your yesterday / And you survived this / You survived us!*" in a peel of church-bell jangle, brass, and choir.

I hum it—a terrible croak. He starts singing it, quietly, alongside me. We sing together. I don't mind singing badly with him. I am comfortable in all things, with him. We live in a world utterly without shame. I would never sing in front of someone else.

He gets to the end of the line, and then says, quite suddenly, "All the greatest songs are made of the same stuff, Dutch. It's something full of light, and energy, and . . . intent. Something that needs to be. And everyone knows this stuff when they hear it. We all know the good stuff. The best stuff. The magic stuff. It is made of a wholly different substance to everything else. Your body reacts. Your hearing becomes sharp; your heart speeds up; the hairs on your arms raise. Your body knows, in the first four seconds. Great songs walk into the room and tell you they are about to change your life. They embed, in those first thirty seconds, and sit, and wait;

and when they get to the chorus, they explode inside. You can feel the impact. That's when you start crying, or dancing, or singing—or simply sit there, mouth open, going, 'But this is . . . it.' Great songs demand that you recognize them."

John takes another swig.

"And then—they are inside you forever. You can never get them out. They become a part of you. And this is their reproductive method—once they are a part of you, you have to play them, over and over; play them to others; and you will spread them across your world. This is how they live. This is how they become immortal.

"And these songs—the truly great ones—I believe come from the same place. It is my belief, although I have no proof, that there is some kind of communal Garden of Eden, in the collective subconsciousness. A place where the water is sweet, and the grass covered in dew, and the soil is as rich and fertile as . . . plum pudding."

"I know you have stolen that description of a magical place from The Wood Between Worlds in *The Magician's Nephew*!" I interrupt. "I just want you to know I have noticed it."

"Oh, it's where *all* the magical places are, darling," John says. "The garden wet with rain, from Van's 'Sweet Thing'; the mountains from 'River Deep, Mountain High,' the ocean from the Beach Boys' 'Til I Die.' This is where all the great songs—the ones glowing and humming with the Stuff—live. Already written. Perfectly formed. Roaming around. And what the writer must do is, somehow, gain entrance to this place, and bring back the song—like a burglar, for mankind."

"Not just songs! Poems! And books! They must come from there, too!" I interject, eagerly.

John nods.

"Or a poem, or a book. And all you have to do, when you're bringing these already perfect things back to Earth, is just make sure you don't . . . knock the mist off it. You can't touch them too much, or handle them too much. You just have to . . . courier them," he says. "And while you're working on it, and recording it, you feed it with something that's in your guts. I don't know how that works. But that's how it feels. Like there's some milky, sugary substance in your guts, that it feeds off. So yes, it has your DNA in it; you give it your strengths, or neuroses, or bacteria. You're in it. It wouldn't be alive, in the world, without you. It smells of you. You dress it, in your preferred production, or strings. That's your privilege, as its parent. But you also know it was around before you were born—in this other world—and that, if you hadn't wandered in there one day, by accident, or design, and stolen it, retrieved it, that someone else would have, some other day. You are in no way irreplaceable. If you dally for just one moment, fucking Neil Young will streak past you, and have it, the bastard."

"And how do you get into the Garden?" I ask. "Where is it?"

I am still looking down at him—his face all lit up, as he talks. God, I love how he talked. When he was at his most drunk, and Welsh, and enthused. It was like sitting under a waterfall of words. He talked like he's speaking to a church full of people on their knees. It made you want to throw open the doors, and drag passersby in. It made you want to pray.

"Well, you never really remember," he says. "You can spend months walking around, desperate for a song, and—nothing. Sitting in a studio with a guitar, begging for something—

just a line, just a chord—and there will be absolute silence. But then suddenly—just as you're going to sleep; or on a train; or when you're drunk, something will just slide into your head. And you know it's from there, because it comes whole—it appears in your head faster than you could sing it. You just have to promise that, whenever one arrives, you will drop everything, and start . . . milking your guts. Because, if you leave it even ten minutes, it will go again. You must be a faithful servant. You must be . . . reliable."

He starts laughing.

"That's rock 'n' roll, ultimately, baby. Being *reliable*."

Then he suddenly puts his head in his heads, and makes a sad, sad sound.

"And that's what's so hard at the moment," he says, from under his big, bear paws. "I can't write. I can't get into the Garden. I've written nothing for the last year. I can't remember where the Garden is—how to get there. It's not anywhere I'm going. It's not in a tour van, or at the side of a stage, or in a hotel, or in a bar, at four a.m. And next week, I go into the studio, to start the new album, and I have . . . nothing. I'm empty."

I think of the last few months, and John's compulsive consumption: food, booze, cigarettes, drugs. Like they're a massive bran tub, in which he might find a song.

I am glad I didn't kiss him. Right now, a kiss would be just another thing he would eat, hoping it might turn into a song. When I finally kiss him, I want him to find nothing in it but *me*.

"You are sleepy," I say, looking down at him. Worn out with talk, and swimming, he is rapidly deflating into unconsciousness.

"John is sleepy, yes," he admits.

I go to the bathroom, and fill the empty champagne bottle with water, from the tap, and put it on his bedside table.

"This—this is your Night Champagne," I say, "so you feel better in the morning. And this, is my present to you."

I take, from my pocket, six sheets of A4 paper, stapled together in the corner. This is the letter I have spent the last month writing to John—to explain to him why he is wrong, so wrong, about his teenage fans. The letter I hope—with all the simple, admirable self-belief of a nineteen-year-old— will instantly make him turn into a better, happier, healthier man, who will then marry me.

"Read it when you wake up," I say, tucking him in, kissing him good night, and leaving his room. "Good night."

I hoped the letter worked quickly. Time was getting on. If John didn't sort himself out soon, I might get to twenty, *still* waiting for my absolutely perfect life to start—and that seemed an intolerably old age.

24

A week later, back at home, two things happen in quick succession.

The first is that I get the worst case of horniness I have *ever* experienced. It's weird, but I have never seen or read a woman really talking about what it's like when you get the horn. They might say something wistful-yet-jocular, like, "It's been a long time. I've almost forgotten how to do it! Maybe it's all sealed up, below!" and then they sigh, and eat a Twix, and maybe buy a new skirt, and that is the extent of their lamentation.

This is not the extent of my lamentation. A Twix will not solve this.

I have not had sex since I had that terrible time with Jerry, back in December. It is now March—which means I have not been kissed, or touched, for three months. I do not want to sound whiny—but this is appalling.

For starters, there is something absolutely needful about being regularly kissed. It's not just a pleasant optional extra, like pudding. It's something that sustains you, like bread, or wine.

We are like pearls, I think, mournfully. If pearls are not touched often, they lose their luster. They become dull—they turn into just bone-colored beads, on a string.

I am losing my luster. I am a bone-colored bead, on a string. I need to be kissed.

The thing about being horny, when you are a girl, is that you feel *hungry*. Hungry "down there." You keep getting telegrams from your knickers, using increasingly urgent syntax: "It has been three months now! We are becoming desperate! Please send penis! Your people are crying out, ma'am!"

I am starving, sexually.

That night in the hotel with John didn't help. Whenever I think of it, I can coldly strip away the fact he was drunk, and unhappy, and that sex would not have been appropriate, and just revel in imagining climbing into the bath with him, and kissing him as the bath overflowed. Or pulling him on top of me, in bed.

Waking up in the morning next to each other, and fucking before we'd even opened our eyes—just rolling into each other, and having a lazy, pre-breakfast screw, before eating breakfast, and then fucking again.

In the dream, I'm wearing hold-up stockings. Dreams can ignore the fact that the only time I wore hold-up stockings, their name turned out to be a lie, and they fell down as

I ran for a train at Euston—with me dragging them behind me, like Peter Pan's shadow, as I bolted for the 10:37 p.m. Wolverhampton train. That's the point of dreams. You can make stockings work in them.

Imagining fucking John in that hotel room has become the greatest sexual stimulus I have ever had. More even than the idea of fucking bears, or Paul McCartney in 1969—when he had the beard, and a baby in his coat.

In the last week, my horniness and wanking have become borderline problematic—in that the wanking doesn't seem to be solving the horniness. Indeed, it seems to be exacerbating the problem—in that as soon as I come, I want to come again. I'm just pouring wank-petrol onto the horny-bonfire.

The root of the problem is that my horniness is now so profound, it's not just about coming anymore. The time for wanking is *over*. It's not *enough*. I simply need a *man*. I need to *make someone want to fuck me*. It's becoming existential—because, if everything has an equal and opposite reaction, and I am this horny—with sparks pouring out of my fingertips, and my skin phosphorescent with lust, and my knickers screaming like a wolf at any passerby with half a face—and there is no equal and opposite reaction from a man, then, ipso facto, *I must not exist.*

"I'm afraid I'm not real," I tell the dog, mournfully. "I'm starting to disappear."

Poignantly, she ignores me.

The second thing that happens, in the middle of the Great Horn Storm, is that Zee comes home, wearing a new jacket.

"That's a nice new jacket," I say, as he dumps his bag on the table, and puts the kettle on.

"Oh, this?" he says, coming back into the room. "Yeah, I went shopping. I've never been shopping before—but I've not seen my mum in a while, and I walked past Gap, looked in the window, and thought, 'Hey! Why not own some clothes that weren't bought for you by your mother!'"

It's not like anything he's ever worn before. Navy, with a Nehru collar.

He looks both proud, and a bit shy, about his new jacket. Like he knows it's a bit hot. Which is hot.

"I got you something," he says, giving me a small paper bag. It's long, and white, with a picture of a Victorian lady in a crinoline on it.

"This is . . ."—I looked again, to confirm—"the bag in ladies' toilets you put sanitary towels in?" I say.

"Look inside."

Inside is . . . gravel.

"I was in Wales," he says, "and I know you love Wales—so I brought you some Wales back. This is from the carpark, in the Travel Lodge."

It is a very Zee present—it is supposed to make me laugh, but it is also quietly, unshowily thoughtful.

I hug him—lovely Zee!—in thanks. And this is when I notice an odd thing: that when I hug him, his body feels unexpectedly awkward. Like it's trying to shout something, which Zee is trying desperately to silence.

I look up at him—about to say, "Are you okay? Have you had lunch?"—when I see the look in his eyes. It's only there for a second—he does a magnificent job of concealing it by quickly saying, "Did you know that, in 1969, the US Army switched off Niagara Falls, to clean it? I just heard that, on

Radio Four"—an admirable deployment of a bewilderingly random fact; a smoke bomb of an anecdote—but I have seen it.

Zee fancies me.

I DON'T KNOW if you've ever suddenly and unexpectedly had sex with a friend at 1:00 p.m. on a Thursday afternoon; stone-cold sober. I have. With Zee, on that day.

It's weird—having sex with someone you know. I'd never done it before. I would definitely say there are a lot more plus points than negative points. The biggest plus point being that I actually *liked* Zee. It was nice to be in a room with him *anyway*—just having a cup of tea, or doing the washing-up—and so taking his clothes off and seeing what happened next was extra-enjoyable. Like, I knew we'd make the best of it, together, and almost certainly he would tidy up any mess, afterward.

I'm kind of confused as to why more friends don't do it, to be honest: it seemed a very simple and straightforwardly fun thing to do—like going on a picnic with someone; or going to the movies. An adventure. With a pal.

The downside was that, because we *were* friends, Zee was very worried we were doing something wrong.

"Dolly, I think you know how I feel about you, but—isn't this too fast?" he says, breaking off midkiss, on the sofa.

I look up at the clock—we have been kissing for six minutes, and I have really enjoyed all of those minutes. I've never kissed anyone in my house before, either—that is another first. It is definitely more relaxing than doing it in a club, at a gig, or outside a pub in the rain. We are warm, dry, and unlikely to have someone drunk scream "GET A ROOM!" at us. We have got a room. "Get a room," it turns out, really is very good, practical advice.

"Shouldn't we—take it a little bit slower?" Zee continues. "I'd really like to, you know, take you out to dinner; talk a bit. I'm just quite old-fashioned . . ."

"*Or,*" I say, very reasonably, "we could just . . . carry on doing this?"

And I kiss him until he stops worrying, and kisses back.

WHEN WE GET into bed, he is still worrying.

"Are you *sure?*" he says, as I unbutton my dress. "I'm not *rushing* you?"

"No—let's be clear: *I'm* rushing *you,*" I say. He's so polite! It's really, really nice. It makes me feel like a cheerful good-time lady, instructing a trembling boy.

On the other side of the door, the dog starts howling. To distract from her annoying noises I roll over on top of Zee.

"Tell me what you like," I say.

"You," he replies, simply.

I unbutton his shirt, as he stares up at me. I can feel how hard he is. Oh, it's a simple pleasure—making someone hard. I never tire of the magic. It's like summoning a dragon, or a platinum, clockwork owl. I've read somewhere—probably *More* magazine—that the best way to move, when fucking someone on top, is in a figure of 8. Making your hips into a switchback. In the spirit of novelty, and celebration of the erection, I start to give this a go—but it proves much harder than you would think. I manage maybe a figure of 5 before the crotch of my tights snags in Zee's flies, and I have to detangle them. *More* has not taken into account the potentially troublesome nature of hosiery.

As I detangle my tights, I notice that Zee is staring up at the ceiling. I stop.

"What's up?" I ask.

"I've never done this before," he finally whispers, to my lampshade.

"Never done what?"

"This."

"You've never . . . *never*?"

"No," he says. He looks worried. Like I might shout at him, for being a virgin.

A virgin! I have a virgin in my bed!

Oh, I am thrilled!

I've never understood why so many men love the idea of fucking virgin girls. For a girl, losing your virginity is often painful, so the notion that there are guys who want to turn up for *that* fuck—rather than coming along later, when all the upsetting hymen-admin has been taken care of, and it's fun all the way—seems baffling. "Yeah—the fuck I fetishize, above all others, is the one with the bleeding and wincing in? That's my goal!"

I secretly suspect those guys might be murderers.

But the idea of taking a *man's* virginity—of being the first person to say "Well, *hello*, handsome," to their penis; the first to make them unable to speak, as they come—*that* seems like a total win/win situation. Why does no one fetishize taking a man's virginity? I totally am, right now. I feel like some amazing Goddess of Fucking. Maybe this will be my thing? I'll be a writer, muse—and Five-Star Virginity-Taker!

"Oh sweetheart," I say, very turned on. "Let me show you. Welcome to fucking, baby."

So this must be the best fuck ever, for my lovely Zee. I must do all my best sexings, ever. I have been entrusted as his guide to the world of Doing It—I'm like the Dungeon Master, in *Dungeons and Dragons*. I try to imagine what *I* would like, if I were a man, and was about to lose my virginity.

"All men love blow jobs," a character in a Jilly Cooper novel once said. And I had, indeed, observed this to be true.

"You have to treat his cock like it's the most amazing thing *ever*." I read that somewhere, too. I can't remember where. Maybe *The Book of Obvious*.

Luckily, I think cocks *are* amazing. I've never understood all the women and girls who kind of wrinkle up their faces, when they talk about them. I think they're ace. Like, I don't want to anthropomorphize a man's throbbing sex part, but they always seem like some kind of fabulous pet. They're soft to stroke, and they love you to play with them, and they spring up eagerly if it looks like you're up for a good, long, hard walk in the country. They're basically spaniels. If they could live separately from men, and I could keep one in a box, on my table, I would. I'd chat to it, when I was lonely, and play with it, and when I got stuck, writing, I'd absently pop it in my mouth and suck on it, instead of eating loads of snacks, or smoking. It would be healthy for me! A pet penis!

"You're stuck in your oral phase," Suzanne once told me, when I told her that. "Your mother breastfed you too long."

"What's the phase after oral?" I asked.

"Anal," she replied.

"I think I'll stay on oral," I said. "I don't want to move on. I'm just not into bums."

I start giving Zee his first-ever blow job. This is a novel thing for me—to be in charge of the sex. To not be fending off someone else's agenda—but to be doing what *I* like. Everything feels different. For starters, there's no *rush*—there's no presumption we should be working to the usual sex agenda, wherein a man tries to have sex with me as soon as possible. I could just do this for *hours*—because I am the Sex Boss! Wow—why isn't *all* sex like this? I am *good* at being the Sex Boss!

I'm just thinking this—"Hey, we could do this *all day*!"—when Zee says, "I'm sorry!," in a very tiny voice, and comes.

"Don't say sorry!" I say. "This is what happens! Didn't anyone tell you?"

And he starts half laughing, half crying.

"Oh, my word," he says, putting his hands over his face. "Oh, my word."

I crawl up the bed, and kiss his forehead. He looks up.

"You're *amazing*," he says. Which is correct. I *am* amazing!

He's looking at me like I'm made of stars.

"You are very good at that. You must have had a lot of practice. Oh God! Not that I'm saying you're like . . ." and he looks flustered.

"I enjoy my work," I say simply. And then I kiss him on the lips, because I've always wanted to kiss someone after they've come in my mouth, but I never could before, because I wasn't the Sex Boss. It feels brilliantly filthy—like I've just invented the most lubricious porn ever. And because Zee has never had sex before, and he doesn't know that blow-job kisses are a thing boys aren't supposed to like, he likes it.

"But what about you?" he asks, gently, after the kissing has subsided.

"Watch," I say, and take my tights off, thinking, "What a great day this will be for Zee! He will get to watch a woman make herself come!"

I am very, very turned on. Everything's so slippery, it's like ice-skating. "The interesting thing," I say, looking at him, "is that there is no word for this."

"For what?" he says, softly, watching.

"This," I say, stopping for a minute, and showing him my shiny fingers. "In books, they just say, 'She is wet'—but wet with what? It has no name. That's the only other word for it. *You*—men—have spunk, and jizz, and cum, and wad, but we have no nicknames for this. It is unnamed."

I go back to my work.

"You are so educational," he says, still watching. "Like *Blue Peter*."

"It should have a name," I say, watching him watching me. "What shall we call it? How about, 'The Virgin Mary's Tears'?"

"Very Catholic," Zee says. "Very *guilty*."

I note, with amusement, that the word "guilty" has made him start to get hard again.

"'Vageline,'" Zee says, pressing up against me. "Like, Vaseline, but down below."

"The French say 'cassolette,'" I continue, informatively. "That's what Napoleon called it. Napoleon Bonerparte."

"Obviously, I've never had sex before," Zee says, stroking my hair, still watching. "But—are all girls like you?"

"Like what?" I ask. I'm so close to coming.

"Like . . . making jokes, whilst fucking?" he asks. "Kind of like Roger Moore, being James Bond?"

The idea of being a lady James Bond is so excellent that I take a condom from the bedside drawer, and put it on Zee.

"I'm so sorry, but you are about to lose your virginity whilst wearing a Carter the Unstoppable Sex Machine promotional condom," I say, fiddling it into place. "It's the only one I have."

"I am starting to see them in a much more favorable light," Zee says, gasping as I roll on top of him.

I put the tip of his cock right on the edge of my excellence, and say, "You're still a virgin, still a virgin, still a virgin . . . *not* a virgin." On the word "not," I push myself down, and take him inside me.

"Congratulations," I say, and then slowly, slowly start to fuck him.

I am so glad I am the one Zee is losing his virginity to! I am making this fuck both of a technically high standard, but also a light-hearted and welcoming experience. I wish someone had made my virginity-loss this friendly. I'm so full of sexual philanthropy and generosity toward my friend! I am being very *useful*.

Zee starts laughing, gasps, "I'm sorry!" and comes again.

"We need to work on this whole 'I'm sorry' thing when you come," I say, beaming down at him. "There's nothing to be sorry about. You need to learn some man-noises. Can you do a roaring sound, like a sexy tiger?"

I've decided that when shagging Zee, my persona is going to be that of a sexy matron in an all-boys' boarding school, quietly yet firmly teaching the nice boys about joy, in the sanatorium, late at night. That's a kind thing to be.

"Rargh!" he says—messy, but happy. "That was . . . I never thought . . . I mean, today is quite a surprise."

"Do you think you like fucking, then?" I ask.

He kisses me.

"It's even better than record shops," he says, with a sigh.

WE SPEND THE next hour in bed—eating bread and mugs of soup, and chatting cheerful balls. It feels like we have had a very solid hour of friendliness.

We're just talking about the Afghan Whigs single when Zee suddenly says: "I don't know what to call you."

"What?"

"Like, your real name's not . . . Dolly, is it? It must feel weird when people call you Dolly."

I think about this. I suppose it is.

"What do . . . other people call you?"

He means, "What do the people who love you call you?" but he can't say "love," because that is a totally inappropriate word here, for us, that will cause fright. I think, instantly, of John: John calls me "Duchess." But that is inappropriate, too. For here. For him.

"I mean, if I was naked in bed with Boy George, I wouldn't want to call him 'Boy George,'" Zee continues. "It's a work name. I don't want to be at work. Dolly is your work name."

He kisses me.

"I'm not at work."

He kisses again.

"I'm Johanna," I say. "My family call me 'Jo.'"

"You have a very, very soft mouth, Johanna," he says. "Very, very soft."

He kisses me again—very, very gently, like he's thinking about it. Like he's saying the word "kiss," very slowly, on me.

"Johanna. So soft. Jo."

And that was how I had, for the first time, some sex that was nice, with someone I liked. Sex that was non-dramatic—and comfortable—like going for a walk in the park, or settling down to watch a rerun of *Top Hat* with a cup of tea. Three years after I lost my virginity. Seven men down the line. I had still not had a man make me come—every pleasure I had ever had was by my own, by-now expert hand—and I knew, with certainty, that Zee and I had no future. Although I adored him, I had no hunger for him—and you must want to eat your loves, I think. You must want to just grab them and then lie on top of them, shouting, "I've got you! I've got you! This means I have won the world!" over and over again. And I did not feel that about Zee at all. But that afternoon in bed with him was the first sexual memory I had that didn't make me laugh, or wince, but just *smile*. Smiling about sex is very underrated.

Girls should smile, when they think about their sex lives. That is the greatest wish I could have for them.

25

Of course, the problem with being sexually impulsive is that you never really think of the *consequences*. Like, Zee was my oldest friend, my lodger, *and* my business partner—if he really meant that thing about shares in his company.

"So what does it *mean*?" I asked Suzanne, the next day. "What does it mean—now that I've fucked him?"

It's Suzanne's day off from the studio, and we are in a pub off Holloway Road, called the Black Horse. It's pissing down with rain outside—but in here, there's a fire, and a jukebox, and no more than three old men, sitting around, staring at their feet. It is the platonic ideal of a pub.

I've been looking forward to having this conversation with Suzanne, as she is my Sex Expertise Bureau and Consulting Service. I have had four whiskies, so I am ready to plunge into this topic with her, for elucidation.

"I can't believe you've fucked the Boss," Suzanne says again, lighting a cigarette. "I mean, no offense, but I really didn't think he had a penis. He's a human cardigan. Or duffel coat. Are you sure you weren't just humping a toggle? It's like you've just banged Paddington, man."

Despite her wide-ranging imagination, Suzanne is having difficulty in accepting my truth.

"I mean," she continues, "he just doesn't come across as a Bang Monster—you know? Coming into your bedroom at two a.m., going 'I can't contain my feelings any longer—I've baked you a delicious lasagna'—yes, I can imagine that. But getting a stiffy?"

She dissolves into hysterics.

"He had quite a large penis, actually," I say, semi-offended. "And he was very nice. I like him a lot. He's a lovely person, Suzanne."

"Yes yes yes," Suzanne says, waving her cigarette around. "Lovely sexy nonthreatening Flump. I get you."

"The thing is," I say, leaning across the table, "the thing is—I don't know what to do now. What does it *mean*? I mean, I live with him. And he fancies me. And we had some nice sex. I've never had nice sex before."

"Do you want to fuck him again?" Suzanne says.

I think.

"I mean, it's *there*," I say, eventually. "And it was really lovely, you know? And I liked teaching him stuff. It's the first time I've had sex that was, like, *my* idea. I'm definitely up for giving it another go. But I just don't know if that's a good idea or not."

"Do you or do you not want to bang his brains out?" Suzanne says, briskly. One of the old men in the corner looks up for a minute. Suzanne stares at him. He looks back down again. "Like, when you think about him, does your mouth water, and your vag goes all fizzy, and you want to punch the Moon, and, like, marry him, whether he wants to or not? Do you want to kidnap him, and keep him in your cellar? Do you want to Gimp him, hard?"

It's a novel definition. It's not how I feel about Zee. It is, however, definitely how I feel about John Kite.

"Okay, here's how I feel," I say, lighting a cigarette. "I'm trying to work out what sex *means*. Because it's lots of things, isn't it? When I started coming down to London, I wanted to be a Lady Sex Adventurer, or a Swashfuckler—I've just always felt I could find myself through stoating around, and ending up in bed with a Pick'n'Mix of likely fellows. It's the only way you can get people *alone*. It's the only way you can find out *who they really are*."

"I have a problem with that theory—but continue," Suzanne says, raising one finger on her hand, to indicate this is a topic we would return to, when I have finished speaking.

"But what I realized is that there's no such thing as 'sex,' really," I continue. "Like, from what I've done, and what I've observed, it's a million different things at different times. There are people out there doing it as a business. There are people out there doing it as revenge. There are people out there doing it for power, or because they're evil, or because they're hollow inside. Sometimes, it's burglary. They *steal* sex from you."

"Jerry Sharp," Suzanne says, nodding.

"Jerry Sharp," I confirm. "And for yourself—sometimes you're doing it because you feel amazing; sometimes you're doing it because you feel bad about yourself; sometimes it's an experiment, or an act of pity, or an act of friendship, or an act of consolation, or a game, or a competition, or a show. Other times, you're using it as a weapon, or leverage, or just a way to introduce yourself. And so now I don't really understand it as a *process*. Is it just like . . . learning French? Something you have to practice regularly, whenever you get the chance, to get good at? Or, is everyone so different that there's no *point* in having sex with lots of people, because there is no 'good in bed,' because everyone wants something different, and you might as well learn from scratch with 'The One'?"

Suzanne looks at me.

"What are you really trying to say here?" she said.

"I guess," I say, admiring the clear brevity of the question, and resolving to ask it myself, a lot, in the future, "I guess I'm saying that no one else seemed to think about sex like I do. I thought it was all a jolly game, we were all entering into, in the spirit of fun, to get better at it. But no men I've fucked seem to be trying to get better at it. *They* didn't want to learn. They just wanted to bang. They just saw sex as something you . . . *win* at. Like a sport."

"So . . . ?" Suzanne prompts.

"So that's why I'm only banging my friends now," I laugh.

But it is true. I realize, with a sudden jolt, I don't want to fuck around anymore. I don't want to sexually experiment. This experiment is over, with the conclusion that everyone has been very . . . *disappointing*. I feel like George Harrison did when he went to Haight-Ashbury, at the height of hippydom, thinking he would meet free spirits. Years later, he talked about how he was expecting to find "groovy gypsy people making works of art and paintings and carvings in little workshops. But it was full of horrible spotty drop-out

kids on drugs, and it turned me right off the whole scene."
That is how I feel about all the sex-men of London. I had
been trying to have championship-level one-night stands—I
have really been bringing my vaginal A-game—and they
have just been shuffling onto the pitch, late, in a dirty kit,
and half-heartedly knocking the balls around a bit. There
has been no *professional pride* in their shuffling around. They
have been lackluster amateurs. I have been trying to impress
them but they have not been trying to impress me. My sexual brilliance has been wasted.

I tell Suzanne all this. She laughs.

"So, what's your end point, then?" she asks. "What do you
actually *want?* What's your sex dream?"

I think.

"John Kite."

She yelps.

"I *knew* it. You fancy John Kite."

"No," I say. "I *love* John Kite."

I have never said those words out loud! It sounds—
amazing. And very stupid.

"For three years," I add. "And very profoundly." That makes
it sound even stupider. I think of us meeting for the first time,
in Dublin, and talking nonstop for twelve hours; racketing
around pubs, talking about how we'll change the world; sitting in front of the TV, screaming conundrums at *Countdown;*
John threatening to punch the guy who was sleazy to me;
John jumping in the sea, and then falling asleep with his head
on my chest as I wrote a three-thousand-word essay I hoped
would re-program his heart, and make him marry me.

"I feel normal with him," I say, finally.

Suzanne looks at me. I am aware my face is the Face of Love—it feels all hot, possibly on fire, and I'm doing one of those smiles that is so wide it hurts. She shakes her head.

"Dolly, don't make things complicated. You need to go back and dump the Flump."

WHEN I GOT back that night, slightly drunk, I found Zee reading in the front room. He was waiting up for me. There was the slight awkwardness of us not knowing exactly where we stood, after yesterday's sex. He looked at me with big eyes— eyes that said, "So—what's going on?"

"I made us a lasagna," he added, which obviously made me laugh, because of what Suzanne had said, but I couldn't explain why.

"I'm afraid I'm about to say, 'We need to talk,'" I said.

OH, IT WAS awful. If you take the virginity of a dear friend and then say, the next day, "We shouldn't do that again," it can't help but get emotional. At one point, he apologized— "I'm sorry. I shouldn't have."—which made me shout at him: "You did nothing wrong!"—and then hug him, hard. We both cried. Then we made jokes about it—"But it was a lovely shag. I would give you five stars out of five stars. Thumbs-up!"—and then cried some more.

"I think I'll go and stay with my mum for a bit," he said, at the end, and packed his bag. "That seems like a good idea. Otherwise things might get more complicated. Goodbye, Jo."

And he kissed me on the lips one last time.

SO THIS WAS my low point, right? I'd always thought sex would make my world bigger, but it had made it much smaller, instead. John had gone into the studio. Zee was back in Birmingham, with his mum. I still, theoretically, had Krissi—but I was trying to avoid his calls, as things with Dad seemed to be getting worse.

Yesterday, Krissi rang me, voice high with fury.

"The disgusting fucker's given us all ringworm," he screamed.

"Oh my God. Is that—sexual?"

"Jesus, Johanna—NO! It's a fungal infection. You get it from contact with wet towels. He's infected all our towels."

"You've got worms? You've all got worms?"

"It's not a worm, Johanna—it's a fungal infection. You get red, itchy circles."

"He's given you skin mushrooms? Oh, my word."

"We're all having to use a fucking cream and boil all our towels, and I look like I've got the plague," Krissi wailed. "Jeffrey won't fuck me, because he's worried about catching something *from my dad*. It's beyond wrong. It's your turn to have him, Johanna. You have to take custody of him, or I will take you to *court*. I will get a law degree, and I will *sue you* for bad sisterment."

I gently put the phone down. I just wasn't in a my-dad place at that time.

26

And so I entered the Season of Suzanne. It was the beginning of spring—with all that daffodil fol-de-rol, and Suzanne had finished her album, and reentered my life with a bang.

"These are my last few weeks before I'm famous," she said, in all seriousness, turning up on the doorstep one Tuesday. "I want to enjoy my last few weeks of being a common person; and *you've* managed to fuck everyone out of your life. So come on—let's go have some innocent *fun* together."

And Suzanne was very good at having fun. She had the knack of it. She introduced me to the game "Bus Fuck"—where, when you get on a bus, you have to look at all the passengers, and decide which order you'd fuck them in. If you had to.

You had to do this discreetly—by nodding toward them,

and putting one finger on your cheek, to indicate that they would be the first; then nod at the second, with two fingers on your cheek, and so on.

She also introduced me to the game "Withnail"—named in honor of the bit in the film where Withnail leans out of the window of his car, and shouts "SCRUBBERS!" at a group of schoolgirls.

"GROW SOME LEGS!" she would shout, from a taxi window, as we passed a short man.

"GET A TAXI!" she would roar, as we passed a posh woman, jogging.

In turn, I introduced her to the concept of "Journey Juice": the idea that when you're traveling to somewhere you're going to drink, such as a party, gig, or pub, you have your "Journey Juice" on the way: a pop bottle filled with vodka. Just to "save time." This was my greatest invention with Krissi, back in Wolverhampton. Suzanne took to Journey Juice with aplomb: "It makes public transport *tolerable*!" she said, swigging appreciatively on the top deck of the number 4 bus.

At parties, Suzanne would enter like a Viking—roaring "LET THE FUN COMMENCE!"—invariably getting into a scuffle with someone from another band whom she believed wasn't treating her with enough deference.

In the morning, we would all wake at her house, and Suzanne would stagger into the front room, hungover, in a silk kimono, and say, "Julia—issue all the usual apologies to all the usual people," with an airy wave of her hand.

Suzanne was in a hypermanic phase—recording the album, on such a tight deadline, had kind of . . . *whirlwinded* her up, inside, and now she couldn't stop.

"I feel like I'm growing a new part of my *brain*," she said repeatedly. "I can *feel* where it is. Just here," and she made me touch the part of her head, where she thought the growth had occurred. I could feel nothing, with my fingers, but I could see the gleam in her eyes, and sometimes, it scared me.

"Soon, everyone will know me," she said, happily, in a café, eating toast. "I will change the room, just by walking into it. I wonder when I'll see the first girl who's dressed like me? I wonder when I'll *happen*?"

And whatever we did in the day—Camden Market, looking for boots; the British Museum, listing which objects we'd most like to steal; Battersea Cats & Dogs Home, picking our favorite cat—the nights always ended the same: Suzanne, drunk, in my house, or hers, banging her hands on the table, and shouting, "The revolution is coming! Wait till you hear the album! The world is going to change!"

In amongst all this, Suzanne did something unexpected: she noticed I had a body.

Here's how I felt about me, in the early spring of 1995. I was quietly happy with my face—I *liked* how pale, and round, it was; because when I drew around my eyes, with eyeliner, I looked like I was a painting of a girl I had dreamed of, and invented. Suzanne was very pro-eyeliner.

"It's the smart working-class girl's look," she said, approvingly, as I carefully brushed the thick, jet-black wings onto my lids. "It's bold, it's cheap, and it tells people to look you in the eyes—because that's where everything's going on."

And I loved my hair, too. I had finally discovered how to back-comb it, into a huge, tumbling mass, and Suzanne was approving of that, too. "Big hair is the accessory you can't lose," she told me, spritzing me with her Chanel No. 5. "Unless your head falls off, in the back of a taxi."

So, from the neck up, I liked me. That's where my hairdo, and mouth, and eyes, and brain lived. That was where all the good stuff was.

But from the neck down—oh, from the neck down, it was all sorrow. I would never, ever mention my body in a conversation—not even my shoulder, or my bones.

I would mention my vagina, of course—because that is a thing with worth. Men want to have sex with vaginas—they make this clear all the time. They will even refer to women solely as vaginas—"Look at all the poon," they say, looking at hundreds of whole women, and seeing only the hole. So I knew my vagina was a hot topic, and would often chuck it into a chat, metaphorically speaking.

But the rest of me—the rest of me had no worth, in the outside world. I knew this as a fact.

It gave me a despair so deep I could not acknowledge it—for the sorrow of being a teenage girl who is not slender, and sexy, and hot is so great . . . so fundamentally the opposite of what a teenage girl should be—that I could not go near it. To have confessed it would have been to be instantly overcome. It would mean finally admitting that I am not as I should be; that I fail at being what you should be, at nineteen: lithe-limbed, tiny-waisted, and living in shorts and cutoff tops. That's what the teenage girls on TV look like—Californian girls, who can wear anything, and go anywhere, and do anything, with their proper bodies.

I was supposed to hate these girls. Fat girls are supposed to hate skinny girls. That is a law—they are our designated enemy. That is the law—based on the subconscious under-standing that because they are skinny, I have to be fat. That's how it works. In some way, all women's bodies are linked—and those skinny girls can only go roller-skating, in ra-ra skirts, because I am carrying their weight for them, under this huge dress, not roller-skating.

In this incarnation, I carried the fat of many other women. It was my duty. It was my fate. I had been given this shame, as punishment for some transgression I didn't understand. My fat was my karma.

And so, ironically, given its size, my body lived in a very small world. It could sit and write, it could sit and drink, it could sit and smoke, it could fuck, and it could sleep. That was it. That was its world. It was like an unhappy, housebound pet. And because I could not think about it, or acknowledge it—because I would speak for a thousand hours before ever mentioning my body—I couldn't change it. You have to name the problem before you can solve it. And I would not name this problem, because I didn't have the time, or the inclina-tion, to feel embarrassed, and then cry for a thousand years. So—it did not change. You can't become unfat, if you will not admit—rigidly, terrifiedly, proudly, despairingly—you are fat in the first place. Because I was silent, I was untransformable. I was stuck.

I had thought of one way out. Just one. Every day, when I took my clothes off, and got into a hot bath, I lay there, look-ing down at all the soft rolls—the floating belly, the dou-ble thighs—and daydreamed that I get into an horrific car crash. One where my body was totally mangled. And, when I finally awoke from the coma, NHS surgeons had repaired everything, and cut away all the extra fat and skin, and I was reborn, as a thin girl. I was nine stone, covered in neat lines of stitches, and my proper life as a teenage girl could finally begin. I would have been remade. The authorities had taken over, and solved the problem of me. But I would never tell anyone that dream. I would never tell anyone anything I think of my body. I was too proud. I was too scared. I was locked in absolute, rigid denial.

And—sensing something in me—no one ever mentioned my body. It's amazing how well you can completely avoid the subject of thirteen stone of pale girl, if the girl in question has, in her eyes, a look that warns you that the universe will explode, instantly, if you ever mention it.

And so my body was invisible, and undiscussed. It might as well have not existed.

Then into this lifelong silence, Suzanne crashed.

"You love dancing, huh?" she said, one morning, as we sat around in her flat. We were supposed to be having "Working Wednesday," where I wrote my column, whilst she wrote her manifesto—but, as usual, we had made tea, and started chatting, and now three hours had gone by.

"Dancing?"

"Yeah. Whenever you get drunk at my place, you dance."

I didn't know how to respond to this.

"As soon as I put Madonna on, you're grinding up all over the place, like a mad Midlands stripper. You were humping my sofa last Tuesday."

Oh my God.

"I'm—sorry?"

"Sorry? SORRY? Oh sweet Jesus—fuck this fucking girl.

I love you dancing, Wilde. Tell me—what do you love about dancing? LET'S GET DEEP!"

This conversation felt a bit dangerous—as it was about my body, and I worried where it might go. I did not want to cry in front of Suzanne.

"'Only when I'm dancing can I feel this free'?" I hazarded. When in doubt, quote Madonna.

"Do you know what I think you'd like?" Suzanne said. On previous occasions where she's asked this question—"Do you know what I think you'd like?"—her answer has been, variously, "Barcelona," "going down on a woman," "steak tartare," and "John-Paul Sartre," so I have no idea where this is going.

"*Adrenaline*," Suzanne said. "I think you'd love *adrenaline*."

Before I could think of anything to say, she grabbed my hand, and said, "Come on—let's go get some," and led me out of the house.

"Adrenaline?" I asked, struggling to keep up with her; she was walking at a fair old pace down Kentish Town High Road, toward Parliament Hill Fields. I knew how Suzanne operated. I presumed we were walking to her dealer's house.

"Where do we get adrenaline?" I asked. "Do you know someone who sells it? How much is it? Will it make me freak out? You know I don't like anything that makes me hallucinate. I will draw a line there."

"We're not going to buy it—we're going to *make* it," she said, as we started walking up steep, leafy Swain's Lane.

Although I looked, subsequently, on maps, and in the *A–Z*, curiously, none of them mentioned that Swain's Lane is the steepest hill in the world. But it definitely is. Within four minutes, I was a hyperventilating wreck. I stopped, like a mule, jerking Suzanne back. She let go of my hand.

"Just . . . resting . . ." I said, leaning against a wall.

My throat hurt. Why did my throat hurt? I could only presume that my body—having used, and exhausted, all the muscles in my legs, torso, and arms—had then tried to use my neck to get up this fucking Eiger.

"You can have a ciggie when you get to the top," Suzanne said, temptingly, taking my hand, and pulling me again.

In the end, my pace was so slow and agonized—and my mortification so obvious—that Suzanne strode on ahead, whilst I trudged behind: all muscles firing, and yet still so pitifully slow and puddingy.

When I finally reached the top, I found Suzanne had gone through the gates, into Waterlow Park, and was waiting for me, on a bench.

"Lie down there," she said, pointing to the ground. I wrapped my leopard skin around me, lay down, and stared up at the sky, breathing like an asthmatic train.

"And?" I said.

"Wait," she said.

And, as I lay there, I got a sudden, ice-cold whoosh in my belly, that flamed across my body. My head felt like I'd just stuck it under a tap, on a hot day—clear, and almost empty. As if decades of clutter had been removed, in one stroke.

I sat up, to tell Suzanne this news—and noticed that sitting up felt really easy, as if my entire body were four stone lighter. Moving felt easy! I had never experienced this before. I waved my arms around, delightedly—they felt amazing. I was, suddenly, so into having arms! These arms were sources of intense pleasure.

Suzanne looked at me.

"*That's* adrenaline," she said. "You have just tricked your body into flooding with adrenaline. You have just got very, very high for free. You're welcome."

"Oh," I said. Then: "It makes me want to poo."

"That's my girl," Suzanne said, proudly.

AFTER ADRENALINE DAY, as I thought of it in my head, Suzanne would regularly force me into further hits. "I'm the pusherman," she would say, delightedly, walking me, like a dog: across the Heath; from Camden to Soho; along the river, to Hammersmith . . . looking delighted every time I would suddenly straighten up, twenty minutes in, and cry, "I feel it! I'm getting the rush!"

As we spent that spring walking, and talking, I became aware of a gradual shift, in my head. I slowly started to . . . like my body. A bit. Just a bit. After a long day, I lay on the bed, and felt something completely new: total physical exhaustion. And it felt *amazing*. My legs and thighs glowed with the springy ache of exertion. Lying in a hot bath, looking down at my legs, I felt *fondness* for them, for all the work they had done.

"I am *proud* of you, old friends," I said, patting them, like a horse. "Well done, you."

I told Suzanne this, about the patting. About the fondness. About how I'd stopped describing my body, to myself, as "the problem."

"A body is something that should *never* be described," she said, firmly. "That way lies insanity. A body is a thing that should *do*."

It was a novel feeling, to look at my body, and see it not as a problem—a shame, to be covered, and ignored, like the

statue of a discredited dictator who had failed his people—
but a source of satisfaction, instead. A new thing to do. A new
world—just below my neck. Suddenly, I was so *into* me. I was
so into me, doing things. I wanted to run into rooms, naked,
and point at my arse, shouting, "Listen! I have a muscle here!
It did not exist a month ago—but now, it can walk me all the
way from Victoria to Richmond Park! I am the mother of
arse-muscles! I have created them! I know you cannot see it,
for I am still luxuriously padded, but push your finger in here!
Feel it! Feel all these secret pistons I am building!"

In the midst of this physical renaissance, on the first truly
hot day of spring, at the start of April, Suzanne turned up at
my house holding a 1950s bathing suit—all jolly sailor frills,
bows, and stripes—and said: "Today, we're going UP a level.
You are Kate Bush's shoes."

When I looked at her, confused, she explained: "I'm going to throoooow you in a lake!"

We took the bus up to the Heath, and she took me down
the newly greening lane, to the Ladies' Bathing Pond.

"I don't like water I can't see through. I'm scared of what's in
there," I moaned, as we stood in the changing hut, pulling on our
costumes. "There might be fish. Or eels. They might go inside
me. I swear to God, if something touches me, I will scream."

"In Jungian archetypery, water is your subconscious," Suzanne said, pulling up her shoulder straps. "You're just scared
of your subconscious. Of what you're repressing."

"Well, if there's eels in my subconscious, then yes, I'm very
scared of them," I say, shivering. "I don't want eels in my head.
Of course I'm going to repress them. Who wouldn't repress eels?"

We stood on the pontoon, looking out at the lake. It was a

dark, soft green—like liquid fertilizer, or nettle soup. Three or four women skulled around, in fabulous bathing caps. They all looked like bluestocking High Court judges. This was very much the pond of matriarchs.

Suzanne took my hand.

"The advice is, on your first visit here, to lower yourself in slowly, to acclimatize to the temperature," she said, stepping toward the ladder, and gripping my hand tightly. She looked at me for a second—then jumped in, pulling me after her.

When I surfaced—coughing and gasping from the cold—her face was right next to me, beaming.

"But this is more *fun*, isn't it?"

The cold was like vivid electrical burning: a transformative extreme. I'd never felt this kind of cold—the kind of cold that feels like a living force.

"Swim!" Suzanne commanded, striking out. "You need to generate heat! Or you'll go into hypothermic shock!"

I started swimming, hard—finding it difficult to breathe as the cold pummeled my lungs, and crushed them into tiny pods. After thirty seconds of hard, desperate front crawl, I started to feel a warm, buzzy membrane forming over me—like I had the Ready Brek glow. I felt very, very high. Cathedral-high. Word-confuse high.

"Amazing, huh?" Suzanne said, looking over her shoulder at my clearly ecstatic face.

"I'm so high!" I said, perhaps unnecessarily, relaxing into breaststroke. The water felt like an ocean of warm lube.

"I know a former heroin addict who says swimming in cold water gets you as high as smack," Suzanne said, flipping over, and staring up at the sky. A heron skimmed past.

"I'm on heron," I said. In my heightened state, I was pretty sure it was the greatest joke ever made. Suzanne ignored it.

I paddled around the perimeter—next to the water lilies, and overhanging branches—whilst Suzanne did a showy backstroke up and down the center.

"You're such a writer!" she called out, at one point. "Skulking around the margins, watching."

"And you're such a lead singer," I called back. "Right in the middle, making everyone swim round you."

"You know it, baby," she said, powering past me.

"HOW DO YOU know about . . . sport?" I asked, later, when we were lying in the meadow. We'd dried off, and dressed, and were lying in growing spring grass, listening to the birds.

It sounded like an idiot's way of asking a question, but I was so relaxed from the swim, I appeared to have turned into a child.

"You know—physical activities?"

No one I knew walked up steep hills, or swam in cold ponds. Apart from festivals, the music industry conducted its business entirely indoors. Everyone lived the lives of indolent vampires.

"From school, babe," Suzanne replied, pulling her fur coat around her, and lighting a cigarette. "Put a fat but competitive girl in a boarding school for five years, and she will leave as captain of the lacrosse, cross-country, and swimming teams. And be bisexual."

"You went to boarding school?" I asked, amazed. I had never met anyone who went to boarding school. To be honest, I wasn't sure if they still existed—I'd read about them in Enid Blyton novels, and had vaguely presumed they disappeared at the same time as golliwogs, "swarthy" gypsies, and lemonade in stone bottles.

Suzanne suddenly looked a bit shifty.

"Yeah, I went to boarding school," she said, before turning over onto her belly, and glaring. "Look, you can't tell anyone, okay? It would be really bad for business. I am not going to spend the next four years being asked by some chippy prick from *Melody Maker* if my parents had servants."

"Did you have servants?"

"You don't call them servants, babe," she said, gently.

"You call them . . . *slaves?*"

"They're staff! It's a proper job!"

This was very weird. Before I became a writer, I had often thought about becoming a "domestic." It seemed like one of the most viable jobs for a girl on a council-estate who believed she would look good in a mob cap. I would look in the copy of *The Lady* in the library, and read the small ads: "Hampshire family looking for cheerful, hardworking housekeeper, own room, £100 per week."

I'd read *Jane Eyre*, nine times; becoming a governess for a sexy-but-repressed castle owner was totally on my "possible futures for a working-class girl" list. But Suzanne . . . Suzanne had been the kind of person who could employ me.

"What was it like?" I asked. "Did they have uniforms? Did they call you 'Miss'? Did they bow? Did they live with you?"

Suzanne sighed.

"Look—you must never, ever tell anyone. I'm as serious as cancer. What I tell you does not go beyond us."

And so Suzanne told me about what it's like to grow up rich.

Her father traveled a lot, for work—"He's in supermarkets," she said, vaguely—and her mother was "madly obsessed with him: like, she couldn't bear to be away from him. It was intense"—and so traveled with him. Inevitably, when Suzanne was eleven, they put her in a boarding school, "for stability."

"Before then, I'd been in six schools in six years," she said. "So it was kinda nice to see more than one year in the same place."

This peripatetic childhood explains a lot about Suzanne— her habit of walking into a new room, full of strangers, and starting a conversation seemingly in midsentence. I guess that's what it felt like, when she was young. Snatched away from one place, in midflow, and thrust into another one.

"I've always thought boarding schools are barbaric," I tell her, as she laid half her fur coat across me, to stop my shivering. "People only think they're normal, or desirable, because it's a thing rich people do? If the working classes sent their children away to be raised by . . . institutions, social services would close them down in a week."

"Well, I kinda liked it, to be honest," Suzanne said. "I mean, I ran away quite a lot, because I was bored, but I was never *lonely*. I'd been very lonely before."

She told me how, when her parents used to travel with her, they refused to alter their lifestyle, which involved a lot of opera.

"They'd leave me in the presidential suite of, like, the Hilton, with the chauffeur to keep an eye on me," she said, staring at my feet, which were slightly blue with cold.

"Did he wear a chauffeur's cap?"

"He wore a chauffeur's cap." Suzanne seemed quite amused by this question.

In the hotel, Suzanne would read, or watch old movies, whilst the chauffeur sat on a chair, bored out of his mind. I imagined her—a little girl, staring out of a huge, plate-glass window, down onto Tokyo, or Manhattan.

I thought of my childhood—insane, anxious, and riddled with terrible smells; but never lonely. Always someone to lie on top of, fight with, get in a bath with, climb a tree with. Always someone to look you in the eye, and react to you.

My father, in all his class-war rants—"They're cunts, Johanna. Parasites!"—had never warned me that, one day, you might meet someone rich, and feel sorry for them.

"Don't you feel sorry for me!" Suzanne yelled, when I did my sympathetic face. "I had a pool, I fucked an earl, and I had access to all my mother's medication. There is nothing sweeter than being fifteen, and floating, on a lilo, in your own back garden, on Valium. I'd bring friends back, during summer holidays, and we'd all lie around getting high, or low, or however you'd describe it. I scuba dive, water-ski, and ride a horse, man. Fuck you. Don't you dare fucking pity me!"

We lay there for a while, thinking about our different childhoods. In the end, Suzanne stood up.

"Come on," she said, holding out a hand. "All this talk of my childhood makes me want to go to Daddy's favorite restaurant."

I mutely followed her out of the meadow, hair dripping onto my shoulders.

27

addy's favorite restaurant," it turned out, was Scott's, in Mayfair. We'd gone back to Suzanne's to change—she lending me a glamorous silk dressing gown that she insisted would double, with the application of a belt, as a dress, and Suzanne putting on an electric blue dress, and her flat, red velvet shoes.

As we walked into Scott's—the doorman nodding at Suzanne—I knew I had never been anywhere so posh before. I instantly felt like I was in the wrong place. Like my body was a clown car, and would collapse, with a series of honking sounds. The tablecloths were as cushiony as duvets, the flower arrangements like ones you'd see at weddings, and everyone there moved differently.

Posh people have a very distinct walk. It's an upright,

confident stride—like they're used to walking around castles. Like to walk from one side of the living room to the
other would take several distinct steps; rather than it being
a room so small you could sit on the sofa, and change chan-
nels on the TV using a stick. These people needed their legs.
Maybe that was why their legs were so thin.

I think the food made them thin, as well. Rich people eat
different food.

"I want something comforting," Suzanne said, and ordered a lobster.

My understanding of comfort food had always been that
it would be something creamy, and carby—a tub of mashed
potato, or pasta. When the lobster arrived—the first I'd ever
seen—it looked like an angry red spider holding maracas.
Like something from *Fantasia*. I couldn't see how it could
possibly be comforting.

"Mmm, the taste of childhood," Suzanne said, wielding
what looked like some kind of podiatry tool, and ramming it
up the beast's hands.

My ordering had been troublesome—there are so many
things I don't know how to pronounce. The menu seemed
to double as some manner of Class Sieve—designed to filter
out people who didn't know how to say "tartare," "carpac-
cio," "foccacia," "Bearnaise," "turbot," or "bisque" to a waiter.
In addition, the numbers next to each dish were so high, I
couldn't work out what they meant. For instance, the number
"24" was next to the turbot. Did that mean you got twenty-
four turbots? I have a strong work ethic when it comes to
eating a lot of food—ignoring when I'm full is one of my
speciality skills—but even I didn't think I could eat twenty-

four turbots. When I realized the "24" referred to how many pounds it cost, I spiraled into terror.

"Suzanne, I'm not that hungry. I'll just have the bread."

The bread was a mere "2." Two pounds! For bread! I made bread! I knew a couple of slices cost no more than a penny to make! Was this magic bread?

By that point, however, Suzanne had airily ordered a bottle of Chablis, and as I could think of no way of explaining to her that this was a meal I could not afford to go halves on, I sadly resigned myself to ending the meal writing a check that would, eventually, bounce, and cost me a £20 fine. I ate the bread as slowly as possible, in order to try and enjoy the world's most expensive side order. And when the wine waiter poured the Chablis, I did not demure from drinking my half—as I was paying for it, albeit against my will.

"Oh, that is beautiful," Suzanne said, taking the first sip, and appreciatively smudging the condensation on the side of the glass with her finger. "You like Chablis?"

"Yeah?" I said. In truth, it tasted bitter, to me; my drinking revolved around sugary, kiddy booze . . . peach schnapps, cider and black currant, whisky and Coke. They were delicious drinks, that kept you peppy.

Wine, I soon discovered—and with little more to mop it up than bread—was a more druggy experience. It was like being coshed—half of your brain closed down halfway through the first glass. It made you feel quite . . . stupid. It was like a bottle of stupid. The first time I laughed, drunk on wine, it was an odd, horse bray that I'd never made before—a sound other drunk people in the room were making too. I whinnied. I wine-ied.

Oh my God, I thought, as the waiter topped up my glass, and I eagerly drank it. "I'm Pinocchio. I'm on Pleasure Island. I'm turning into a donkey."

As it turned out, being a wine donkey is quite enjoyable. It makes you liquid, and fuzzy—within twenty minutes, I was holding Suzanne's hand, and telling her how amazing she was. I was full of hot love. The wine had set it alight. The wine had made me want to say everything I had ever thought. It filled my mouth with words.

"You're like . . . the eye of the hurricane," I told her, stroking her fingers as she beamed at me, delightedly. "You rearrange everything in the room, just by walking into it."

"I know, baby," she said, delightedly. "And you do, too. This is why I *adore you*. You *inspire* me, you know that? You are my muse. This album *reeks* of you. You know who I wrote it for? *You*. Every time I got stuck, I'd just write something I could imagine you dancing to. *My muse*."

It was okay to hold hands with Suzanne in a restaurant, because the wine narrows your peripheral vision; you can't really see anyone else. It's like entering a private booth. It was like looking at her down the wrong end of a telescope . . . all I could see was her face. The rest of the world had floated far, far away. Every so often, I was aware of the wine waiter topping up my glass, and my hand reaching out for it, but Suzanne and I were swimming around in our little wine tank, separated from everyone else by the cold glass of the bottle.

As the second bottle of wine arrived—which I didn't remember us ordering, but, clearly, we had—I got up, very carefully, and asked the waiter, in my best and most stable voice, "Where are the lavatories?" Because I had read in Jilly

Cooper's *Class* that this is what the upper classes call the toilet, and that saying "toilet" would probably get you thrown out of a restaurant such as this.

Sitting on the lavatory—which felt exactly like a toilet, to be honest—I rested my face on my knees.

"I am so drunk," I told me.

"I know," I replied. "I can tell from the way you have put your head on my knees."

"This place is so posh," I whispered, to me, "that I am surprised they do not have tablecloths on the toilet. *Lavatory.*"

And then I laughed at me, for a bit, because my humor was so strong.

As I sat there, swaying from side to side, I heard something that caught my ear. My name. Someone was saying my name.

"Dolly Wilde," a woman was saying. "Did you see her? At the table by the window? She's here."

"Ah, this is a moment," I told myself, quietly. "You are famous! You are being recognized in posh restaurants! Someone is admiring your work in *The Face*! You are the *famous writer*, Dolly Wilde."

And I sat there, enjoying being famous. All my years of work, now paying off. My words had made me known. I smiled at me. It was a lovely thirty seconds.

"Well done, me," I said, and patted my legs, in a celebratory manner.

"Do you think she knows?" one of the women was saying.

"God knows," the other replied. "Has Jockie seen it?"

"No—but Work Phil has. He says it's just . . . I mean, he didn't know what to do. All the other guys were laughing, but it's such a weird thing to do? Why would you invite your mates round and put that on??"

I didn't like this. What were they talking about?

"What do men *do* in those situations? Are they all sitting there with stiffies?"

"Apparently it's quite a common thing. With normal porn, anyway. Did you hear the worst bit?"

"Do I want to?"

"It's awful. Apparently she just keeps saying 'Fuck me harder,' but in a Birmingham accent. I mean, it's just not a very pornographic accent."

The other woman laughed, and then, over the sound of them washing their hands, I heard them try a variety of frankly offensive Midlands accents, whilst saying pornographic things: "Tek me up my Bull Ring, babba!" and laughing more. They're drunk, I thought, disparagingly, with my melting face pressed against the cool glass wall tiles. They cannot tell the difference between a Wolverhampton accent, and a Birmingham one.

Then, as they left: "She's not the only one. Apparently, he's building up quite a collection. Did you hear about Sara? Jerry's so fucked-up."

"So fucked-up."

And the door slammed closed.

I sat there for a while, digesting all of this. I tried very hard—*so* hard: like my life depended on it—to think of anything else this exchange could have meant, but I kept circling back, in tighter, and more painfully certain circles, to just one, single conclusion: Jerry Sharp had been showing his video of me having sex to his mates.

WHEN I GOT back to our table, Suzanne was in the middle of a contretemps with the people next to us.

"We don't mind smoking," they were saying. "We smoke ourselves!" They gestured to their ashtray. "But you delightful ladies are smoking so much, we can't actually taste our food, hahaha!"

I looked at our ashtray. It *was* kind of appalling. A mountain of butts with three almost entirely unsmoked cigarettes thrust in, at the top—looking like those GIs planting the flag at Iwo Jima.

"I got the bill, babe," Suzanne said. "Well, Daddy did. I put it on his tab. Let's drink to Daddy." She raised her glass—and then looked at me. "Oh my God—what's up?"

I could tell my face looked strange—my jaw was sticking out, because it felt like there were tendons that connected it to my eyes, and, if I kept the tendons taut, I wouldn't cry.

"Just got some bad news," I said, gesturing to the toilet.

"Oh my God—you're pregnant!" Suzanne said.

"No! No. Well, pregnant—with horror. Can we leave?" I said. My jaw was aching, from the thrusting.

We reclaimed our coats from the concierge, in a drunken fumble of putting the wrong arms in the wrong sleeves, as he patiently held them up.

"Thank God you don't have to help us into our trousers!" Suzanne said, at one point, after nearly punching him in the chest with a wildly flailing hand. He merely rolled his eyes.

When we got out into the street, Suzanne grabbed my lapels, and said: "What?"

I told her. It took some time, as I was crying so hard I

had hiccups, and the words were all chopped up, like babies' spaghetti.

"Oh my baby," Suzanne said, hugging me close to her, when I finished. "Oh my baby. It's okay. You can cry. You can cry."

She squeezed me hard. I fought my way out of the hug.

"No!" I said. "I'm not sad!"

Suzanne looked at me, in surprise.

"What?"

"I'm not sad! I'm *not sad.*"

Because what I was feeling was something I'd never felt before. In all my nineteen years, whenever anything had gone wrong, or been bad, I had been sad, or I had crushed my feelings, or I had tried to put a brave face on them, as Judy Garland would, in a musical.

But today—today, for the first time, I was feeling something else—something which was making my face burn and my chest explode . . . something which was pumping the same adrenaline into me I felt whenever Suzanne and I marched up a huge hill, or jumped into a cold lake. A huge, new, terrible, amazing feeling.

"I am . . . *angry,*" I said. I have never said those words before. "I am ANGRY. This is *angry* cry."

I pointed to my face. "*Angry* cry," I clarify. "ANGRY."

Suzanne whooped.

"Baby just got her Angry Wings!" she hollered, putting an arm around me. "Oh, babe—it's always a festal day, when a woman finally gets *angry* for the first time. I'm so happy for you."

And she took a camera out of her handbag, and snapped

a picture of me, right there—angry and crying on the pavement.

"You'll want to remember this forever," she said, fondly, putting it back in her bag. "The day you finally let yourself get angry. I'll send you a copy when I get it developed. Tell me. Tell me what you're thinking."

"That I'm being punished for having sex, even though I didn't do anything wrong," I said, blowing my nose on my sleeve. "*I didn't do anything wrong. I gave* him some sex—the thing all men want—so why's he being *a shit* about it?"

"Yes yes *yes*," Suzanne said, putting out her arm for a cab, and hustling me toward it. "This is the *right* thing to feel. That's what I've been *saying*. Women have to get *angry*. Come on. Come back to mine—I want to whip your anger into fury. And then—onwards to murder!"

Back at Suzanne's, Julia was sitting in front of the TV in her pajamas, watching *Mastermind*. Her Afro was up in a turban, and she was wearing glasses that made her look automatically disapproving of everything.

"Dolly's *angry*," Suzanne announced, dumping her handbag on the table, and pouring drinks.

"Harold Wilson!" Julia shouted at the TV, then turned to us. "My God, you're both paralytic. Have they evacuated the Booze Hospital?"

"Tell her, Dolly," Suzanne ordered, as I flopped onto the sofa.

I told Julia the whole story about Jerry, from beginning to end. Halfway through—around the first, aborted blow job—she started drinking, too: "I can't do this sober." When I got to the end—having been interrupted, at various times, by Julia shouting "NO! HE DIDN'T!" and "MICHAEL STIPE?" and Suzanne going "You didn't tell me THAT bit!"—both Julia and Suzanne were almost levitating with indignation.

"So, to recap," Julia said, swigging on a glass of red wine, "you bin this guy off, he uses Michael Stipe as a weapon to revenge-fuck you, tapes it, and is now screening it, at Pervert Parties?"

"And everyone in London's talking about it," Suzanne added. "Dolly is the news."

I winced. "Yes," I said. "Now you put it like that, I can see why I have been failing to turn this into an amusing anecdote."

"What are you going to do?" Suzanne asked, fiddling with her lighter.

I thought. I'd been thinking about this for the last half hour.

"Well," I started. "In *What Katy Did at School*—the lesser-read sequel to *What Katy Did*—our formerly disabled heroine Katy Carr is accused by the punitive headmistress, Mrs. Florence, of flirting with boys from the neighboring boarding school, even though she is wholly innocent. And for a whole term she is ostracized, gossiped about, and punished by the school, and many of her classmates, until, finally, her shiningly good character wins them all over, and they apologize for ever doubting her. She knows it doesn't matter what everyone else is saying about her—she knows she's a good person. That this gossip will go away, in the end. Her righteous anger at the injustice keeps her going. And that's what I'm going to do. Fueled by righteous anger, I am going to live through this, with my head held high, and outlive the storm, saying nothing."

"I love that book!" Suzanne shouted, just as Julia said, "That's a shit idea."

"Why's it a shit idea?" I asked.

"Because Jerry doesn't get punished, and you just have to suffer, and become stronger, and I *hate* stories where the conclusion is that women just have to suffer and get stronger," Julia said. "Those are the worst stories."

Suzanne nodded, somberly. "Good point. Even though it *is* a great book."

"The bit where they get the Christmas boxes, and they're full of cake, and jumbles!" I said.

"The jumbles!" Suzanne said. Then: "What *are* jumbles?"

"I dunno," I said. "A kind of biscuit?"

"There *must* be another way through this," Julia said, who was still considerably more sober than Suzanne and I. "Come on—we must be able to make a plan here, and not derail on fucking *jumbles.*"

And we talked about it for the next two hours—drinking wine, where appropriate—but at the end, when Suzanne had taken a pill, and fallen asleep, facedown, on the floor, it was still the only option I had: to simply be strong, and noble, and get through this on my shiningly good character. That's all a woman *can* do, and therefore the best plan.

28

Two weeks later, at the *NME*'s annual Brat Awards, I realized that this plan wouldn't work.

It started well. I was in a gang, which is always comforting. The Branks had finished their album, and the first single—"God Is a Girl," the song Suzanne sang to us at the salon—is currently at Number 12 in the charts. Whenever anyone congratulated Suzanne on this, she said—almost offended—"But this was always going to happen?" She has never doubted her stardom.

This week, she is on the cover of the *NME*—something that delighted her in a way I didn't think possible. When I turned up at her house, earlier, to pick her up, she was as excited as I've ever seen her—full-frontal mania, and bouncing off the walls.

"I've just HAD SOME COKE!" she said, as I came through the door. I found Suzanne's way of taking drugs very endearing. Everyone else would be very clandestine, and mysterious—referring to it in oblique code; nodding and winking. Suzanne just shouted, "I'M GOING TO HAVE SOME DRUGS NOW! ANYONE ELSE WANT SOME?" It made cool boys angry. Nearly everything Suzanne did made cool boys angry.

"Coke? Oh—that explains it," I said, noting that she was opening and closing her fists so rapidly, the knuckles were white.

"NO, NO!" she shouted. "You don't UNDERSTAND! When my guy dropped it off, the wrap it was in—IT WAS ME!"

I didn't understand, so she showed me the now-empty coke wrap. It was made from the front cover of the *NME*. It was a portion of her face.

"IT'S ME COKE!" she shouted. "I'M A WRAP! THAT'S WHEN YOU KNOW YOU'VE MADE IT!"

"Be sure to tell them that's what you've taken, when you OD, and the medics arrive," Julia said, sitting peaceably on the sofa, eating a sandwich. "Me-coke."

"Ambulances are for amateurs," Suzanne replied cheerfully.

With The Branks now in the charts, they have been invited along to the Brat Awards, to provide a bit of excitement. Suzanne has rapidly become known for her reliably entertaining interviews. Appearing on *The Word* last week, she had repeated the thing she'd said to me, months ago— "It's 1995. Everyone's bisexual after eleven p.m."—and then kissed a girl in the front row of the audience. And her first interview in the *D&ME* had ended up with her getting drunk, and high, in the pub, with Rob, chatting to a girl on the next table, and insisting on giving her a makeover: taking off her top, pulling off the girl's, and swapping them.

"You belong to The Branks now," she'd cackled.

The headline was: "HIGH. STREET. *BRANKS*."

There was also the interview where she punched the journalist who called her "a classic angry feminist"—shouting "Go buy a vagina, Richard"—but that barely seems worth mentioning.

THE CAB DECANTS us at the venue, in Camden, where a red carpet leads up to the door.

"Oh my God—let's *throw shapes*!" Suzanne says, delightedly, dragging Julia and me down the red carpet, in the same manner Cruella De Vil drags her Dalmatian-fur stole behind her in *101 Dalmations*. Our role is, definitely, as "living accessories."

Not surprisingly, Julia does not happily take to the red carpet. She is dressed in a cutoff silver boiler suit, tights, and work boots, and has brought a satchel full of cider: "Champagne makes me gassy," she'd explained, flatly, as she'd packed her bag. "And, let's face it—it tastes like piss."

On the red carpet, she looks very angsty. As they take pictures, she retrieves her first can of cider and takes a swig as everyone snaps away.

"Ah, fuck this," she says, after a minute, as Suzanne poses gleefully for the photographers. "I'm not being paid to stand here doing a 'surprised' face."

She wriggles us free of Suzanne's grasp—to Suzanne's glee, as it enables her to start doing "arm-posing," too.

"Inside," Julia says, heading toward the entrance. "I've put on my bad tights. The crotch keeps dropping, and I need to hoik them up."

She turns just as I heard a voice shouting, "Hey! Dolly!"

I turn around, and see someone I vaguely recognize from *Loaded*. I start to wave, as he says, maliciously: "So where's Jerry?"

I turn to Julia, in horror.

"Still hanging out the back of you?" he continues, in a horrible, faux-matey tone. For the first time ever in my life, I actually gasp. The brutality of the question, in daylight, sober, is shocking. That he's seen me—with my friends, in my nice dress, smiling; just a girl, having her day—and the thought of me fucking has inspired him to wound me. To crush me. To coat me in the sticky black tar of shame. This is the machinery of his thoughts. This is how he has processed me. That is what he needed to do to me, when he saw me walking past him. The hatred is raw, inexplicable, and brutal.

"He's busy fucking your mum in the eye, dickless!" Suzanne shouts back—still posing. "Come on. Screw this."

I was still shaking as she put her arm around me, and marched me inside.

IT'S A STANDARD awards ceremony: tables, chairs, a stage. And now me, charging through the doorway.

"It's okay," I say, as Julia and Suzanne crowd around me—like as woodland animals around a fellow woodland animal who's just been shot in the face. "It's just some gossip, that will pass. I am still noble, and angry. I don't care what anyone thinks, apart from my friends."

"What other people think is none of your business," Julia nods. "A drag queen called Sarah Cunt told me that."

I sit down at our table—back ramrod straight—as Julia hands me a can of cider. I am burning with nobility. I am a martyr candle. I am so ready to be better than everyone else in the room.

"I wouldn't normally share my cider," Julia says. "But you— you've earned this."

TONIGHT'S SHOW IS being presented by another of the rock 'n' roll comedians, of whom London has a surfeit, at the moment: Tim Brazier, who also has a lot of material about liking cool bands, and not being able to find a girlfriend.

"Is there a factory that's making these cunts?" Suzanne asks, as he launches into his opening monologue, about how he'd recently gone on a date with a girl who was beautiful, and hot, but liked Madonna, and thought that Black Francis from the Pixies was called "Fat Francis," and so he'd dumped her.

"*Never* trust a man who doesn't like pop music," Julia says, lighting a cigarette. "For there, most assuredly, is a bore."

The atmosphere is blokey; coke-y: "One out of two isn't bad," Suzanne says, who's just dabbed some more coke under the table, after announcing to everyone else, "I think it might be time for some more drugs!"

She tries to persuade me to have some: "Just think of it

as 'powdered booze,' " she says, handing me a wrap. "Like in the war? Powdered eggs, powdered booze. Saves you having to go for a piss every half hour."

"It's a powerful recommendation," I reply, giving her the wrap back, "and I'm sure you could sell it to the elderly, and incontinent, and possibly the military, on that basis, but it's just not my game."

"What's not your game, babe?" a voice from behind me says. I turn around. It's John.

"You're here!" I cry, standing up, and hugging him.

I look at him—half expecting to see the same puffy, unhappy shambles I'd left in Eastbourne. But being locked away in a studio in Wales, recording, has clearly been good for him. His eyes no longer look like those of Sauron, he's lost what looks to be nearly a stone, and his posture has gone from that of a victim, to that of someone about to start dancing.

"You're *back*," I say, waving an appreciative hand at his hotness.

Tonight, he has been nominated for Album of the Year, Single of the Year, *and* Solo Artist of the Year. Tomorrow, he begins a tour of America.

"I've been practicing my gracious face, for when I lose to Blur, Oasis, and Paul Weller," he says, lighting a cigarette. "I've had a good early tip-off on one category—Kurt Cobain's won something."

"What for?" I ask.

"Bummer of the Year."

"They've described the suicide of Kurt Cobain as 'Bummer of the Year'?" I ask. "Blowing his brains out with a shotgun was . . . *a bummer*?"

"This is what will kill Britpop, in the end," Suzanne says darkly. "An inability to process or express any emotion more complex than, 'Oi oi, savaloy! Nice tits! Bummer!'"

"I dimly recall," John says, "that in 1989, in the Readers' End-of-Year Poll, the Reading Festival nudged the Number One slot over the fall of the Berlin Wall."

He shrugs.

"In many ways, we are engaged in an arena of fools. This is not Avalon, but a knavery."

I would like to say that Suzanne was grotesquely over-stating the blokey, triumphal, emotionally-reductive mood in London in spring 1995—but she was not. As the evening went on, it became more and more apparent that this city—and particularly this industry, in this room—was now in a delirium of degeneration. What had, last summer, been a cheerful cultural excursion into simpler, childlike times—all the sunshine, Chopper bikes, bacon sandwiches, great blokes and top birds—had, nine months later, morphed into a shriller, willful regression. I guess you cannot stay a child, high on sweets, staying out late, forever. You eventually grow into a teenager—a sullen teenage boy, scared of girls; and it seemed like those teenage boys were running the show tonight.

There were two "sexy" female models onstage—one in a skintight PVC bodysuit, the other in tiny PVC shorts—who were there to hand out the awards. Their presence, we were assured, was "ironic"—but, as Suzanne pointed out, "A vagina in PVC hot pants cannot be ironic. It's either here, or it's not. It hasn't got fucking quote marks around it."

There were very few other women in the room, and so

the presence of the models became ever-more disturbing, as man after man in jeans, or wearing a parka, went up onstage to collect their award. Just two years after everything was PJ Harvey, Björk, Alanis Morissette, Courtney Love, and Riot Grrrl—clever, funny warrior women, smarter and bolder and faster than any man in this room—this queasy, silent return of "sexy silent lady models" was jarring. Not least because, as the evening went on, it became increasingly clear that the only woman who had won an award that night was Kylie Minogue, for "Most Desirable Person in the World"—and that she would, therefore, be the only woman who spoke all evening.

"This room is just a massive testicularium," Suzanne said, gaping, as Kylie went up to get her award, to whistles, and shouts of "Alright darlin'?" She turned to me. "There's only one thing to do: let's go and take drugs in the toilet."

In the toilet, I simply treat myself to going to the toilet, whilst Suzanne and, unusually for her, Julia do coke, in the cubicle next to me.

When we all come out, there is a drunken woman standing there, staring intensely.

"I'm afraid I don't have any left," Suzanne says, automatically, showing her the empty wrapper. "You can . . . lick it, if you need to?"

"You're Suzanne Banks and Dolly Wilde, aren't you?" the woman says, carefully. Quietly. Now I look again, I recognize her—she is a PR for Polydor. I've seen her around, at parties—I had her filed under "good-time girl."

"Almost all the time," Suzanne says, slightly unsteady on her feet.

"Jerry Sharp," the PR says. Isla. That's her name. Isla.

She lets out a painful, ragged breath, then says:

"*Me too*," in a very small voice.

"He filmed it?" I ask.

"Yes," she replies. "And now I've seen what's happened with you, I am so, *so* scared."

I hug her, stop—and then hug her again. There's something unexpectedly . . . *reassuring* about hugging a woman who's been through the same thing you have. The simple fact that you are both still here. So far.

"What can we do?" she asks.

I look at her.

"I'm so sorry," I say. "But I don't think there is anything."

She nods, as if she expected that answer, squares her shoulders, and leaves the room.

When I come out of the toilets, two things happen at once. The first is that I bump straight into John Kite, who is standing, agitated, next to the door. He's clearly been there some time.

"Babe, word in private," he says, pulling me into a dark corner. "I wouldn't normally report this kind of thing back, but the table I'm on has just been told, loudly, by an enormously confident prick from my record company with the hair of an *actual* rapist, that Jerry Sharp got you your job on *The Face* because you shagged him."

I wince, and start to say, "But that would have been imposs—"

"Babe, you don't need to explain anything to me. Ever. I just wanted to make sure I was correct in telling him that, if I ever heard him repeat that spiteful bullshit about my friend again, to anyone, that I would personally break every fucking finger on his hands; and that *he* would be well-advised to go fuck Jerry Sharp now, and ask him for a job at another record company—because I was going to call the head of Warner's tomorrow, and insist he fire him."

He puts his arm around me.

"Are you okay, honey? I've heard a lot of weird stuff tonight. There's a bad buzz going round."

I am just about to reply to John, when the compere starts introducing the next award.

"Now it's time for Video of the Year. Women in the audience—and you know who you are—rumor has it, this could be won by *any of a number of you.*"

There's a small pause, and a gasp—and then the kind of laughter that I thought only existed as a sound effect when all the evil goblins laughed in *Labyrinth*. It has a particular tone to it—when men know they're laughing at something wrong, it sounds a little like wolves. It is not a kind sound. And I know they are laughing at *me*. Dozens of them have turned to stare at me.

I bury my face in John's jacket—I want to hold my face from them, somewhere safe—only to hear the laughter change, suddenly, into a confused, baying, "Oooooooooh!"

There is an almighty kerfuffle, down the front. I look up—and see that a furious-looking Suzanne is now climbing, effortfully, onto the stage—knickers flashing, although she clearly doesn't care.

"Ah, I see Suzanne Banks has not had enough attention tonight. Big round of applause for Suzanne Banks, everyone!" the compere shouts.

Suzanne gains the stage, pulls her dress down with a sexy wiggle, lights a fag, and walks casually over to the microphone.

"Would you like me to adjust the mic stand for you, Suzanne?" the compere asks, patronizingly.

"Well, given that it appears to have been positioned so low down it's broadcasting whatever your penis is thinking, yes," Suzanne says, expertly adjusting the mic herself, to laughter, and then staring out at the audience.

"So, guys, guys, *literally* guys," she says, over occasional shouts, "I thought I would come up here—in case you'd forgotten that women can actually talk?"

There is uncomfortable laughter.

"I am a physical reminder that we do still exist? That we are fifty-two percent of the population—that we are fifty-two percent of your *consumer base*, music industry," she continues, squinting out into the crowd.

"I just asked one of the staff here how many people are here tonight. Two hundred and fifty-eight, apparently. Of which, approximately, sixty are women. Or seventy, if you include the waiting staff. All the ladies in aprons having men click their fingers at them, give me a 'Fuck you, assholes!'"

The room remains silent. No waitress in the world will shout, "Fuck you, assholes" until her paycheck is cashed. Waitresses aren't stupid.

"Tough crowd. But then, that's the problem, isn't it? In a room full of powerful men, lesser-paid women tend to stay silent. Look, I'm too loaded to be nuanced about this. I just took some coke from a wrapper with my face on, so I'm kind of quite high right now, which is cool. Although I can see my label manager saying, 'Don't say that, Suzanne!' Hi, Zee!"

She waves at Zee, who arrived five minutes ago—just in time to watch his key artist slag off the entire music industry from the stage. He has his head in his hands.

"Don't do drugs, kids," Suzanne says. There's more laughter. "And here's another thing not to do—don't be a cunt, yeah?" The room goes silent. "Do you know how fucking exhausting it is being a woman? Every woman here—we've had to fight four times as hard to get here, we've spent five times longer than you getting dressed, our feet already hurt because of our fucking shoes"—here, Suzanne takes off one of her shoes, and throws it into the audience—"and then, when we finally get in the room—when we get to be in the room where all the winners are; where all the deals are being made—we find that all women seem to be good for is winning a prize for 'Most Wanked Over'—no offense, Kylie; I've flicked one off thinking about you too, babe. Or being Hester Prynned by gossip. This is a classic hostile work environment. You," she says, turning to the compere, who looks genuinely discomforted, "have created a classic hostile work environment. You know, you're not cheekily referring to the 'elephant in the room' when you talk about the 'Video of the Year.' *You* brought it up. *You* just brought the elephant into the room. You're an . . . *elephant pimp*, you dick."

She takes a swig of her drink, and stumbles a bit. She is absolutely trashed. By this point, I've run to Zee, who is quietly wailing, "What should I do? As her friend, I think I should get her down now. But a man can't remove a woman from the stage when she's talking about the patriarchy!"

Julia sighs, and walks over to the stage.

"Suzanne!" she calls, loudly.

"My colleague wants to talk to me. Hang on a minute. Just be cunts amongst yourselves," Suzanne says into the mic—then bends down to listen to Julia. Julia speaks to her for thirty seconds, and then Suzanne comes back to the mic.

"Julia wants to remind you all our debut album, *God Is a Girl*, is out next month on Jubilee Records, and that she thinks you're all cunts too. I'm Suzanne Banks, fuck you all very, very much. Good night!"

Suzanne carefully climbs back down from the stage, as the compere walks back to the mic, and says, "It's so embarrassing when your mum turns up at work, drunk," to explosive laughter, and relieved cheers.

Suzanne—not breaking her stride—kicks her other shoe off and up, into her hand, turns, throws it at the compere's face, and carries on walking out, whilst shouting, "I AM TWENTY-FIVE!"

As she leaves the room—us running in her wake—half the photographers are photographing her, and half are photographing the host, standing onstage, bleeding profusely from his nose, as the glamour girls stare at him with a cold, hard blankness.

WE STAND OUTSIDE the venue for a minute—Suzanne, Zee, Julia, John, and I—not knowing what to do. I have a ringing in my ears—like when you've been hit on the side of the head. The others look similarly stunned. Except Suzanne. She lights a cigarette and stands there, shoeless, looking unperturbed.

"Well, I think that went well," she says, leaning against the wall.

I don't know what to say. On the one hand, my dear

friend has just got up in front of a room of people and de-
fended me—whilst, in the process, losing two good shoes.
So I feel very *loved*.

But on the other hand, by defending me against a couple
of dicks, she has—of course—ensured that *everyone* in that
room will now be talking about me.

Gossip is a virus, for which there is no treatment, and
contact serves to spread it. If there was anyone in that room
who had *not* known what the compere was insinuating, they
would—even now—be asking the person next to them.
"Video—*what* video? What woman was he talking about?
Dolly Wilde? *No!*"

And then, later, they will tell others, and others, and others. I can imagine London lighting up with this story—the
computer circuits running overtime. And then—the printer
springing into action. For this is, now, surely, going to be
written about, in reports of the night.

"Suzanne," I begin. "What you just did there was amazing—
don't get me wrong—but I think maybe talking about it was the
wrong thing?"

"I'm an ENTJ," Suzanne shrugs. "My personality type is
all about *getting things done*. Lance the boil!"

"I think Dolly's personality type is more 'never complain,
never explain,'" Julia says. "Silent, dignified suffering—like
Jesus."

"You know how much I love you, don't you, babe?" Suzanne says, ignoring Julia. "Something had to be *done*. You
know what Audre Lorde says."

I do not know what Audre Lorde says.

"'*Your silence will not protect you.*'" She kisses me. I'm still
stunned.

Julia takes over.

"I think Suzanne is very high right now," she says, matter-of-factly, "so I'm going to take her back to the Phantom Zone, like Zod, to have a little think about what she's done."

She puts her arm out, for a cab, and bundles Suzanne into it. "You, come," she says to Zee, who is still standing there, looking helpless. "We're going to get the press calling us—we need to talk strategy. John—look after Dolly."

The cab disappears up Parkway, with Suzanne hollering, from the window, "THIS TOWN IS RUN BY SEXUAL CRIMINALS" until it disappears from view.

SO—I HAVE AN unsolvable problem.

I have just had the horrible realization that it doesn't matter how noble I am, or how much I know I'm a good person—because I must now walk around in a city where to hundreds—maybe thousands, I don't know—of people, I am the punch line to a joke. It's all very well saying that it doesn't matter what other people think of you—because the simple truth is, it really *does* matter.

The category of humanity I have just been placed in is: "A thing to make comments about; to have opinions about; to be pointed at." You always wonder, when you're growing up, what your "thing" will be—what people will remember you for, what you'll be the shorthand of. You live your life, and you work hard, always wondering, "Is this my defining moment? Is *this* the first thing someone would say about me? 'She was a really kind person.' 'She was really funny.' 'She was a great writer.' 'She was a true friend.'"

And all of that has gone by the wayside now—because, all the time I was working hard, and trying to be decent, Jerry was waiting in the wings, to *steal the idea of me*. To most people, I'm not "me" anymore. I'm just a thing that happened in his life, instead. I'm a dirty footnote. I'm the beginning of the salacious sentence, "Did you hear?"

And that is devastating, because: all I have is me. I have no money, or powerful friends, or well-connected family, or status. All I ever had was the idea of me. That was all I had to invest. All I had to live off. My creation of me had been so painstaking—so hard-won. I have tried, *so hard*, to be good! And now Jerry—Jerry has stolen it.

I see what he did, that night, when Suzanne and I confronted him at the John Kite gig. Even as I walked away, he jumped on my back, and now he won't let go. I will have to carry him around forever. He's hijacked me.

This is what I try to say to John, in between all the crying, as John offers increasingly violent ideas for solving the problem: "I'll do an interview, where I tell the truth. I'll break into his house, and steal the video, and smash it to bits. I'll hit him, Dutch. I'll break his fucking neck. I'll do time for you."

And even as I laugh-cry at his increasing, desperate fury, I explain to him that there's nothing he can do, because the problem is that story is now spreading, like a plague, and the only way to defeat it would be to set fire to this entire city, and kill everyone in it.

John immediately takes his lighter out. "Say the word, babe, and I'm good to go. I'll burn this fucker to the ground."

"Oh, I can never leave the house again," I wail, hysterically.

"People are out there, rating my sexual performance—like I'm Fuckoslavakia in the Eurovision Song Contest. I shall have to become a hermit, and communicate only by phone and letter. I can never look another person in the eye again—in case I look at them, and *know they know*."

"Or," John says, grabbing me by the shoulders, "you could just . . . come with me."

"What—to your house?" I ask.

"No—*America*," he replies. "I am getting onto a plane in seven hours, to a country where no one knows who you are. Come with me. It would be such a delight to have you. I want you with me. Sometimes, the only, best thing to do is just—run away."

"I can't just *go to America*," I say—even as I fill with absolute joy at the idea of it.

"Of course you fucking can. Andy! ANDY!"

John's PR, Andy Wolf, emerges from the shadows, where he's been lurking.

"Andy, you can sort this, can't you? Bring the duchess to America with me?"

"I would be absolutely fucking delighted to," Andy says, with the air of someone who would like to kill everyone in the world, one by one, starting with me.

"First class, yeah?" John continues. "No small seats. We don't *do* small seats," he says, putting his arm around me. "Always evacuate a burning life in style."

PART IV

29

It's amazing how quick money makes things happen. Seven hours later, I am on a plane to New York—suitcase stowed above, rucksack under the chair in front, and Kite in the big seat next to me.

I look at him. He is wearing his usual shabby suit; cheap gold signet ring flashing on his finger. His hair is still wet from the shower—early-morning comb marks through it, like neat furrows in a field. He's not a person—he's a place you travel to. Everything changes when you're with him. He is the mayor of good times.

I remember a quote I read: "It was no man you wanted, believe me—it was a world." I have always, unreasonably, wanted a whole world. And there he is.

As soon as we got on the plane, we were offered champagne with orange juice in. I'd never seen it before.

"What is it?" I asked John.

"Buck's Fizz. *Breakfast* alcohol," he said, taking one. "They invented that, the fucking geniuses."

"Then I would love some—yes."

I drink my breakfast champagne—looking around at all the other people in first class, settling in their seats. Everyone else is a white man, in a suit. Businessmen. First class is a simple visual representation of who has all the money in the world: guys who look like this. When John told me how much this flight cost—£4,000—I couldn't believe it.

"Just to sit in a chair for ten hours? You could buy our house in Wolvo for ten grand. Who can afford that?"

"Well, them—" John says, nodding at all the businessmen. "And me. The music industry is the third-biggest industry in the UK, babe."

"Is it?" I had no idea.

"Yeah. The only two ways to get into first class is either set fire to the rain forest, or sing sad songs. Everyone else sits in the Losers' Cupboard at the back." And he jerks his ringed thumb toward coach.

In the air, I take a second proffered breakfast champagne, and then a third. John—who is still sipping his first—looks at me, askance, as the bottle comes round again.

"Babe—you're drinking like you think it'll make you better," he says, wonderingly.

"Maybe it will," I say, with bravado. Last night has rattled me to my bones—I feel a palpable need to change the chemistry in my body, which is toxic with adrenaline, and I can't walk up a hill, or jump into a lake, to work it off. Alcohol is the only drug I have access to. I explain this to John.

"I hear you. I have an alternative," John says, rootling around in his rucksack. "Here."

And he hands me a Walkman—a chunky, clunky yellow Walkman, with scratches on the side.

"You ever had one of these?" he asks.

I haven't.

"This can change your chemistry, too. This is a portable crucible for the heart," he says, looking at the cassette inside. "Ah, Joni. Do you know Joni Mitchell?"

I shake my head.

"Perfect. Dolly Wilde—I want you to meet Joni Mitchell. Joni Mitchell—meet Dolly Wilde. I think you're going to get on."

He puts the headphones on my head—carefully moving my hair out of the way—and nods.

"Hit it," he says.

I press the "play" button. There is the clunk, and hiss, of header tape, and then—as Britain falls away behind us, and we head out over Ireland—my head fills with Joni Mitchell's silvered spiraling carol, singing about wanting a river, that she can skate away on.

It is perfectly beautiful and painful—like pulling a long, black thorn from your palm in one easy move, and having a shiny barb in one hand, and a small, empty hole in the other. It is the right time to cry, now, so I wrap my scarf around my head, so I am hidden, and cry.

John nods.

"Joni will see you right," he whispers.

After a minute or two, I put my Buck's Fizz down, and lean my head on John's shoulder, still quietly crying. He reclines our seats, and spreads a blanket over me, and I eventually fall asleep, curled up against John, flying over the Atlantic, with Joni's voice in my head. If I could have stayed up here forever, I would have been perfectly happy. I had found a river to skate away on.

AS A CHILD, when I saw New York on my TV, or in the cinema, I'd just presumed it was a film set—a dream-imagining of a city. No one *actually* lived somewhere that looked like that. The city of *Ghostbusters*; the Sharks and the Jets; *Fame.*

But—there it is, as we come in to land. I see the water towers, fire escapes, intersections, and blocks—just as they are, in movies. Fire hydrants, steam escaping from vents, and the skyscrapers—the Empire State Building, the Chrysler Building, the World Trade Center—standing there, as tall, handsome, and famous as a cocktail party consisting of Cary Grant, James Stewart, and Humphrey Bogart.

As we shuffle through security, and then into a cab— John managing to smoke *three* cigarettes between getting through Customs and into the car—I can't stop exclaiming at all the *America-ness:* the flags, the pretzels, the New Jersey accents, the businesswomen in immaculate skirt suits, wearing trainers—just like in *Working Girl*!

There is no Britpop here—no Adidas, no tracksuit tops, no lads, no parkas. London—Camden—suddenly seems like a very small, limited dream, in the heads of half a dozen people. Here, you can feel that you're on the edge of a vast continent, full of kids in the Midwest who are into metal, and country, and Michael Jackson, and who would simply boggle if you shouted "PARKLIFE!" at them.

No one here will *ever* care who I am, or what I have done. I have run away from terrible persecution in the Old World to start, anew, here—like the Pilgrim Fathers, but with a sex tape.

In the cab—face pressed against the window, so I don't miss a *second* of America—I think of how everyone knows New York is one of the best places in the world, "up there" with the modernist hustle of Berlin, the cobbles of Prague, and the sheer, raw power of Mumbai. It's known it's one of the best places.

But they are understating it all. New York, I thought, is *obviously* humanity's favorite child. It's *the* best. Every parent says they don't have a favorite child, but they lie; and everyone pretends that other cities have a chance of catching up with New York, but they don't.

I realized all this in under thirty seconds, as the taxi flew over the Brooklyn Bridge—each metal thread of its suspension cables harp shining gold, in the sun—and threw us straight into Manhattan, at chest height to the skyscrapers. John had tipped the driver $50 to requisition the car stereo, and blasted Julian Cope's "Double Vegetation" at top volume, thin metal window frames rattling with the bass.

There are five, huge, swinging chords in the very center of it—played on a guitar that sounds like a 747 on vertical takeoff—and John had timed it perfectly, so that those were the chords that blasted us over the bridge.

As we entered Manhattan, I felt like my hair was trailing out behind me, from the gloriousness of our entrance.

"Did you do that on purpose?" I asked, drunk on how astonishing it had been.

"Very much so," he replied. "God, I love showing you new things."

ON THE PLANE, John had asked me two questions: "Do you want to talk about it yet?"

To which I had replied: "No. Later."

And: "What do you want America to be, babe?"

To which I'd replied: "Two friends, having an amazing dreamtime interlude?"

"Two friends. Gotcha," he'd said, cheerfully.

"How long can I stay?" I'd asked, in a tiny voice.

"How long can you *stay*?" he'd repeated, incredulously. "As long as you want."

AT THE HOTEL, after we checked in—rooms adjoining, bags dumped, showers had, to wash off the mysterious plane sweat—John met me in the lobby.

"Babe, it's three p.m., and you're in New York. I've got to go off and be a bit of a rock star wanker for a bit—so I got you this."

He gives me one of the tourist maps off reception. He's drawn circles around various things.

"A walk in Central Park is always awesome, or you could get a taxi to Greenwich Village, and feel the Dylan vibes. There's the Empire State, of course, but I thought you might save that, and we could go together, later . . . ?"

He says it doubtfully—like he doesn't want to presume.

"I'm staying with you, you fool!" I laugh. "What are you going to do?"

"Just the usual twattery—honestly, I bore myself with it. Just go—have fun!"

"I will not do New York until we can go halves on it," I say, walking him toward the door. "Come on. Let's get a cab. I want to watch you at work."

IN THE CAB, John is oddly restless—like he's nervous about what he is going to do. I've never seen him being nervous about his job before. Mind you, I've never seen him do his job sober before. Something has, clearly, changed.

When we get to the venue, he goes to the boot of the cab, takes out his guitar with one hand, takes my hand with the other, and walks toward the venue. Then suddenly, he stops.

"You know that thing?" he says, looking at me. "That you wrote for me? About fans? Teenage girls? It has . . . changed things."

He starts walking again.

"I hope I get it right."

THERE ARE MAYBE two hundred and fifty, three hundred people here, all very young, and—oddly for a gig—more than half of them are girls. The kind of girls you don't see on TV, or in magazines.

Fat girls, odd girls, short girls, tall girls, girls in hats, girls with big feet; girls with big faces and clever, witchy eyes.

Girls in clothes they made themselves; their fathers' clothes; their grandfathers' clothes. Girls with cherry-red hair, and green hair; girls holding records they love. Girls with bottle-bottom glasses that speak of reading late at night, under dim lights. And all young. None over the age of twenty. These are half-children, with all the bubbling raw potential and chaos that entails. Girls—like me.

They emit a faint buzz of excitement, as John approaches the stage door. He waves at them—they wave back; some jump up and down, with excitement—and then he is whisked through the door by an assistant.

"The licensing laws on venues here are tight," John explains, as we walk through the venue, and the stage, at the back. "If you're under twenty-one, a lot of venues won't let you in. So we're having what my agent lovingly refers to as 'a Toddlers' Tea Party' here—letting the young ones come to the sound check, before the bar opens."

He climbs up onto the stage, and starts quickly tuning his guitar.

"He also refers to these events as 'Jail-Bait Rock,'" John adds, hitting "G" over and over. "He's a pungent phraseologist. Right! In the words of Paul McCartney, let them in!"

The venue assistants open the doors, and the girls pour in—some running down to the front to get the best position; and some hanging at the back, waiting for friends. Fizzing with the pre-birthday excitement that comes in the silence before music.

As everyone shuffles into place, John leans into the microphone. "Good afternoon, Young America!" he shouts, still fiddling with the guitar. "As you know, New York City does not allow you to rock out at night, so in the spirit of Judy Garland and Mickey Rooney, we're putting the gig on—right here!"

There is a cheer.

"We're only allowed to play for thirty-five minutes"—boos—"so I've chosen the set list by a simple process of democracy. I've studied which are my most popular songs, by way of their chart placings, and am going to play them in ascending order of success. You ready?"

Screams.

"Let's go!"

It isn't the best gig I've ever seen John play—there have been nights where I've seen him lose himself so completely in a song, it's like he's singing along with an invisible choir in the room. Harmonizing with things that don't exist.

But it is the *sweetest* I've ever been to. With the audience so young, and sober—no clusters of drunken men, pushing down the front—the dancing is free and, frankly, silly . . . girls spinning round and round; waltzing with each other.

The first stage diver is a gangly boy of no more than fourteen—when he makes it onstage, he bows, and then dances like Kermit the Frog.

John beams throughout the whole thing. After the first stage diver jumps back into the audience, he shouts, "Anyone else wanna come up here?" and the stage is suddenly flooded with teenagers climbing up; leaping around; kissing him, then jumping back into the crowd.

The gig ends with John, almost hidden in the crowd, handing his guitar to a chubby teenage girl, and saying, "Go for it, babe! SHRED!"

She is absolutely terrible—her playing comes from the Suzanne Banks School of "strings at the *front*"—but, halfway through, she assumes the wide-legged stance of Slash, from Guns N' Roses, and John is laughing so hard, all he can do is hug her.

"Thank you very much, New York," he says, putting his arm around her, as the stage erupts. "I will now be signing records, at that table, over there, for those who wish to marvel over how one man can make the word 'John' look so illegible. Good evening!"

He then jumps straight off the stage, and heads to a table, set up at the back of the venue. The audience forms an orderly queue, and the signing begins.

The first two fans are perfectly straightforward—just asking for a signature, saying, "I love the record! It's beautiful, man!" before going on their way.

The third girl, however, is visibly shaking as she walks toward John—and then bursts into tears. She's a girl not much older than me, in truth—and with the same ratty dye job, and Doc Marten boots, but pierced everywhere: ear, nose, tongue. The kind of piercings that look like each one was made, like a pin pushed into a war map, to mark a battle that was fought. She hums with bad history.

As soon as she starts crying, John comes out from behind the table and hugs her—murmuring "Don't cry, sweetness—don't cry. You'll start me off!"

"I can't believe I'm meeting you!" she sobs. "I thought of so many things to say, and I can't remember any of them now. I love you so much."

She is absolutely inconsolable—shaking and crying.

"And now I'm crying in front of all these people," she says, mortified.

John hugs her hard, to his chest. "You all think crying is cool, yes?" he asks the crowd.

They all cheer.

"See?" he says, gently, to the girl. "Crying is cool. You've started a trend. Look—I'm going to write that on your record—then it's official."

He scrawls "CRYING IS COOL—OFFICIAL" with a Sharpie on the CD, and signs it, with a flourish.

"You've got me through so many bad days," the girl says, in a rush, as John gently wipes the tears off her face with his sleeve. "My parents broke up last year, and it got really dark, and I just shut myself in my room, and listened to you over and over."

"Sometimes, that's just what we've got to do, man," John says, quietly. "Just got to chrysalis in our rooms, waiting for summer."

There is a queue of over two hundred people, and I know, from John's schedule, that he has only an hour here.

But, somehow, he manages to spend time with every one of the troubled, broken kids who comes up to him—signing their records, arms, and diaries, talking to them, telling them they look hot, or beautiful, or—in the case of two kids, a boy and a girl, who have a certain energy about them, "You know what, my darlings—you have an *air of destiny* about you."

As soon as one person is ushered away, another takes their place, so John does not see the reactions of those he's just met. But I do.

Most leave smiling—clutching their records like treasure.

Many run into the arms of waiting friends, like they've just scored a goal, or met God. Some punch the air. One runs round and round, clearly unable to control their adrenaline high. And one goes over to her waiting parents and collapses, weeping "I love him so much!" as her parents crowd around her, like deer around a sad Bambi.

I think about how brave it is, to do this: to queue up, and meet your hero. There's something incredibly intimate about reading, or listening, or looking at someone else's art. When it truly moves you—when you whoop when Prince whoops in *Purple Rain*; or cry when Bastian cries in *The NeverEnding Story*, it is as if you have *been them*, for a while. You traveled inside them, in their shoes, breathing their breath. Moving with their pulse. A faint ghost of them imprinted, inside you, forever—it responds when you meet them, as if it recognizes its own reflection.

And this is why meeting an artist you admire is always such an uneven, unfair thing. For they—they don't recognize *you* at all. You shake their hand, feeling as if you are seeing a dear, old friend again—remembering all the times you shared, together—and they look back at you, as if you are a stranger, and say, quizzically, "And what name would you like me to sign it to?" And you remember: *they* did not share those times at all. You were there—but they were not.

You can't meet your heroes—because they are, in the end, just an idea, that lives inside you.

This is why I feel such love for John—watching what he is doing, with all these fans. They are not meeting *him*—he is meeting *them*. He is looking them in the eye, conspiratorially; he is hugging them, like they have imagined hugging him. He is saying, "We meet—at last!" He is telling them they *are* as wonderful as they feel when they listen to him. He has . . . completed the circle of putting art out, into the world. He sent those songs out into the world, not knowing who would receive them, and now, one by one, they are coming to him, and saying, "I found it. I get it. It worked. It made a piece of me—just here."

And he is saying, "And I see it has made you glorious. *Thank you.* That was just what it was supposed to do."

WHEN WE GET back to the dressing room, after the signing, John's arms are full of presents, given to him by his fans. A book, a poster, some badges—a packet of cigarettes, a miniature of whisky, smuggled in. A doll—a John doll, made of felt, and wool.

"I hope this has not been used for voodoo," John says, turning it over, in his hands. "Although it would be comforting to learn my hangovers were not alcohol poisoning, but witchcraft."

"That was—that was *so lovely*," I say—gesturing out to the now-empty auditorium. "You made those people so happy."

"Well, I had some good advice," John says, looking over at me. He goes over to his guitar case, and takes from it six, very crumpled, very stained sheets of A4 paper.

It's the piece I wrote for him, and left in his hotel room, in Eastbourne.

"I have read this many, many times," he said, looking down at it. "At first, I have to admit, I was peevish about it. 'I am a rock star!' I thought. 'I know how to do my job! I have won awards! I have had hits! I have been drinking with Richard Madeley! I have been a guest on *Steve Wright in the Afternoon!* I don't need *advice*. A rock star does not take *advice*—unless it is on matters of off-shore tax breaks. A rock star *broadcasts*—he does not receive.

"But then I read it—and got to the end, and read it again; and then again, the next day—and thought, perhaps, all rock stars *do* need advice. Perhaps this is why so many go mad, or die, or become monstrous. They are all, generally, godless children, badly parented, bullied, friendless. Odd. Then they become famous, and they start talking—and they never stop. They are suddenly, God help them, *authority figures* to people just a couple of years younger than them. They're constantly asked for opinions, and advice—when they're just toddlers, leading babies. People stop *telling* them things. They stop learning. They go unquestioned."

He gestures to the paper. "But you—you told me things. You questioned me."

He hugs me.

"I once read how the primary problem is that developmentally, you freeze at the age you become famous," I say, face buried in his coat. "It's very interesting."

I really *do* find it interesting. But unfortunately, at this point, as if to disprove my assertion, I start yawning. I am so, so tired. The last forty-eight hours feel like long years. John takes stock of the situation.

"You look like shit, Dutch," he says, gently. "When was the last time you properly slept?"

I'm so tired, I can't even work it out.

"Baby, I'm going to get you a cab. You need to get back to the hotel, and sleep."

"I'll get my second wind," I say, feebly.

"I think you're already on your fifth, babe," he says, gently, putting his head out into the corridor, and calling his tour manager. "I'm just going to deal with some rock 'n' roll business here, and then I'll be back at the hotel by eleven. I'll see you in the morning. Don't die in the night. Breakfast in America is one of the very greatest things."

He kisses the top of my head, and I walk out to the cab, sleep drunk, in the rain, with his arm around me.

He tells the cabdriver which hotel to take me to, and hands him $30. "She's precious cargo," he says. "The world absolutely pivots on her survival. Drive with care."

He takes off his fur coat, and wraps it around me, like a blanket.

My head is already lolling on the car seat as we do a U-turn, and pull away—John standing, in his shirtsleeves, in the rain, waving.

30

Letter to John Kite, March 7th, 1995

John, I did a lot of thinking—about what it must be like to stand on a stage; and what it must be like to have people you've never met love you. And I wrote you this. D xxxx

There is one terrible weakness you can have, if you amusedly and self-deprecatingly describe yourself as an artist, and become famous. One letdown if you become loved by millions, and your work is meaningful work. And that is if some of the millions who know, and love you, are teenage girls.

There is nothing more shaming than to be loved by teenage girls. The love of teenage girls is not merely substandard, or worthless—it is an active mortification to an artist. Our language is full of how little we think of artists who are loved by teenage girls: we talk of "mad fans," and "teenyboppers," and "little girls wetting their knickers."

Oh, you can take those girls' money, and become elevated on their devotion, and enjoy them putting you at Number 1—you can do all those things; no band ever refused them—but you do not *respect* those girls. You do not want to talk to them, or look them in the eye, or hang out with them, or love them back. You do not talk about them—unless it is to turn to your "cool" fans—the men—and mouth, *Sorry. These mad girls have crashed the party. So embarrassing. Of course, they don't get it. Only you get it.* Men are the *right* fans to have.

This is why rock is cooler than pop; acid house is cooler than disco; prog cooler than boy bands. Things that boys love are cooler than things girls love. That is a simple fact. Boys love clever things, cleverly. Girls love foolish things, foolishly. How awful it would be to love bands like teenage girls do. How awful it would be to be the wrong kind of fan—a girl. How awful it would be to be a dumb, hysterical, screaming, teenage girl.

How amazing it is to be a dumb, hysterical, screaming, teenage girl. How amazing to go to a gig thinking of nothing but how loud you will shout; how hard you will dance; how much you will sweat; how tightly you will hug your friends, as your favorite song plays. How amazing to react to music in the way the music wants you—to become an ecstatic animal. To murmurate, in your millions, through the cities—calling to each other, in billows of girls, as you head to a gig, to exult.

How amazing to scream at the top of your voice, and see

the band respond to your call: they play faster, they play harder, they look sexier, they look out into the audience, and smile. How amazing to give yourself completely, expecting nothing in return.

Later on, maybe, in the dressing room, or in an interview, they might apologize, to other men, for the screaming girls: "It was a bit mad out there!" "Blimey—St. Trinian's were mental tonight!"

But they know, and you know, that tonight, your screaming was the most important thing to them. It was the energy that they fed on. It was the vortex they levitated in. They could not have been amazing without you. You have blessed them with your magic. You made them holy, and endless, and hot—and, in return, they played in a febrile way they could never attain in front of an audience of motionless men, murmuring, "Nice middle eight. Good reference."

Bands need to be screamed at. In their hearts, they know that. They know there is a power they will never attain until they have stood in the white-light noise of a theater of devotion, and seen girls down the front collapse in ecstatic tears.

And this is true even when it's the biggest scream in the world. Even when the mythology is that the screaming was what killed your band. When the Beatles played Shea Stadium, they turned up to a vast cauldron of howling, wild, melting girls, and might as well have mimed for all anyone could hear. That was when they decided to stop touring—that was what drove them to the studio, to write *Sgt. Pepper*. They were so tired of being screamed at—of being chased down streets— that they turned into another band: all decked out in Day-Glo army uniforms. They joined the army to escape all the girls.

But when *I* watch the Beatles at Shea Stadium—after I have

sighed over the beautiful podginess of John, his belly strain-
ing at the buttons on his jacket, which begs to be taken off;
once I stop swooning over the impossible cow-lashed eyes of
Paul, and his pale, milky skin—I watch the girls. I watch the
audience—those thousands of girls, dressed like their mothers;
dressed like *Far Side* ladies, in glasses and pencil skirts, and
rigid hair. I watch those girls, in those rigid decades, before
contraception; before feminism; before women were seen as
people—fucking *freaking out*. At first, because they are looking
at the Beatles—who would not freak out looking at a Beatle?
So podgy! So milky!—but soon, freaking out because *they are
the girls*. Fifty-seven thousand girls—will they ever have seen so
many of their own? Have there ever been so many girls in one
room, united? United in the very thing girls are not supposed
to do: losing their minds—in forgetting everything, and everyone; the unprecedented power of being able to scream, cry, wail;
overwhelming the security, untouchable by their own parents.

They are a power grid of energy—they are splitting their
own atoms with love and exploding, over and over.

They cannot hear the Beatles—the band plays through the
Tannoy, as distant and tinny as an ice-cream van, five streets
away—so these girls are making their *own* music. They scream.
All they can hear is their vast chorus of their own, ecstatic
wilding. They all scream at different pitches, notes, and tone—
sliding up and down the scales like the orchestra in "Day in
the Life" will, a few months later, when the Beatles record it.
The girls are singing their wild, high, feral-love seagull songs
to the Beatles, and the Beatles embed it in their songs, and
give it right back to them. It was a communal composition.

How, we ask ourselves, over and over, do we understand
the miracle of the Beatles? How could one band—four

men—have done all they did, at such velocity, with such density, and with a complexity so hot and elastic it feels like the simplest, most obvious thing in the world . . . until you try to do it yourself. Until you stand, in a silent room, and feel for one minute how impossible it would be to pull "Strawberry Fields"—that dark, fizzing, heartfelt oil wheel—out of the self-same, empty English sky John Lennon found it in?

When we talk of genius—of seizing a moment—these are man-words used when people are too scared to say "magic," and "witchcraft." We are too scared to talk about what we cannot see. We fear we might find God at the end of that sentence—some galactic passion that chooses its vessels, and gifts to them the universe's most totemic joys.

But here's the magic that the Beatles had—the unprecedented energy surge that blew out all the cultural circuits in the world. *They had girls.* They had the love of teenage girls. An audience who were neglected, belittled, hungry—they spoke to those girls, and unleashed the kind of power that can change the world.

And why did girls love them so much? Because the Beatles loved girls. The Beatles were saturated in girl culture—they loved black American girl groups; they had dandy outfits and uncomfortable pointy shoes, like girls. They went out of their way to write about girls in their songs—"She Loves You" is the Beatles siding with a girl in love . . . acting as her sexy envoys. They grew their hair long—like girls: an act of alliance in a time when femininity was implicitly inferior. All the teasing they got, all the outrage they caused, but they wanted their hair to look like *girls' hair.*

At a time when the difference between genders was never

more rigidly enforced, they rebelled into soft, clannish, sly, joyful femininity. Never combative, like boy gangs usually are; instead, their weapons were the weapons of girls: humor, sexiness, slyness, flirty wit.

So much is written about how all boys want to be, then kill, their fathers: Freud has gifted us decades of Luke vs. Darth. But the joy of the Beatles, as a gang, is that rather than becoming men by killing their fathers, they became men by turning into their dead mothers. John and Paul—both motherless at an early age—married single mothers; wrote songs about dead mothers and their living mother-wives; left the maelstrom of the Beatles to live the lives of wives: buying farms, making bread, raising children. They rioted into their femininity. They switched the polarity. They lived the unseen half of life.

How can you be as extraordinary as the Beatles? How can you change so much, in such a short period of time, with seemingly nothing—no capital, no contacts, no education—on your side? By tapping into the untouched cultural capital of humanity: girls. To be on the side of girls. To look girls in the eye, and declare yourself on our team. To copy girls. To acknowledge girls. To learn from girls. To accept what we give you—screaming, loving, singing, dancing—and let it set you free.

The great pity of my lifetime is that, still, no one notices this is what happens. Girls are invisible. The power source goes unacknowledged.

But not to other girls. I see you, girls. I see you, in history.

And all anyone has to do—to have our impossible energy, and love, given willingly, forever—is say, "I see you, too."

Love, Duchess

31

The next few days are like starting a new life, as a new person. All the traveling I've ever done before has been either work—twenty-four hours in a European city: plane/hotel/hour interview with the band/gig/hotel/plane home; or with my family—arguments in caravans, and tents, in Wales.

I have never been away with someone who is just joyous, uncomplicated, fascinating *fun*: who, over breakfast, will say, "Right. It's about time we went and met van Gogh's *Starry Night*, isn't it?" and take me to MoMA; or stand at the top of the Empire State Building whilst I sing the appropriate songs from *On the Town*; or push me into a cinema where they serve you margaritas *in your chair*, then lean over to hiss, with barely repressed Welsh fury, to the man who kept rustling his crisps: "Or perhaps, my love, it would be quieter to just *eat a tuba*?"

But the main thing is—we talk. We talk whole books, every day. What we say over breakfast *alone* is two chapters—John telling me about how he's rated his roadies, over the years: "Lesbians at Number Two—they're faster than anarchists, but slower than men."

Me telling my favorite story about writing: Henry James being asked to write a two-thousand-word book review, and submitting thirty thousand words. When the editor pointed out it might be a trifle too long, James cut one sentence and sent it back with a furious note, reading, "Here—take back the *mangled remains*."

This makes John laugh until he wheezes, and his eyes crease into just three lines—like when people laugh in the *Mr. Men* books. This is his best laugh. It is my favorite thing to make happen. I feel like I am collecting everything we say, and every honking laugh that bursts forth, in a series of leather-bound volumes, on a shelf, in my head, marked, "Continuing Fun," and that this is the library I shall browse through, remembering, when I'm ill, and dying. These are memories you can live in.

In Philadelphia, on the third night—in a hotel that, winningly, has a massive fiberglass Liberty Bell in the lobby—John plays me the songs from his new album. Lying on the bed, guitar balanced on his belly, fat fingers bouncing on and off the strings, like rain on a tin roof.

"After I read your letter," he says—still playing, as he speaks—"I went into the studio, which I had been dreading; as I'd believed I had run out of songs."

He shakes his head as he fumbles a chord—corrects it, smiles, and continues.

"And I found out that—I was wrong. That, actually, I had *plenty* of songs. It's just . . . I had thought they were the *wrong* kind of songs. So I'd ignored them."

He pauses speaking for a minute, to play a particularly complex flurry of chords. Task completed, he continues.

"I had been ashamed of all the new songs that were coming to me—because they were all so bloody *bright*, and shiny. Hahaha! They're so *commercial*, Dutch. They couldn't *be* more pop. I could hear the bloody Radio One jingle coming in at the end of them. And I hated it. *Hated* it. I could just imagine all the terrible balls your Tony Rich at the *D&ME* would say about them."

The name "Tony Rich" sounds so out of place, and long ago, here. And redundant. It is as if John had just mentioned the medieval practice of setting fire to bags full of cats.

"But then, I read your letter"—and, here, he smiles his best smile: the one that feels like sunshine on my arms, and face, and the streets around—"and I realized what a rotten bastard I was. I was! I was! *Why* do I care more about the opinion of half a dozen miserable, old journalists, than the opinion of *thousands* of brilliant, bright girls? What was I *doing*? What was I running away from? Whoever, in this world, *turns down love?*"

His fingers slide down the guitar neck, as his strumming hand turns into a blur. "This is the chorus!" he shouts, over six bars that cartwheel with joy, through meadow-rich melody. He beams as he plays it. "Isn't it fucking brilliant? That's down to *you*, babe. This one's on *you*."

Normally, at this point—in this kind of conversation—we would then hug. I would go over to him, and say, "It's my pleasure, you terrible murderer! Please write a song about me now," and we would do our brother-sister kissing, on the cheek, or in the hair; the brother-sister kissing that has sustained me for the last two years.

But instead, I stay where I am sitting—on my chair, by the window, smoking. And John stays on the bed—looking at me warily.

I feel safe here. I cannot move any nearer to him.

For since we have come to America, things have changed. There is mutual understanding that we should not be . . . too close. That if one of us steps forward, the other should step back. When we accidentally touch each other—in a lift; squished up together in a cab—we both hold our breath, for a second, until we move, safely, apart; and then we breathe again.

We have stayed up all night in dozens of hotels, over the years—lying on the bed, talking until dawn.

But here, we do not lie on the bed—we avoid it as if it were unstable, or electrified.

We have run away together, to America. We know what should happen next. I catch John often looking at me for a beat too long, a degree too hot. I am aware of him watching me as I brush my hair; as I drink my wine; as I walk into the room, with the new button-up green suede boots I bought in Greenwich Village.

"Those are the kind of boots that could make a man dizzy," he said, appreciatively, as I smiled at him—and then sat on the chair farthest from him, at the table.

I know the way John thinks about me has changed. I see him waiting. He is waiting and watching for the slightest sign from me—a look, a word—and he would then take that one step toward me, and that will be it. All this static electricity will find its path to the ground, and the kissing will begin, and never stop.

But I can't go near him. It feels like a bad idea, right now. And I don't know why. I presume it's because of Jerry.

John, of course, knows *something* bad has happened, but not the full story—for the first two days in America, I was too ashamed to tell him. I do not like telling sad, awful stories about myself. I do not know how to end them. How *do* you finish a story that cannot swing up into a triumphal joke, or conclusion?

When I finally tell him tonight, I end it suddenly—"So he filmed it, and now he shows it to people at parties. And that's the story of my sex-tape shame."

I look down, and notice I have torn the room service menu into three hundred tiny pieces—my lap is filled with confetti that says "urger" and "yonnaise."

The story makes John so angry, and distraught—"How could he *do* that?"—that I think he might actually wail, as if injured.

"When his karma comes, I hope it's painful, and testicular," he concludes, at the end of a white-fury rant. "I wouldn't even bother burying him, after I'd killed him. I'd just throw him up a tree, and let the birds fuck him up. Oh my love, what can I do? I'll do *anything*."

"I don't know," I say, still looking down at my lapful of paper. "I don't *know* what can be done. I think about it all the time. At first I was in denial, and then I was angry, and now . . . now I'm in this odd place, between emotions. I feel like I'm . . . *waiting* for something. You know how, in *The Railway Children*, Bobbie wakes up one day, and *knows* something's going to happen? Everything feels really dream-like, and disconnected—and then, at the railway station, her father appears?"

"'Daddy, my daddy!'" John exclaims. "God. If you ever wanted to bawl like a baby."

"I feel like that," I say. "That I'm waiting for something. That I'm waiting for something to happen."

John nods, but stays on the bed. I stay on the chair. Waiting.

WEDNESDAY IS WASHINGTON, DC, where John has a whole day of press to do.

"I'm sorry bube," he says, over breakfast. He was right—about American breakfast. They *are* amazing. I'd never had a hash brown before.

"It's like some chips had an orgy," I say, wonderingly, as the waiter puts it in front of me. "Don't worry about abandoning me. I have a plan."

"Bar? Strip clubs? Bongo flicks? Crack den? America is bounteous with its diversions for the troubled," John says, finishing his eggs, and lighting up a fag.

"Oh no," I say, cheerfully. "The Smithsonian Institution. I've always wanted to go."

"Your nerd pilgrimage continues," John says, tenderly, putting down a hefty $10 tip.

He kisses me on the hand, and goes out to his cab. "Four p.m., back here. We will be handy dandies on the brandies."

THE TRUTH IS, whenever I am abroad, and alone, I always go to museums, and art galleries. Museums and art galleries are by way of a worldwide network of places a teenage girl can go, when she has time on her hands, and no friends to speak of, and be both safe, and uplifted. Where she can *think*. Where she is *shown things* that will, undoubtedly, be useful to her. And museums always, *always* have great cafés. It is one of the things I admire about the liberal, middle-class elite: if they make a place of culture, it will be *unthinkable* to them that such a place would not also have a shit-hot selection of soups, cakes, and sandwiches. It's very clear that their take-home message is, "What history has taught us, is that lunch is *very important*."

As I walk the ten blocks from our hotel—on a day where the wind is brisk enough to make all the Stars and Stripes, hung from flagpoles, unfold graciously, and the sky is as blue as the blue upon them—I am heading toward where Krissi and I always go, when we hit up a museum: Geology, Gems, & Minerals.

In the beginning, it was, of course, because we wanted to look at diamonds. Diamonds, and emeralds; sapphires, amethysts, and rubies. Why would a poor child not want to see the most glittering and expensive things on Earth—trapped in a glass case; inches away from changing our lives, if we smashed it, and ran? We would walk around, deciding which one we would have, if the museum decided to gift us one single thing from their cabinets.

We felt it very important to know which jewels we would take, if we were ever asked. We wanted to be *ready*, should Daddy Warbucks walk in, and feel generous. We didn't want to be caught on the hop, and go home with . . . *garnets*. Garnets are just shit. Muddy rubies, for sad Aquarians.

But to get to the precious jewels, you have to walk through the "lesser minerals" first—the browner ones; the duller ones—it's like eating your Yorkshire puddings, before you get to the roast in a roast dinner. Over the years and the hours we have spent there, we have come, eventually, to love these best. They *are* the best, once you stop, and look at them. Once you stop valuing sparkle—and start coveting mysteries, instead.

It takes a minute for my eyes, and brain, to adjust to the room—museum quiet, and dark, with the cabinets lit up, like stars on a stage—but once I do, the old magic starts. Rocks shaped like stars; like Buddhas; like temples; like daggers. Rocks as fine as hair; or which glow in the dark. Rocks that look like bubbles, or hearts, or molten spacecraft.

I wander over to the maps, on the wall, which detail where all the finds have come from. And I note, with slow wonder, how every single amazing thing in this room—everything that is precious, or glittering; everything that glows; everything that is *notable*—comes from somewhere awful. Terrible. Terrifying. Somewhere where tectonic plates have ground up against each other; or things have exploded. Places of chaos, or intolerable pressure. Volcanoes and landslides. Earthquakes, and floods. Asteroids, slamming into the Earth. Without exception, the way wondrous things are made is through trauma.

Pressure and explosions, I think, slowly—starting to feel

excited, like a very useful thought is happening—make the extraordinary things.

And as with these minerals in the ground, so with the minerals in *us*. Surely. For we are made of the same stuff as the Earth, after all—and so *we* must alchemize when *we* are pressurized, or when things explode, too.

This is why certain places in the world—Nashville, New York, Liverpool, Berlin, London, Detriot, Vienna—keep producing voices, and geniuses; storytellers, and singers. Things exploded there—politically, economically, socially. There were fires, or bombs, or floods, or plagues—and so the chemical compositions of their citizens change. This is the geology of creativity. Pressure, and heat, make astonishing people.

And sometimes the cataclysms are smaller, though just as painful. Terrible, life-changing cataclysms happen on every scale—from an entire continent, down to a single house, or heart.

I think of Suzanne's early years—the hotel rooms, alone.

Or John's childhood—his mother ill, then dying.

As I reach the cabinet containing a supposedly cursed diamond, I think, finally, of what is happening to me. I stared at it, lit up from all sides. This was, once, just carbon. It went through an almost intolerable pressure—the world literally bore down on it—and now, there are untouchable red-blue fires in it; tiny pink and green comets streaking across its core. A whole galaxy, in something the size of a baby's fist.

This is what happens, when it feels like the weight of the world is crushing right down on you.

You fear it's going to change you forever.

And you're right. It is.

It's going to turn you into something that is both beautiful, and the most indestructible thing on the planet.

I am both touched, and amused, by how apt its name is: Hope.

"I relate to you," I say to the Hope Diamond, as I stand there, staring at it. "I get what you are saying. You are the sparkliest metaphor I have ever seen."

"WE CAN STAY away forever, if you like," John says, after a week, as we sit on the balcony of his hotel room in Savannah, Georgia.

John's tone is very casual, but when I look up from my poached eggs on a silver plate, with the weird, light, insubstantial toast America inexplicably fucks itself with—his look is earnest.

"What?"

"If you don't want to go back," he says, voice still breezy. "We don't ever have to go back, if we don't want to. I could make one call now, and by this evening, they'd have a year-long tour laid out for me. You could go anywhere you wanted. Canada. New Zealand. Japan."

"India?" I say. "I've always wanted to see the palaces of the last maharajahs!"

"That's not one of my key territories—so, no," Kite says, looking comically pained. "I've sold absolutely fuck all there."

"Mexico, then? That's astonishingly beautiful."

"No—no, I sell fuck all there also."

"They're not going to care about you in Nepal, either, are they?"

"No."

He lights a cigarette.

"But you do see the *general principle* of what I am saying—which you are fucking with your arcane travel preferences for countries that, by and large, have little-to-no appetite for angst-stricken white singer-songwriters from Wales? We could just—fuck off from Britain. It's finished. We need never go back there. Take off, and nuke it from space. If you don't want to go back. We can stay away forever."

I've finished my eggs. I drink my coffee. The cups are pleasingly white, and chunky. In my equally white robe and slippers, I feel like I am in an advert for a satisfying new life.

The idea of simply trotting around the world with John, for a year or more, is, obviously, what Willy Wonka would have put in a special chocolate bar for *me*, if he knew how bad I would be at the day-to-day admin of running a chocolate factory—but, nonetheless, still wished to reward me.

And yet—I know I can't.

"Well. The thing is. All this. It isn't . . . real, is it?" I begin, musingly. This conversation is an experiment—as I am still trying to work out, exactly, what the problem is. And the only way I could do that was—as I explained before—by talking. This is why I was often stupid around bad listeners.

"Quid in the box, babe," he says, rattling a tin, and putting it on the table.

We have a "cliché tin," for every time one of us uses a rock 'n' roll cliché.

I put a dollar in the tin.

As I put the dollar in the tin, I suddenly realize what my

reservation was. Finally, everything falls into place—why I can't touch him, why I can't stay.

John is rescuing me.

"You're *rescuing* me!" I shout, because I am so excited that I'd worked it out. "*That's* why I can't do it."

"What do you mean?" he asks, looking confused.

"If I run away on tour with you—which would, of course, be the most extraordinary thing . . . the most perfect and amazing thing—then you will, technically, when you get down to it, have rescued me. And I can't be rescued."

"Oh, you're not *that* bad," John says, ruffling my hair. "It's probably blown over alrea—"

"No, no. You don't understand. I can't be rescued. As in—I will not accept being rescued. It is—not my thing."

John looks hurt. I really don't want him to feel hurt. But I am so excited that I've just worked out what this persistent, chirping worry in my guts was, that I had to share it with him. I feel like a professor, sharing a new theorem with a colleague. I expect him to be proud of me. He always is, when I work a thing out.

"Jerry did a thing which made me vulnerable, and sad. Now you have done a thing which has made me safe, and happy. But what if you stopped doing the thing that was making me safe, and happy?"

John looks absolutely bewildered. "That could never, ever happen! Unless it was funny. And only then for, like, two minutes. I am you. You are me. How could I *ever* stop wanting to make you happy?"

"You might die."

"Balls. I will absolutely never die."

"You will die at *some* point."

"Impossible. You think *I* am going to die?"

He laughs, lights another cigarette, and then coughs, furiously. "Fucking hell—is coughing exercise? It feels like it."

He drinks his orange juice down in one.

"There. I am healthy again. Easy."

I light a cigarette, and lean back in my chair. The sunshine is bath warm; it is so beautiful on this balcony with John; and, as a sidebar, he has never looked more wonderful—the mess of his hair, the swell of his belly, his clever, fast fingers on the lighter. His eyes, so full of love and amusement. It is so perfect.

And somehow, it is the loveliness of the morning that makes it easier to say: "It's a long story, but I saw this diamond, and it's me. I have to go back now."

We have never argued once, in all the time we have known each other, and it isn't an argument now. Just John, being baffled—even as he rings his manager to arrange plane tickets—and me unable to say anything other than, "I just have to go now. I'm so sorry. Thank you for everything."

"You can't thank someone for something that has made them inordinately happy," John says, miserably, watching as I packed my suitcase. "I am with you for wholly selfish reasons."

I left for the airport two hours later.

32

Back in London, as I walked through my door, I noticed two things, in quick succession. The first was that the dog was running toward me. The second was that the house smelled of curry. Delicious, cinnamon curry.

Both of these were confusing, as I'd left the dog with Suzanne, at her flat, while I was away; and, as far as I knew, the dog did not know how to make curry—and so the combination of dog and curry was incredibly disconcerting.

For a moment, I wondered if I'd walked into the wrong house—but then Julia emerged from the kitchen, drying her hands on a tea towel.

"You're home," she said, implacably. Nothing ever seemed to surprise Julia. She picked up the phone, and dialed a number.

"Dolly's here. Come," she said. There was a pause, and then, patiently: "They're under your tights. No—UNDER your TIGHTS. Look properly. No, don't do that. Why? Because last time you did, you passed out for sixteen hours. Okay. See you in ten. Bye."

She put the phone down.

"Welcome," she said. "Tea?"

I dumped my suitcase, and followed her into the kitchen—utterly bewildered.

"I thought the dog was staying at yours?" I started.

"Yeah," Julia said, putting the kettle on. "That didn't really work out. Our flat's not really geared up for dogs. She kept eating things, like a hairbrush, and a fur hat. So I thought I'd stay here, with her. Your dad made her a basket."

She gestured to a bread crate with . . . with one of *my* coats in it, as a blanket.

"My *dad*?" This morning was getting more surreal by the minute. "Is *he* here?"

"No," Julia said, plonking the tea down in front of me. "We had a good chat, and, in the end, we agreed it would be for the best if he went back to your mum, and just . . . said sorry."

I put my head on the table. Nothing was making any sense, and my body still thought it was in Georgia. Julia took pity on me.

"Right. So. I moved in, with the dog. Then your dad turned up—said your brother had told him you were going through a bad time, and might need the loving help of a father."

Krissi! He'd used *my* sex scandal to off-load Dad! I knew that when you had lemons, you had to make lemonade—but

Krissi had stolen *my* trauma lemons to make *his* lemonade! What a bastard!

"We had a good chat, me and your dad. Once I realized he wasn't a burglar, and put the cricket bat down."

"I don't *have* a cricket bat!" I wailed.

"Oh, I always travel with one," Julia said, gesturing to the cricket bat propped up in the corner.

I drank my tea. I needed it.

"Anyway, we got chatting, and in the end, he told me about how things have gotten a bit . . . edgy with your mum."

I nodded.

"He's a fascinating man, your dad," Julia said, musingly. "Bright, charismatic, funny, keen on drugs, selfish, insane. Reminded me of someone."

Right on cue, the doorbell rang.

"That's Suzanne," Julia said, going over to open the door. Suzanne was standing there, in a nightie with a fur coat over the top, smoking a cigarette.

"We were just talking about you," Julia said, pushing a cup of tea in front of Suzanne, as she sat down. "About how Dolly's dad is like you."

"Pat? Yeah. He's a darling," Suzanne said, cheerfully.

"And from everything he told me about your mum—downbeat, sensible, keeping the wheels on—she sounded—"

"Well, she's you, Julia," Suzanne interrupted. "She's totally you. We all know she's you."

"So I told your dad what had kept me and Suzanne together, in our relationship."

"Is it mutual love and respect?" I asked.

"Not so much," Julia replied. "It's *cash*. Love and respect are so much easier if you both just . . . have the same amount of cash. You can put up with an enormous amount of balls if you have an equal ability to buy shoes."

Suzanne nodded wisely.

"So I told him to either sell the stupid car, and split the proceeds with your mum; or let *her* take out a loan, too, and let *her* spunk it on whatever she wanted."

Apparently, my father's reaction to that had been to start heffing and peffing about the size of the potential repayments, to which Julia had replied, "Well, now you know the APR for equality, Pat. That's the marriage maths," and he'd quietly agreed to sell the car and split the money, and then gone home.

"So that's it?" I asked, faintly. "You've sorted out my dad? Is that why you're here?"

"Oh no," Suzanne said. "That's just a sidebar."

"Curry, anyone?" Julia asked, going over to the hob. In answer, Suzanne rattled her bottle of pills—"They *were* under the tights! You were right!"—and I gratefully received a plate.

"I'm here for the *real* business," Suzanne said, putting her feet up on the table, and promptly having them pushed back off by Julia.

For the next half hour, Suzanne and Julia told me of everything that had happened since I'd left.

The press had, obviously, been interested in the story, but were unable—for legal reasons—to speculate in print that it was anything to do with me.

"So, they've been hinting," Julia sighed. "Lots of blind items. Zee's been great—put out press releases about how Suzanne's speech was 'addressing general misogyny and abuse in the industry.' It's been a *big* topic."

"I got the headline 'THIS CITY IS RUN BY SEXUAL CRIMINALS' in the *Evening Standard*," Suzanne said, proudly. "*And* they ran a plug for the album at the end."

"I'm so pleased for you," I said, faintly. "Has all that . . . stopped it?"

"Oh no," Suzanne said, regretfully. "I'm so sorry, babe. Everyone in the industry is still talking about you. And it's been pretty disgusting. I'm so sorry."

My heart felt sick. For one beautiful minute, I thought the problem might have solved itself.

"But we have not been idle!" Suzanne said, gleefully. "Since that night, and all the pieces in the press, I've had *other* women getting in contact with me. Dolly, there's *so many*."

She shivered.

"There are so many women Jerry has wronged. He was basically a full-time abuser, and part-time comedian. It's a miracle he ever got any work done, to be honest. And, during my time as the unofficial hotline for all sexual wrongness in London, I managed to procure *this*."

Suzanne put a huge Jiffy bag on the table.

"Go on. Open it," she said, pushing it toward me.

Fumbling, I opened it. Inside—there were a half a dozen video cassettes, with scribbled labels: "SH," "IB," "VR," "DW."

"One of Jerry's current 'girlfriends' called me. Only, she's not his girlfriend anymore. Not after she found these."

Suzanne nodded at the collection of cassettes, and pushed one toward me.

"There was a whole cupboard of these. 'DW' is you," she said.

I looked at the video. God, what an odd thing. A black plastic box that contains a mere half an hour of my life—but a half hour that had threatened to eat up my name, and work, and life, like acid, until there was nothing left.

"Is this the only copy?" I asked, touching it with my fingertips, as if it were dirty.

Suzanne nodded, and put the video on the floor.

Julia handed me the cricket bat.

"So now, you can get rid of it," she said, with quiet glee. "You can smash it to bits."

I held the cricket bat in my hand. The idea of smashing up the tape seemed deeply, deeply appealing. But I also had a feeling that, if I could just keep talking for a while longer, I would come up with an idea that was even better. I knew I was on the verge of thinking something . . . different.

"Ladies—could you just let me talk at you for a while?" I asked, putting down the bat. "I just need to talk. I just need to talk."

33

The launch party for The Branks' album is at the Astoria—they are going to play the album, live, from beginning to end, and then the plan is to "get more fucked-up than anyone else in creation," as Suzanne puts it, happily.

I go to their dressing room, where Zee is fussing over the cheese and meat plates. As I walk in, Suzanne is exclaiming over something.

"It's so *cute*!" she says.

I go over to see what's in her hand. It's a wrap of pink cocaine.

"Cute?" I say.

"It just came in from L.A.!" she says. "It's what all the L.A. heiresses are taking now." She names a few. "They didn't like the taste of Coke Original—so some fucking *genius* has started cutting it with Strawberry Nesquik. It's *adorable*."

Zee leans over, and takes the wrap off her.

"Shall we call it pudding, and keep it for later?" he says, putting it into his pocket, like a dad.

Suzanne looks at me. "How you feeling about this?" she asks. Julia and Zee put hands on my shoulders.

"Yeah—you okay?" Zee says.

"I don't think there's anything else I *can* do," I say, bravely. "I have my notes."

I wave my pages of A4 around.

I had been writing all week. I have always had faith that you can write your way out of anything, if you think hard enough. That is my primary belief. It got me out of Wolverhampton, it brought me to London, it made John write commercially viable songs without wanting to end himself. It is my comfort, my weapon, my wealth, and my better self. It is all I have, really.

Obviously, right at this moment, I've reached the point in the process where I believe what I've written on these A4 sheets is total dog shit, and that I have made an unbelievable error—but it's too late now.

Suzanne gets up, and hugs me. "Just—stay angry," she whispers. "Anger makes your eyes really blue."

AT NINE TWENTY p.m. I am standing at the side of the stage with Suzanne, levitating with panic, when the house music cuts out. I hadn't noticed I was holding Suzanne's hand until she squeezes it—then lets go, and walks out onstage.

"Good evening, London!" Suzanne says, to whoops and applause. "I am Suzanne Banks—"

More whoops and applause. "And we are The Branks! Thank you for coming tonight!"

Cheering.

"This is the launch party for our album—due to go Top Ten this Sunday!—and it's brilliant to see you all here, ready to rock!"

Screams.

"Before we start, however, there's a little business we must attend to. We are all," she said, unhooking the microphone from the stand, and starting to stalk the stage, "part of a gang; part of a pack. I hope some of you tonight have come here tonight with *your* pack."

More girl screams.

"Well, I have a pack, too. And when one of your pack has been done a great wrong, you have to stop, for a moment, and help your pack member back up again. Which is why, ladies and gentlemen, I want you to welcome to the stage the most burningly brilliant creature, who has a few things she needs to say to the world. I want you to go wild for *my girl*, Dolly Wilde."

There is applause—and as I walk out onto the stage, into the bright, white light, and Suzanne's hug, I marvel, once again, how the simple act of banging two hands together can take on an emotional timbre. This applause sounds . . . confused.

There is one man, however, who isn't confused.

"Suck my cock!" he shouts, from down the front, as is the traditional greeting of men to women, when they walk onto a stage.

"Suck your own goddamn cock—she doesn't have *time*," Suzanne replies, briskly.

There is a ripple of laughter.

"So, Dolly's here to discuss . . ." and then Suzanne, perhaps uniquely in her life, stumbles for words.

"My Sex Tape of Shame," I say, helpfully. "Hands up here who's heard about it?"

There is a confused, abashed pause—and then pretty much the entire audience puts their hands up. It's a horrible moment. The absolutely indisputable evidence my shame is vast, and real.

For ten heartbeats, I feel the most pure terror imaginable. I look at Suzanne, helplessly. She leans in, off-mic.

"Go to work, kid," she whispers.

It was the best thing she could say—for I am never, ever afraid of work.

I take the microphone.

"So. As you have all just confirmed, to me, I am currently famous for having had some sex, one time."

There is applause.

"Given how—for want of a better word—*successful* this sex tape has been, I thought I might capitalize on its success, in the way one does with any popular entertainment," I continue. "This is why, therefore, tonight, I offer you the chance to hear a director's commentary on the *original footage*. Are you ready?"

The audience registers applause, and more confusion. They don't understand what is going on.

I nod to Suzanne's tour manager—and the grainy footage of the Worst Fuck in the World starts projecting onto the screen behind us.

I look at it for one second. There I am—in my sexual

hopefulness, lying on Jerry Sharp's bed. And there—moving away from the camera, that he's just turned on—is Jerry.

"Let's see your dark side, Dolly Wilde," he says, on screen.

"This," I say, "is the footage from that night, supplied by a friend from a hard-core feminist collective. This is me being fucked by Jerry Sharp."

Absolute pandemonium breaks out in the audience. They cannot believe I am showing my sex tape on a big screen. To be honest, neither can I.

On the screen, we hear Jerry saying, "So—shall we find out what you can take, you dirty bitch?" as he comes back to me on the bed. And that's not a happy thing to hear someone say to you. I freeze again.

Looking across, Suzanne sees my terror, and steps in. With the casual air of a Las Vegas MC, she leans on her mic stand, and asks, "So, my lady, what's going on here?"

I stare at her.

"Come on. What's Mr. Chips doing up there?"

She points to me, on the screen.

"Just *say what you see*. Show me on the doll what he did to you."

She hands me a whisky bottle. I take a swig.

"So, if we could pause here, for one second?" I ask the tour manager. He pauses the video.

I am caught in midframe—staring, slack-jawed, at the camera—with Jerry looming over me. The video camera on his dressing table captures the whole tableau: his bed, the bedside lamps blazing—and Jerry pointedly maneuvering me into the best position, so I am wholly visible to his future audiences. He looks like a contestant at Crufts, manhandling their dog so that it looks at its best for the judges. I am that dog. I am a Cock Spaniel. I am a Golden Receiver. I am a Labiarador.

It is not a scene of glory.

I stare at the screen for a moment. There is a reason most people have sex in the dark, I think. It's because they all look as awful as this. I look at Suzanne. She hands me a lit cigarette. I take a deep drag.

"Okay. So. Just in case some of you don't know, I am going to tell you how women have sex with men. The unwritten rule. Okay. Here it is: you have some of the sex he's having."

I pause, for a moment, and stare out at the audience—so everyone has time to think about it—before resuming.

"Sex is the copyright of men. It's a thing they invented, to do with women—and, once you've gone to their house and taken your clothes off, you're kind of contractually obliged to go along with it.

"Of course, you're allowed to say 'STOP!' if he really hurts or frightens you—it is 1995, after all!—but, as for the rest of it, you've bought your ticket for the ride. You can't get off until the end. A grown woman is supposed to see the sex through to the end—like a sexual soldier, on a mission. You get into bed, are given your sexual orders, and you must carry them out. You can't stop now."

I look up at the audience. It is agog. The video starts playing again.

"So here I am, having Jerry's sex. Because that's what coming to his house means."

On the screen, Jerry's slightly-out-of-focus mouth is on my slightly-out-of-focus breast.

"So, we're starting with the breasts. I'll be honest—I've never understood all the hoo-ha here. For me, someone fiddling around with my nipples is a bit like a drum solo—the person doing it always seems to be enjoying it more than everyone else in the room."

On the screen, Jerry lumberingly crawls behind me.

"Still, I'm not bored for long because, as you can see, all the foreplay is over now—that clocked in at just under a minute, for anyone keeping notes—and it's time for Jerry to get down to the *real* business. It's the beginning of the actual sex!"

I let the video run for a while. Jerry is pumping away, behind me, as I stare at the wall, with an expression that is . . . stoic. I look like an eighteenth-century shepherdess, walking through a storm to find my sheep.

The audience is alternately laughing and gasping.

"So, what we have here is some classic sex," I say. Suzanne hands me a pointer stick.

"As we all know, the key erogenous zone of a woman is here—"

I point to my clitoral area.

"It is, odds on, pressure on *this* area that will make me orgasm. As Jerry is not touching it, we can conclude he does not wish me to orgasm. What Jerry's doing, instead, is having the kind of sex he has seen in porn films."

Jerry, still pumping hard, slaps my arse. My face on screen registers shock. The audience gasps.

"There's a lot of slapping in porn films. Personally, I've never understood it. Perhaps all men hope they have found a delightful, one-off freak, whose clitoris is on their bum cheek. Like the plot to *Deep Throat*, but with a bum. *Deep Bum*. Sadly, I am not Deep Bum. When he slaps my arse, it very much feels like he's just slapping my arse. You know—like parents do, with children. In my case, this is the first time I've had my arse slapped since I was nine, and accidentally taped over my mum's copy of *Yentl*. So it's not terribly sexual for me."

Jerry, pumping harder, spanks me again. My face looks oddly blank—punctuated with the odd grimace.

"That grimace," I note, "is because I am now thinking of my mum. Oh Mum! I don't want you in my head right now! I'm going to think about Barbra Streisand, instead. That will make it marginally better."

On screen, you can see the brief ghost of a smile on my face.

"That's my Barbra Smile," I say. "I am now thinking about her wearing a gold lamé dress in *Hello, Dolly!* And now I am thinking about me wearing a gold lamé dress. These are nice distractions. These are what I am thinking about while this sex happens."

The audience laughs. I continue.

"So, with Jerry not even attempting to make this pleasurable for me, and me pretending I'm not there, the question we have to ask here, ladies and gentlemen, is—*is this actually sexual intercourse?*"

I point at the bad fucking going on behind me, and then open the dictionary I am carrying.

"Sadly, according to the dictionary, it *is*: 'Sexual intercourse: sexual contact between individuals involving penetration, especially the insertion of a man's erect penis into a woman's vagina, typically culminating in the ejaculation of semen.' There is, you will note, no mention of *female* arousal, or orgasm. Is there little wonder that Jerry does not think of my sexual pleasure, when *it's not even in the dictionary?* Ladies—*our sex is not even in the dictionary.*"

The women in the audience boo/cheer. I point at the screen, where Jerry and I are still humping. Me on all fours; Jerry behind me, still spanking. He looks like a horny jockey, trying to win the Grand National.

"And so the description of what's going on here depends on who you are. Men, you are absolutely watching sexual intercourse. For you, this is a sex tape. Women, on the other hand—what we are watching is, in fact, a man having a wank into a woman. I'm not having sex here. Someone is just having sex on me. I know that now. Since this fuck occurred, I have—to be wanky for a moment—discovered my own body. I know what makes it feel happy. I know it would be far, far happier, at this moment, walking in the rain, or jumping into a lake, or even just lying in bed with a friend. If my body could talk, it would tell me it does not want to be in this room, having this one-night stand. My body is getting nothing out of this. Oh, body! I am sorry I put you there!"

On screen, pumping so fast he's almost a blur, Jerry reaches over, grabs my hair in his fist, and pulls it. My head jerks back—my throat is exposed. I wince as I watch it. It just feels . . . *sad* to see him do this to me. For there to be a record of this joyless event.

"Don't worry, ladies!" I say. "I know in any other filmed medium, if you saw this, it would be just before someone had their throat slit, in a battle scene. But that's not what's happening here! This isn't *Conan the Barbarian*! This is just 'rough sex.' Except, if the woman doesn't feel like she's having sex, then all we're left with is . . . rough. That's what I'm having. Some rough."

On screen, Jerry has started pulling my hair so hard that I begin to slip across the bed. On the muffled soundtrack, you can hear me say, "Fuck me harder."

"Could we pause the video again for a second?"

The video pauses, freeze-framed.

"So the one thing I want to make very clear here is: this *is* consensual sex. Absolutely. As you can hear, I have just asked Jerry to 'fuck me harder.' So I am consenting. I believe, for many people, me saying 'fuck me harder'—in a *Wolvo* accent, not a Birmingham one, you ignoramuses—is the bit they talk about most. The moment where they really laugh. When I'm asking to be fucked. Women asking to be fucked is funny. Awful, and funny. I don't know why."

I take another drag on my fag.

"But here's a secret: I am saying 'fuck me harder' not because I'm enjoying this—but just because *I want it to end.* And saying 'fuck me harder' is the only way I can think this will happen. Anyone else here ever do that?"

Sheepishly, about three hundred women put up their hands.

"Right? It is a well-known technique. I wasn't crazy for more of Jerry's sweet loving. *I just wanted to go home.*"

I sigh.

"Look. I don't want to take up any more of your time. I just want to thank you for letting me show you this film, because—now it's not a secret anymore—now I've shown it to the entire Astoria—now I have stood here and described every second of it—*no one has anything on me anymore.* You know everything about me. And that makes me—free. If you are a man presenting an awards show, and you have a joke about me fucking Jerry Sharp that's better than *Deep Bum*, come at me. Otherwise, I think this is done. I have carried around a weight of shame that has crushed me. Before it turned me into something harder—and I am harder now—it almost broke me."

And here, I start crying. Not sobs. Just hot, angry tears.

"But then! But then I realized—I should *never have been carrying this shame.* No woman who has had this happen to her should. The idea that women carry the shame for shameful things that have been done to them is Bible old, and Bible black. This shame is yours, Jerry Sharp. You may have it back. It is not mine, and it never was."

I put out my cigarette, and leave the stage.

On the screen, the video comes to an end—with Jerry flipping me over onto my back, saying, "Open your mouth," and drowning what I was trying to say, as he comes.

I have no idea how the audience is responding, because the whooshing sound in my head has returned. I appear to have gone deaf from trauma.

I reel into the wings, where Zee catches me. "I want to go home," I say. I am suddenly so, so tired—tired in a way that takes your legs out from under you.

I can see he's talking to me—"Dolly. Jo. That was amazing"—but it's like when the teacher talks to Charlie Brown, and all he can hear is a wah-wah trombone.

"I need to go home," I say again.

The floor has started shaking, so I presume The Branks have begun their set.

I say, "I would really like to go home now" to him five times, until he finally nods, takes me outside, and puts me in a cab, mouthing the words, *"Are you okay? I will come to see you, later,"* and I nod, because I need this car to go. I just need to go home, immediately. I have burned up a whole life onstage. Whether it was mine or Jerry's, I still cannot tell.

In the cab, I curl up on the backseat. The driver is alarmed.

"Hey—you're not going to be sick, are you?" he says.

"No," I reply. "The night's catharsis has been emotional, rather than emetic."

He doesn't like that reply.

"You're not going to be sick?" he repeats, more urgently.

"It's only my shame that has been voided," I say. I seem to be stuck in the 1700s. "My gorge will not rise."

I think he just presumes I am foreign at this point.

"DO. IT. OUT. THE. WINDOW," he says, loudly. "OUT. THE. WINDOW."

From my prone position, I give him a cheerful wave.

"Will do," I say.

We track the way from Kentish Town to Camden, the driver complaining, all the way, about some bad driver who's "up my arse."

We arrive outside my flat, and I get out of the cab, slowly. I feel very old, and frail, as I hand him a tenner.

"Christ, this clown again. Pardon my language," the driver says, as a minicab pulls up abruptly behind us.

And from out of it, running: John.

34

In my front room, I sat on the sofa, still mute from the evening, shaking.

Without saying a word, John put a blanket around me, got the dog to sit next to me, and gave me a shot of whisky.

"I hope you're enjoying my enforced presence," he said, gently. "I thought you might want some company."

I couldn't say anything. I felt like I'd run out of words.

John—seeing I was in shock—quietly put the TV on, put a cushion behind my head, and then sat next to me, in silence.

It was the snooker. I've never understood snooker, but it *looks* pretty—a man dressed up for ballroom dancing, gently nudging pretty-colored balls with a stick. The gentle applause. The quiet murmurs of anticipation as the blue bounces off the cushion, and rolls toward a hole. It's comforting.

"The blue one's my favorite," I said, conversationally, leaning my head on John's chest. Now, it felt right to be near him. Now, I was allowed to touch him. He stroked my hair.

"I like the blue one too, baby," he said, companionably.

We sat like this for ten, fifteen minutes. It felt like I'd been sucked out of an exploding plane, and had now landed in a field, in France, stunned and winded.

We continued sitting, like this, as the phone rang and rang.

In the end, John reached over, and pulled it out of the wall.

I settled closer to him, and sighed.

It was after a particularly, soothingly uneventful ten minutes—where the men had failed to get in any balls—that I said, quietly: "John. Have I just done the maddest thing ever?"

"Absolutely," John replied, stroking my head. "You are demonstrably insane. In those situations, you're just supposed to stay silent, push all your emotions down into a toxic ball in the bottom of your stomach for twenty years, and die of a furious, inoperable cancer. Couldn't you just be normal, like everyone else?"

"No," I said. We were still staring at the TV. It felt very peaceful.

"Why did you do it?" he finally asked, gently. Curiously.

It was a big question. There were a million things I could say. About how angry I am, that I had something stolen from me. The unfairness—the terrible unfairness—that others got to judge me. The horror of realizing how disgusted the world is by women. A desire to haul Jerry into my shit. Some not yet fully formed awareness that, out there, there are other girls, who shouldn't think that it's acceptable that this happens. I opened my mouth to start this huge, tumbling, impassioned rant, but what came out was:

"The idea made me laugh."

And that was actually the main reason. Letting secrets go makes you laugh. Showing everyone your terrible fuck makes everything . . . lighter, in the end.

"I feel—better now."

And I did. I felt as if I had just stepped out of endless darkness, into the light.

I started laughing—because it was over, and I was happy. And because nothing makes you laugh more than someone else laughing, John started laughing too. We became quite hysterical for a while—in the way you often are, after dramatic events. Weeping, and gasping for breath, before finally subsiding, exhausted.

"Oh, my darling," John said, taking my hand. "I have never been under the impression that you are anything other than the most amazing, amusing, singular, determined woman I have ever met. That much is empirical fact. Even the blind could see it."

He paused for a minute—clearly about to say something, but wondering if he should.

He shifted on the sofa, so that he was still holding my hand, but facing me. "But watching you, tonight, up there on the stage, utterly alone, breaking down all that is wrong with the precision of a High Court judge, made me realize something more. You are the new religion. You are the new craze. You are the next stage in evolution. You are so palpably my superior, in every way, that I tremble like a child in your presence. You make my head spin. You make my heart burst. You make my soul explode, every fucking minute I am with you. What I am inescapably heading toward, in this monologue, which might be the last thing I ever say, is: Dutch, I'm in love with you."

His face was as open and wondering as a child, looking at snow.

"I love you, Jo."

A KISS, I sometimes think, isn't really instigated by one person, or another. A kiss is a third party that floats through the room, if the atmosphere is correct, and just involves whoever's around in its mad kissing schemes.

One second before, we were not in a kiss. We were in the pre-kissing world.

A second later, and my old life was over, and I know—as I had always suspected—that kissing John Kite is the greatest luxury there is.

"Your mouth is so soft," he said, at the end of the first kiss; before he began the second.

This kissing was clever, and intense—it was like finding a new way to talk. He did . . . *this*, and I did . . . *this* back, and we were both delighted, and then thought of a new thing to do.

"Oh sweetness! Sweetness!" he said, burying his head in my hair.

And I was saying to him, "You are so beautiful; you are so beautiful," over and over, because men are never told they are beautiful, are they? And he was. Handsomeness does not look soft-eyed when it kisses; handsomeness does not kiss the palm of your hand. He is *beautiful*.

In bed, we started again. There were suddenly too many clothes involved in this kissing now—I made him lie down while I unbuttoned his shirt. He lay there, staring at me, smiling.

"Why are you smiling?" I said. I had never seen anyone smile when they were being kissed.

"I'm happy," he said. "I always smile when I'm happy."

He smiled like a stoned dolphin.

I said: "Tell me—what do you want me to do?"

I was ready to find out what sex John wants. I was totally up for it. I took his shirt off. I kissed his chest. I felt like the Pope kissing the airport tarmac, after he's landed. Thank you, God! Thank you for this!

"I want you to . . . talk," he said.

"Talk? Like—dirty talk?"

"No—like, talking talk. I want you to tell me *everything* you're thinking."

I was still confused.

He started to unbutton the rest of my dress, now. Oh! Fingers on collarbone! His fingers on my collarbone were the most perfect thing—I jolted so hard at his touch that he laughed.

"Darling, we have talked our stupid bloody heads off since the day we met. There is no one I find more fascinating. Why—when I finally have you in bed; when I finally get to take your clothes off, and make you jump like that—would I suddenly want you to stop telling me what you're thinking?"

I looked at him. He was staring at me so intently that I felt I could, now, finally, tell him what has really *terrified* me about sex, all these years.

"Tell me what you're thinking," he said again, cajolingly.

"Okay," I said. I looked him right in the eye. "Okay— here's the deal. Here's what I *really* think about sex. No man has ever made me come. You know that. But I am too scared to let anyone *try* to make me come."

"Why?" John said, wonderingly.

I let out a painful sigh. "In case it takes *too long*. So long that your hand gets tired, and you get a terrible cramp, and stop, because you're in pain, and you'll think I have a greedy vagina, and leave me. I'm worried," I said, "that I need too much. *I'm worried that I'm too much.*"

John looked at me. All through my speech, he'd been smiling at me in a happy, lazy way, which was also, at the same time, quite intent.

"Is that everything?" he asked. "Is that *everything* you're worried about?"

I thought.

"Yes," I said. "Those are the sum total of my fears, right now."

Whilst still looking me in the eye, he put his hand inside my tights.

"May I?" he said, with great courtesy.

"You may," I said, jaw dropping open the second he started touching me. He was straight to the place that aches most. I was so slippery for him.

"The thing is," he said, with unbelievably hot, slow resolve, "is that I can do this all day, honey. My hand will *never* tire."

His hand started moving.

I suddenly realized why I had always loved boys who play guitar. All that delicate repetition. All that timing. I watched his hand. The precision was astonishing. He'd been touching me for less than a minute, and yet very, very soon, if this continued, I would be shouting out his name.

Then he stopped. There was a small hole in my tights. His attention was drawn to it—he kissed the tiny burst of thigh pushing through it, before sucking it all into his mouth. That dislocated the remaining 20 percent of my brain. It was the single hottest thing to have ever happened to me. Oh, he was so good at sucking on tiny skin! He looked up at me—and the expression was, "You know why I'm doing this, don't you?"

"My worries are really waning," I said, weakly.

"Good. Because I am a lifelong fan of 'too much,'" he said, putting his fingers in the hole, and ripping it, until it was the size of his hand.

"Those were three ninety-nine from Boots!" I said, outraged.

"Baby, if you don't think what happens next was worth it, I'll personally refund you at the end of the night," he said, ripping them right up to the crotch, and burying his head between my legs.

THE REASON THE next eight hours of fucking were so amazing is because we never stopped talking. John had a lot of great ideas, which I was very enthusiastic about, on how we could come as many times as possible—but it was very much a collaborative effort. We would both describe to each other what was happening, while we did it—a technique which, for two very verbal people, makes everything so dizzyingly intense, it feels like you've set the world on fire, and are busily fucking your way to another planet.

"I've got my cock inside you, and my fingers in your mouth, and it feels like you're eating me alive," he said at one point, as I sucked down on his knuckle, almost crying with how feverish it felt.

Twenty minutes later, and I was on top of him, hands in his, pinning them to the pillow, and crying out, "Never stop, never stop, never stop, never stop," whilst he said, with solemn assurance, "I promise you, I absolutely promise you, I will fuck you for as long as you need it."

That was a lie, because he suddenly came two minutes later—"Sorry baby. You're just too hot for me not to"—but he made up for it by gently eating every drop from me, and then continuing to eat me out so slowly, and with such precision—almost stopping, and then starting again—that I couldn't talk anymore.

"I'm going to talk to you," he said, looking up. "I'm going to tell you what's happening. You are hot, and slippery, and swollen, and that is because I've fucked you very, very hard. Because I have wanted to for a long, long time."

Those words made me levitate.

"Say it again," I said. "Please."

"You are hot, and slippery, and swollen," he said, very slowly, "and that is because I've fucked you very, very hard. Because I have wanted to for a long, long time."

Oh, those words! There is nothing else!

"And now," he said, climbing back up, and easing himself in, "I'm going to fuck you again."

I suddenly understood what people meant when they say, "You should always fuck as if it's the first time."

I'd always got it wrong. I thought they'd meant you should fuck as if you're a virgin—slightly afraid, and unknowing.

But what they really meant is that you should always fuck like it's the first time *in the world*. As if you were inventing it, right then. And, when you'd finished, you'd want to go out and tell everyone what you'd just discovered.

"What do you like, sweetness?" he asked, quietly, right at the start, face buried in my hair, unbuttoning my velvet dress. "What shall we do?"

"I don't know, yet," I replied. "But: everything."

IT'S AMAZING HOW easy it is to have great sex when you're doing it with someone you really want to fuck. As I held on to John's thighs and kissed the underside of his belly—gently rounded, like Silbury Hill—I realized I hadn't wanted any of the people I'd fucked before. Not like this. Not like every minute means something, and every millimeter of them is a prize, and you want to drink the sweat from their temples, and turn them inside out to make them come. To drive them like you stole them.

"This is the best sex in the world, isn't it?" I said, happily, during a break in proceedings. John had brought back a mug of red wine, and some cheese, and we were having a picnic in the bed. A fuck-nic. "I mean, can you believe we don't have to pay for this? That it's absolutely free? If we had to pay for this, I would definitely go as high as fifty quid. It is enjoyable."

"You are humanity's greatest upgrade," John said, touching my face. I rubbed against his hand, like a cat, when it is petted by a loved one.

I lay back on the pillow, resting my mug of wine on my belly. I kept waiting to feel embarrassed about being naked in front of John—to want to coyly wrap a sheet around myself, like ladies in the movies—but it seemed ridiculous to do this with someone who, twenty minutes ago, had their face rammed between my bum cheeks. John's appreciation of my flesh was so palpable—he had wobbled, grabbed, and buried himself in me—that it would seem like a rejection of his values to now hide my mighty, hog-stopping thighs. He was the hog I'd stopped. And it was brilliant. Also, I had barely six brain cells left. I couldn't worry about anything. He'd fucked me stupid. It was awesome. I was so, so happy.

"So," I asked, reaching out and gently touching his hair. "How long have you wanted to do that?"

With a hand gesture, I pointed to all the sex we'd had in the last four hours.

"Oh, since the moment I saw you," he said, lying next to me, and kissing the top of my head. "In that bar, in Dublin—I looked up and you were standing there, with your cherry-red hair, and your top hat, stolen from a duke, and your blue, blue eyes. You really will have to stop having eyes the color of the sky, woman, because it means I see you everywhere. I've gone across the whole world, trying to get on with things, and wherever I go, I look up, and you're staring down at me.

Sky eyes. Once you meet a girl with eyes the color of the sky, you're doomed."

"Why did you fancy me?" I ask. I have my hand on his chest, over his heart, as he tells me he has always loved me. There is no greater joy than this in the world.

"You were," John said, with infinite love, "talking such absolute toss."

"Fuck you!"

"Such absolute toss," John said again, gleefully. "I'd never met anyone—man or woman—who could just talk, and talk, and talk like you do. I'm an easily bored man who wears uncomfortable shoes, and all I ever really want to do is sit down and talk to a bunch of interesting people about everything and nothing. And they," he said, simply, "were you. You're a bunch of interesting people."

"I didn't think you liked me!" I wailed. "Not like that! You never flirted! I did flirting! I winked at you several times—but you never responded, so I stopped."

"Sweetness," John said, gently. Since we kissed, I am "Sweetness," it seems. I am sweetness. "When I first met you, you had never drunk an alcoholic drink. You had never smoked a cigarette. It was the first night you'd ever slept away from home. It was the first time you'd been in a plane. It was the first time you'd slept in a hotel. It was the first time you'd ever interviewed anyone—which would explain why you were so terrible at it. And would I be right in thinking," he says this tenderly, "that you had maybe never slept with anyone, either?"

"Oh, I'd never even kissed anyone," I said, cheerfully. "Unless you count making a hand-mouth out of your hand, and kissing that. I'd done that a lot. With tongues."

"Well, there is a word for the kind of man who makes a move on a sixteen-year-old girl like that—however amazing, unusual, and sui generis she might be," John said, winding a piece of my hair round and round his finger. "Especially if he's the kind of man who spends most of his time roaming the Earth, on a variety of planes, and buses, and spending quite a while getting very fucked-up, and unhappy. You were a thing I really, really did not want to hurt, or change in any way. There is a terrible narcissism in the kind of man who wants to be the one to be with, and change, a young woman. I wanted you to be *you*. I wanted you to wholly continue in making yourself.

"You know why I never wrote a song about you—even though you begged me, a million times? Because songwriters lie and steal, Johanna. You are a writer, too, and you should never, ever let some other fucker steal your you. That's all you got. Every breath of you is material. I respected," he says, starting to laugh, "your copyright. I don't think I will ever say anything more romantic than that. *I respected you as an artist.* That's why tonight, I could not wait any longer. I stood there, watching you onstage, and thought, 'I am in the presence of an actual genius.' There is nothing hotter than that.

"Of course, I'm making this seem a lot more thought-out and noble than it was at the time," he said, reaching past me for the cigarettes, on the bedside table, and kissing me as he went past. "At the time, I simply thought, 'Do not fuck this weird, bollocks-talking child drinking Coca-Cola.' The rest I kind of . . . worked out later. I had a lot of time to think about it. Oh, I spent a lot of time thinking of you. You've been with me, all over the world. You come into my head a lot. Every seven seconds."

And because we were in bed now—because this is the place where we can, finally, say everything, I asked: "How? What do you think of?"

And he told me. And I see why he did not tell me when I was younger.

Because, when someone tells you why they love you—someone whose love you want; someone whose love feels like the wisest, most-craved eye—in a way, it's like attending your own wake. You hear your eulogy.

He tells you why he loves you, while you lie there—he tells you all the secrets of you; how you walk in a room; how you laugh in the best way; how you say the most unexpected things; how you never give in; that, when your hair is piled up on your head, your neck is a thing he wants to kiss. He tells you of the expression you have when you're thinking, tongue clamped between your teeth; and the way you say "Hel-*loooooo*, you!" the first time you meet someone, and you look at them so delightedly, like you're thrilled that they exist. You hear the tributes to yourself. You get to read your reviews.

And then of course, ever after that—in the minutes, and days, and years ahead—you are never really innocent again: because you know why you are wonderful. You know your best bits. You see the highlights of your set list. You know the value of your presence. You learn the things that you do which work. You become—unconsciously, but unstoppably—slightly calculating.

You are like a performer who, one night, spontaneously—

high, and happy, and wired—throws himself into the audience, and swims across a sea of outstretched hands—and who the next day, makes a news story, on page 4, for having done so. "It was the most exciting thing I've ever seen!" . . . "That was her defining moment!"

And so, the next night, onstage, you know everyone would like to see it again. You smile to the audience—cheers—and throw your arms wide—more cheers—and launch yourself out onto these new hands, and, this time, it is *not* spontaneous. It's not a dumb, untested, instinctive moment. It is not naive. It is done to please the audience. Because you want to please the audience. Because why would you not want to do your very best things for this loving crowd? The way you do things has changed.

I learned there is a dress I have—"With all the buttons down the back"—that John loved the best (I will buy more dresses like this!); that he loves my "cloud" of hair (I will never cut it!); that he is most amused when I have two drinks and launch into a long, impassioned theory about the Beatles, or sex, or Nabokov (I will do more of these! I will order a thousand more rants like these!).

And so part of the declaring of love means you are working to a commission, now. You are not the sole architect of the person you are building. Someone else is looking over your blueprints—nodding, enthusiastically, over this turret—so you build the turret bigger!—and remaining tactfully silent over an ostentatious fountain, which you immediately and silently scrap. You have entered a new world—in which there are two opinions on what will make the very best you.

And if your partner is wise, and kind, and has the same taste as you, you will make amazing things together.

And if your partner is broken, or impatient, or has darker needs—is unknowingly trying to build you in the shape of another woman he once knew, and lost; is trying to lean into your foundations to make his own stronger—you will build something with rotten walls, and impossible angles, which will, one day in the future, collapse.

But that is all part of becoming an adult. That is the difference between girls and women. That they are finally ready to hear the secret of what makes them them. That they are strong enough—for good, or for ill—to ask someone what is, unexpectedly, the most terrifying, revelatory question, on Earth; one you have to be brave, and ready, to hear: "Why do you love me?"

35

Of course, he didn't tell me *all* that that night. That night, we got sidetracked several times by how naked we were, and then the doorbell rang at 3 a.m., and Suzanne, Zee, and Julia were standing on the doorstep, to "see how you are?" and Suzanne took one look at me said, "Oh my *God*, you inappropriate bitch—you've just HAD SEX! With WHAT?" and then John appeared behind me, and Suzanne said, "Ah. With *that*," as John bowed to her.

And so I ended up holding my second-ever party, as Zee ordered pizza, and John beamed at me like a lighthouse, as I poured out Suzanne's "celebratory champagne."

Soon, the room was a cloud of cigarette smoke, and music, and talk, and at one point, Zee slid a check across the table to me, saying, "Don't cash it for two months—I'm just doing this to be dramatic, and symbolic—but these are your first earnings from The Branks' album," and that paid for John and me to go on holiday; to run away again, but, this time, whilst touching.

And so where he eventually told me why he loved me was in a hotel, perched over a loch, in Scotland; and then an apartment on Cardigan Bay; and then in a B and B in Worcestershire, as the apple blossom frothed down the valley, over a bitter blue-green sea of nettles.

"And you do understand, that this isn't even the start of it," he said, warningly, as we sat in bed, looking out of the window. "I'm very much afraid that I have only just begun the entire business of telling you why I love you. I suspect the whole business may take weeks. Months. Years. Very possibly, a lifetime. I don't wish to demand dominion over your schedule, but I feel I'm onto a very significant story here, and I'd like to go on tour with you, for a while, and report on your phenomena. You are the new craze. You are the storm on Venus that has raged for a million years. You are my safe word. You're my cool priest. You saturate me in love. You make my heart effloresce."

"You sound like a demented, screaming, raging teenage girl-fan," I said, climbing on top of him. "And there is nothing better to be."

ABOUT THE AUTHOR

CAITLIN MORAN's debut book, *How to Be a Woman*, was an instant *New York Times* bestseller. Her first novel, *How to Build a Girl*, received widespread acclaim. She lives in London. You can follow Caitlin on Twitter @caitlinmoran.